Annunciation

By

Ciara Houghton Ruane

Dedicated with love to Grandma and David

Contents

Annunciation

1

Mother of God

Maybelle 'Belle' Carter was chosen. As her story began, she was staring into space behind the counter of the gas station five miles outside Memphis, Tennessee where she worked. Hotdogs twirled beside her in the tray and a loud, fat fly buzzed past her ear occasionally. She was 19, fresh out of high school and had been working at the gas station for a month. Would she like to go to college? Of course, but to study what? She had been pretty good at English and she liked science but didn't consider herself a genius in either field. As she was seeing how many candy bar names she could read from the opposite side of the store, her mind wandered to what it was she could do with her brain.

    She had been described as 'bright' at most parent-teacher evenings. It seemed a pretty vague, catch-all term for 'not stupid' to her. Despite what had just been decided for her, she had no sense of being destined for anything notable. Like everyone, she was bound by the relentless ticking metronome of reality. She went to school and now she had a job. A boring, repetitive, smelly job that involved hot surfaces, an ugly uniform, and bleach. Occasionally she would have to work nights, standing there under the florescent buzz, warming up paninis for truckers who would try and flirt with her, or worse, make casually racist comments. Belle had an unparalleled ability to smile sweetly in the face of such things, before setting the panini grill just a little too high.

That day, as she stood unaware of her destiny, was hot and humid, as the previous few weeks had been. The sun was beginning its descent over the misty, hilly horizon facing the storefront. The gas station was an oasis, somewhere you could get a latte after miles and miles of unbroken farmland. Just fields and trees, fields and trees occasionally punctuated by a red barn or herd of cattle. The front door buzzed. Belle automatically turned to smile at whoever stepped through and to welcome them. It was her boss, so she didn't bother.

"Afternoon, Maybelle." He only ever addressed her by her full name.

"Afternoon Mr Lowe." She answered.
Mr Lowe was a short, stocky man with white hair ahead of his years and a bizarrely outdated handlebar moustache. When she described him to others Belle would call him 'the Walrus of Lowe'.

He set about in a well-worn circle around the store, picking up the same items he always did when he came in. A sugar-free red bull, a supermarket tabloid, and a bag of ranch-flavoured chips. He breathed unusually loudly, and always sounded as though his mouth was full. He brought his purchases to the counter and Belle, a tall and willowy dark-skinned girl who was almost his exact physical opposite, began scanning.

"And how have things been here today Maybelle? Any sign of your friend Doug?"

Doug was an old widower who had taken a shine to Belle and would come in almost every day to talk to her about his uneventful life.

"Not yet, he did say yesterday that he might be getting sick."

"I sure hope not, at his age it could kill him."

As soon as he had handed his money to Belle he cracked open his Red Bull and took a deep swig.

"I almost forgot what I came in to tell you."

"I thought you came in for your snacks?"

He always called his regular purchases 'snacks' even though one was a magazine. He took another swig and wiped some drops off his moustache.

"You got a new coworker tomorrow, this new guy, uh... Gary or Graham or somethin'."

"You hired someone and you don't remember his name?"

"He dropped his resume off Tuesday night just as I was leaving. I didn't even get a chance to interview him, I just had to say yes. Lord knows I need the staff since Matt went to jail."

"You made me take a bunch of math tests before you hired me."

"That was then, this is now, I'm a desperate man, Maybelle. I'll stop by tomorrow to see how you two are getting along. You never know, you may fall madly in love."

She scoffed.

"Next time you wanna hire someone, let me run

some tests and I'll pick out my dream man."
He chuckled as he opened his ranch chips.

"You're funny, Maybelle. I'll see you tomorrow."

She waved at him as he exited, cradling his chips and magazine in one arm and crushing his now-empty red bull with the other hand.

The next two hours of Belle's shift passed by uneventfully. Her Mom pulled up outside five minutes early to take her back home, so they shared a decaf cappuccino while they waited for the night shift girl to show up. In the car back to their little home on the outskirts of Memphis where just the two of them lived, they talked about the mundane days they had both had. Her Mom worked at the city hall, filing and data entry. That day the most exciting thing had been a pigeon flying in through the window by her desk. Belle's Mom was shorter than her and had lighter skin. Belle's Dad was killed by a heart attack when she was eight and had given his daughter his height and his wit and his melanin. Her Mom talked about him sometimes, but for Belle, it was like being born with a limb missing. She was jealous of other people who had living, breathing fathers, but she felt she wasn't entitled to miss someone she had lived without for so long.

Belle mentioned the mysterious new guy starting at work over their mac and cheese dinner.

"Mr Lowe couldn't even remember his name. Called him 'Graham or Gary'"

"So it starts with a G?" replied her Mom.

"Who the hell knows? It might not even be a guy."

"Didn't you have to do a whole bunch of tests and stuff?"

Belle swallowed a mouthful of mac.

"Yeah. That's exactly what I said. Mr Lowe was like 'maybe you two'll fall in love'"

Her Mom snorted.

"Did he get his snacks?"

"Hell yeah, he got his snacks. No Doug today."

"No Doug?"

"No Doug. I hope he's OK."

"He ought to leave you alone, bothering you at work like that."

"Eh, he's just lonely."

"You are like bait for weirdos."

Belle shrugged.

"They don't bother me."

Her Mom leaned back as if she was taking in more of her daughter.

"Your Daddy was the same, he used to talk to everybody. I remember once this old guy on the bus with a twitchy eye sat right next to him, and your Daddy talked away to him like he was his oldest friend. I was always more suspicious of people. He used to say the same as you 'he's just lonely' and I used to say 'there's probably a good reason for that, honey.'"

Belle mopped up her plate with a piece of bread and stacked it on top of her Mom's.

"I'll wash up."

"You even attracted oddballs when you were a baby. Strange people would come up to me when I was holding you and they always used to say 'this one's been here before."

"Is that why you gave me an old lady name?"
Her Mom playfully slapped her arm.

"You were named after Maybelle Wright, one of
the best soul singers around when I was your age."

"I know, I know. I used to tell kids at school I
was named after Belle from Beauty and the Beast.
Didn't really work cos the movie came out after I was
born, but they didn't know that."
Her Mom looked at her watch.

"Shit. I gotta call your aunt."
She left Belle alone in the kitchen, staring out at the
next-door-neighbours living room window and washing
up the remnants of mac and cheese.

The next day when Belle arrived at work Mr
Lowe was already there, with the back of Gary's – or
was it Graham's – head facing her as she walked in. He
and Mr Lowe were deep in conversation, with Mr
Lowe's 'snacks' already paid for on the counter.

"Ah! Good morning Miss Maybelle! I'd like you
to meet Gabe."
Gary or Graham, whose name was actually Gabe,
turned around and flashed her a smile. He was a little
taller than Belle, with dirty blonde hair just past his
ears. He had heavy eyebrows and a pair of the brightest
blue eyes Belle had ever seen. They would have been
creepy, had his smile not been so warm.

"I'm Gabe." He said, with an outstretched hand.
His accent was a little odd, he might have been from the
North. Belle shook his hand.

"Belle. Lowe calls me Maybelle but he's the only
one who does."

"Whatever you say, Belle." He was still smiling at her. Throughout the conversation, which was mainly Mr Lowe explaining the basics of gas station operating, he kept smiling at her. A real genuine, twinkly-eyed smile, as if she was the subject of a surprise birthday party his friends had thrown.

The gas station usually employed teenagers fresh out of high school like herself, or people who were rebuilding their lives. Gabe looked too happy and stable and too old for gas station work.

"I gotta get goin'. I'll be back tonight to check up on you two. Maybelle, you walk him through everything. She knows her stuff, Gabe."

Belle nodded.

"I know all of the stuff."

"Buh-bye!"

Once he had left, Belle turned to her protege, who was still grinning.

"What's first, boss?"

Belle smirked. She hadn't been called that before.

"Well, first I gotta clean out the coffee machine, which is gross, you can watch and I'll talk you through it, and then maybe if you're lucky I'll let you clean up all the disgusting wet coffee grounds."

Gabe took to everything pretty easily. Belle had never had to train anyone before, but she couldn't imagine a better student. He was too smart to be working there. He would occasionally mess up, like screwing up the temperature on the hot dog machine right after being shown how to do it, but it was almost as if he was screwing up on purpose to make her feel as though she had something to do. In the post-lunch lull,

Belle set about demystifying her perky new colleague.

"So where are you from, Gabe?" She asked while absent-mindedly scratching at a coffee stain on her shirt.

"Illinois."

"Just Illinois? Nowhere specific?"

He smiled at her.

"Just far enough out of Chicago to not really say I'm from Chicago."

"Uh-huh, and why are you down in Tennessee? For the heat?"

He smirked.

"I'm not a big fan of heat. My Dad is from around here, he moved back after my Mom died and I came here to care for him."

A customer came and bought a pack of cigarettes from Gabe. When the shop was empty again he asked:

"What about you? You always lived here?"

"Yeah, I can't get enough of humidity or religious freaks." She answered.

"You're not religious?"

She waved her head from side to side.

"Not...especially, I was in debate club at high school and we must have had an argument over the existence of God like twice a week. I can see good points on both sides but it seems like a good idea to keep my options open." Gabe tidied some packs of gum on one side of the counter. "What about you, Gabe, are you happy to leave the big city heathens?"

Gabe paused, considering his answer.

"I think 'God' is too big for humans to understand. Just referring to God as 'he' all the time is a little weird when you think about it. Why would the all-powerful creator of the Universe have a gender? What would they do with it?"

Belle nodded.

"It's like... I was listening to the radio and they were talking about molecules and electrons and how matter is mostly empty space, and half of me thinks 'OK, this is way too complicated to just happen by accident, so there must be a God', and the other half thinks 'we find out how things work all the time, eventually we're just gonna figure out everything on our own." She said.

"That's a pretty good way of looking at it." Agreed Gabe, just as a trucker stepped through the door. Belle straightened up.

"Here I am talking about God and the Universe, it's debate club all over again, good afternoon, sir."

The trucker turned. He had a beer belly and was wearing ridiculous reflective orange shades. Belle noticed a confederate flag pin on his shirt pocket and let the smile fall off her face.

"Just picking up some lunch, girl."

"Mhm."

Gabe's eyes seemed to fix on the guy like he was scoping him out as a threat. He lazily browsed through packets of chips before settling on a bag of chilli Doritos and grabbed an ugly-looking BLT from the fridge. He slapped them on the counter and stared Belle down as she punched them into the register. She purposely avoided eye contact.

"Y'know, you're pretty good looking for a...uh."

"For a what?" She curtly replied

The trucker raised an eyebrow and threw his hands up.

"Just trying to pay you a compliment, honey,"

"I'm good for compliments. That will be $4.99."
He reached into his back pocket and dragged out a
crumpled five-dollar bill, confused as to how a girl 20
years younger than him could possibly resist his
charms. Gabe was still staring the man down, so much
so that he was beginning to squirm.

"Who's this guy? Your bodyguard?"

"I just work here." Replied Gabe, in such a blunt
way the man's eyes widened.

"Well, sorry man." He picked up his purchases
and left, muttering under his breath, something only
Gabe heard.

Belle pretended to dry heave.

"I wish that guy wanted a panini. I always burn
the paninis when they're like that."
Gabe smiled and said 'good', but he still carried a coiled
tension, which made Belle feel like it was her duty to
diffuse the situation with more jokes. The business
picked up shortly afterwards, and the friendliness of the
remaining customers lifted the mood without a comedy
intervention. At around 4 pm Doug showed up, looking
a little under the weather but beaming at a chance to
see his gas station friend.

Belle returned the smile with a larger one.

"Doug! Buddy! We were worried about you here,
how're you feeling?"
Doug shuffled in, his seven-and-a-half decade-old legs
beginning to crumble. He spoke like a real good ole boy,
with none of the retro racism of his trucker co-shopper.

"I'm just wandering, Miss Maybelle." He

coughed, "Nothing more than a cold, it's gonna take more than that to bring me down."

"Damn right."

Gabe was tucked away pricing eggs on a lower shelf of the fridge, listening intently. "Mr Lowe was asking after you, and my Mom."

"Your Mom, have I met her?"

"Yeah, Cynthia, you talked about old soul singers that time."

"That's right! Y'know, I used to go to dances with a lady who looked just like her!"

Belle laughed.

"You sure it wasn't my aunt?"

"Oh no, no, this was back in New Orleans. We used to have to go to underground parties, a lot of the big dances were still segregated back then." He chuckled at the memory. "I used to get some funny looks, I'd be the only white boy in the room."

Belle smiled, making him the latte he always ordered.

"Were you a good dancer?"

"Good enough for her!" Belle handed over his coffee. Gabe stood up from his shelf duties.

"Oh, Doug, this is the new guy, Gabe. He's from Illinois." Gabe strode over and shook Doug's hand.

"Nice to meet you, Doug.

"And you. You got a good handshake."

"Well, thank you."

Doug assessed his new companion.

"Son, you're too good-looking to be working in a place like this."

Belle stifled a laugh, thankful that Doug had brought up why he was working in a gas station. Gabe actually seemed to blush.

"Well I have to take care of my Dad, and this place has good health insurance for a minimum-wage gig."

"Well listen to that, you're like Miss Maybelle. I tell you that girl's an angel, the way she looks after her mama."

Belle curtseyed and batted her lashes.

"And of course, she takes such good care of me when I visit," Doug added to her list of good qualities.

"I'll have to learn from her so I can take care of you when she's not at work."

"Well good, I expect nothing less from this place."

"Yeah, he's a VIC, a very important customer." Added Belle.

After Doug had finished his latte and said his goodbyes, Gabe turned to Belle.

"Should we start counting up, Miss Maybelle?"

Belle scowled.

"To Mr Lowe, I'm Maybelle, to Doug I'm Miss Maybelle, to you and everyone else I'm Belle."

"Like from Beauty and the Beast?"

"Exactly."

Gabe and Belle got the store cleaned up and counted up ready for the night shift. When she waved him off Gabe just seemed to walk in the direction heading away from Franklin, off into the endless fields. Belle craned her neck in search of a car, before giving up and getting into her Mom's.

"Is that Gary?" Her Mom asked.

"His name is Gabe, as it turns out." Replied Belle.

"Ah. And have you two fallen madly in love yet.?" Belle smiled and shook her head.

"He seems nice and all, but he's not my type."

"White?" Asked her Mom.

"Extremely." She replied.

Belle felt a weird, energetic sensation in her body as she crawled into her single bed that night. She had multiple sensations of falling before finally entering her sleep. She plunged into her dream with such a feeling of reality it was as if she had dived straight into a freezing ocean. She found herself standing on a road in the middle of a desolate, icy plain. It was night, and the cold was sharp on her skin. Above her, the northern lights danced with green and violet threads weaving in and out of each other, next to a huge orange moon. She could feel it all as if she was there, a cold breeze whistling past her ears, her bare feet on the asphalt, cool air entering her lungs. There wasn't the detachment she was used to in her dreams, which were usually just a swirl of abstraction. Still, even as she took steps on the road to take in her surroundings, she knew it was a dream.

She heard, as clear as any sound she would hear while she was awake, the mournful, low bellow of a blue whale. It came over the mountains, swimming as if it was in the water, swooping down to the ground the way a dragon would fly. She could count the wrinkles in its huge underbelly and made contact with its beady black eye. Its tail swept down where she could touch it, dappled with light fractured by unseen water. She reached out and felt its rubbery surface and it bellowed in recognition. She began to giggle, relishing in such a gorgeous dream. She had never visited the ocean and had always had a fascination with whales. When her eyes returned to the road, an arctic fox sat patiently in front of her, staring up at her with intent. It spoke to her, in a gentle voice.

"I've been meaning to speak with you for a long time, Belle."
Only now did she notice what she was wearing – a white silk dress woven with minuscule gold threads. She had silver bangles on her wrists and ankles.

"I brought you here for a reason," said the fox.

"And where is here? Besides a really good dreamscape"
The fox laughed. "We are in a place of your choosing. The place we all go to, provided we are worthy of it. The place where everything is as you want it."
She recognised the dress. She had seen it in a catalogue when looking for prom dresses but knew she could never afford it. She wanted to be buried in that dress one day.

"And who are you?"

"I am a messenger."
She knelt down and looked into the fox's steel-blue eyes. They responded to her, looking back with equal understanding like human eyes would. She stroked its ears.

"And what is your message?"

"Be ready, Belle, for you have been called upon."

"Called upon for what?"

"You will know when the announcement is made."

"What announcement? I need more information than that."

The fox turned, and with feathery steps, ran towards the mountains. He looked back at her, his furry ears pricked up.

"Be ready for anything, and be at peace."

He disappeared into the darkness, and Belle woke up.

She told her Mom about the dream over breakfast. All she did in response was raise an eyebrow. Belle never understood why people found other people's dreams boring, it was a window into their unfiltered subconscious, what could be more interesting? The sense of peace that the dream gave her didn't leave, and she felt her mind wander more than usual as her Mom drove her to work. Looking out at the streets and then the fields, she imagined herself running through them, leaping over cars and fences and easily keeping up with the speed of the car. When she arrived at the gas station it was locked and none of the lights were on. She frowned at her watch, sure that Gabe was supposed to open up today. She took out the key Mr Lowe had given her.

The silence and darkness were punctured as the fluorescent lights buzzed and flickered on out of sync, like the store itself was groggily waking up. She clicked on the coffee machine and the register and made herself a latte. Half an hour later and not a soul besides her had set foot in the store. There was no sign of Gabe, and he didn't seem like the kind to skip work. She reasoned that he must be at home sick. The door pinged. She looked over and saw a possum with three babies on its back lazily walking past the door. She snorted and put her head in her arms. Thinking of her dream again, she wondered if she could wish herself back there. She knew there were ways you could induce lucid dreams, something she could google on her break. The door pinged again.

She looked up expecting another possum, but no one and nothing was there. The door was simply wide open, without anything to trigger the sensors. She had never seen that before. Assuming it must be a fault, she walked over to see. She craned her neck outside, expecting to see someone standing by the door with a gun and a ski mask, or for the doors to slam shut on her neck. But there was no one, just the hot air of summer. Then, behind her, the sound of a guitar strumming. She spun around and saw no guitarist, but a record player on a small table in the centre of the store

Oh, where have you been my blue-eyed son,
And where have you been my darling young one

No one was there. Just Bob Dylan singing to her. She stepped softly towards the turntable as it span. She could see no power source, no speaker, just a lazily spinning vinyl. Expecting it to be electrified, she lifted the plastic cover with great care.

I've been out in front of a dozen dead oc-

She lifted the needle and Bob Dylan stopped singing. All she could hear then were birds tweeting and cicadas vibrating. Lots of birds.

"Belle?"

She turned and saw Gabe standing at the door. The sun seemed brighter than it was before behind him.

"You're late." She said, without any of the authority and annoyance she wanted. Gabe didn't say anything. He stepped inside and the door shut behind him. He stood in silence.

"Gabe, you're freaking me out. I've had such a weird morning. I had this dream, and..."

"The one with the fox?"

She cocked her head to one side.

"Now you're really freaking me out."

"I know how you can go back there."

"You know about lucid dreams?"

He smiled and stretched out his hand.

"Come with me."

Any other time some guy she barely knew asked to hold her hand she would have said no, but Gabe was radiating an infectious sense of calm. He took her hand and walked her out the door.

A white light flashed for a second, and she was stood in a forest clearing. She could smell the towering pine trees, hear the crickets chirruping, she could feel the cool yet humid air, feel the soft moss sinking under her work shoes. Her breath stuck and her heart lurched.

"Where are we?"

"Somewhere better to talk." Replied Gabe. "It doesn't have to be here though, it can be anywhere you want, anywhere you feel safe and calm."

She turned to him, a million questions buzzing in her head but unable to pick out a single one.

"This seems...pretty nice."

"Alright then, let's talk."

She felt the fabric of her work clothes shift and looking down she saw the same dress she had been wearing in her dream. A few feet away from her a campfire blazed, but despite her proximity to it, she felt no stinging burn on her skin, just pleasant warmth.

"Gabe what the hell is going on."
He sighed.

"I need you to understand...who I am."
She felt the bark of a tree. It was real, ridged and dry with patches of furry green moss. She cautiously sat down on a stump by the campfire, expecting it to disintegrate beneath her.

"And who are you?"
She turned back to him. He was wearing a burgundy sweater and jeans. He walked towards her and kneeled next to her, matching her eye level like he was breaking the news of a divorce to a child. She remembered a doctor telling her that her father was dead just like that.

"I'm a messenger of God, Belle."
She stared at him for what felt like ten minutes. She stood up at last, and struggled to find a proper response.

"What are you talking about, Gabe?"

"My name is Gabriel. I am an Archangel, a messenger of God."
She stepped back from him.
"That wasn't a dream you had last night, it was a vision, you've been called upon for a very important task."
Belle held up her hand for silence. Her heart was violently pounding. She wanted to laugh in his face but had seen too much to deny that something truly divine was happening. This was no hallucination. It was real. She spent a moment processing what it all meant.

"So there is a God?"

Gabriel shrugged.

"Well, yeah."

Spots clouded her vision and she sank to the floor.

"I need a minute here."

"Take your time."

His voice was muffled and distant. She stared at the ground, looking for answers in the carpet of pine needles and twigs. She breathed deeply and her vision returned to normal.

"So there's a heaven and a hell and angels and an afterlife and...and" her voice began to crack "...and somewhere up there my daddy really IS watching over me??"

Gabe smiled and nodded.

She let out a noise halfway between a laugh and a sob and lay flat on the soft ground. She began laughing.

"All this time I've been freaking out. Ohhhhhmygod. Oh, sorry."

Gabe waved away the light blasphemy. He kneeled beside her again.

"We don't normally reveal ourselves like this, except in very exceptional circumstances. It's only because we believe in you that we're coming to you with this."

She sat up. "Because," he continued "you can say no. We've waited for many millennia, we can wait some more."

"Wait for what?"

He held her hand.

"Maybelle Carter, we want you to be the mother of the world."

"What?"

He looked her right in the eye.

"We want you to carry and give birth to the Son of God."

2

God-Bearer

"I don't understand," said Belle at long last.

"God has been watching. And I've been watching too, for a long time." Explained Gabe "He has seen a world entrenched in chaos. He is willing to offer a great sacrifice to save it." He took her hand. "He has selected you to bear and raise his son."
Belle laughed like a woman possessed.

"Why do they always laugh?" Muttered Gabe.

"There has to be a mistake." She said. "I'm 19, I live with my Mom, I work *part-time* at a gas station. I couldn't take care of a cat."

"But that is precisely the point," Gabe replied, sitting cross-legged next to her.
"We're talking about God here. The all-powerful, all-seeing, all-merciful, all-knowing" he continued. "He is sending his son, essentially himself, down to this.... sick little planet. He needs to understand what it means to be human. To show himself to be human. To be..." he gestured towards her "....human."

"And he chose me," replied Belle, sitting up on her elbows and speaking with more than a little indignation, "...as the pinnacle of human grossness?"
"As the exact opposite." Answered Gabe, placing a hand on her shoulder. "As someone who can raise the Son of

God with humility, and grace, and empathy. Someone who can represent what he means. Someone who can represent what humanity can be."

Belle took a few moments to remember how to breathe.

"And that's me?"

Gabe nodded. She sat up and looked through the trees as if the answer might be there. She saw a female deer pushing its nose through the undergrowth in the distance, searching for berries.

"How can I just drop everything and become..." She threw her arms up, tossing away the words that didn't apply.

"That's why we're asking," replied her angelic guide. "That's why you can say no."

"And if I say no? Does nothing happen? We never get the... saviour or whatever?"

"Not necessarily." He was now facing the same direction, observing the deer. "We can wait. It will take a long time to find another like you. But we can wait."

She hugged herself.

"I just can't.... comprehend it."

Gabe sighed.

"Let me show you something." He turned towards the fire. Walking over, he knelt and reached out to the flame as if it was nothing.

At first, things remained as they were. Then the flames began creeping and climbing up his arm, singing the fibres of his sweater but not touching his skin. Before Belle could say a word, the clearing erupted in a blinding, phosphorous light. As she became adjusted and lowered the arm shielding her eyes, she saw Gabe as a being of stunning radiance and terrifying form. His head was that of a lion, with his same blue eyes, he had four great wings, as wide as he was tall, sprouting from his back. Along the edges of these wings were flaming eyes, staring, unblinking. His cloak was gold, his hands were outstretched. She was speechless. In a voice as soft as cotton but as resonant as an earthquake, he said;

"You will be a mother to the world. Holy amongst women, you will be worshipped."
She walked a step closer, scarcely able to blink. The trees and the deer were all gone, they were surrounded by the light.

"I don't want to be worshipped. I just want to be happy."
Gabe bowed his head and stretched out his hand. Expecting it to burn her, she stood up and reached out slowly to hold it.

Once her hand rested in his, a swell of something primal yet divine came from deep with her. As if it had always been there, buried deep in her subconscious, her DNA, since before she was even born. She felt the surge of a love so strong that it could power her to move a mountain. It buzzed all over her skin and expanded her heart. It lit fire to every synapse in her brain. She knew that it was no directionless love, but the love she would have towards the son she had a chance to accept or deny at that moment. She thought of her mother, her job, of all the small and comforting things that she enjoyed. All of the half-formed plans of a life she had yet to live. The things she had thought of studying, the apprenticeships that had caught her eye. Every aspect of her young life that would never, could never be the same if she accepted Gabe's offer.

He let go of her hand. Without her senses to hold her up, her knees fell beneath her, her body feeling as though someone had plucked out her nervous system, her ears ringing. Her surroundings were still a pure, glowing white, but Gabe was back to looking like an ordinary human being. He knelt again and placed his ordinary hand on her ordinary shoulder.

"Where do you want to be right now, Belle?"
She looked up at him, and behind his head, she saw a flock of birds. Looking around, she recognised the small, somewhat overgrown garden, gently stroked by a springtime breeze. Daisies and dandelions sprung up in the rich green grass, a single cherry tree provided a patchy shade from the warm sun. At the other side of this garden stood the back wall of her house and a homemade porch swing.

"Why didn't we go back to the forest? I thought that was where I was most peaceful?"
Gabe helped her to her feet.

"Perhaps, but this is where you feel most yourself."
Her feet were bare and the soft grass tickled.

"This is everything I'll lose."

"It doesn't have to be," Gabe replied. "It may just have to be adapted."
She paused, taking in the light smell of the cherry blossom.

"You said something about a sacrifice?"
He hung his head.

"That is part of what will happen. The son of God will save the world, but he will have to suffer to do so."

"And me?"

"You will be protected, and blessed."

Belle walked over to the porch swing. She sat down on its canvas seat and heard the familiar creak of the wooden frame her Daddy had spent so much time crafting. She took one big breath.

"There is someone else I wish I could speak to. You know a lot, Gabe, but you don't know what it's like to be a human being."

All was silent for a moment. Just the rustling of the grass in the wind and the occasional chirrup of a bird. Then, she heard a phone ring.

She looked around and saw that Gabe was gone. Next to her was an old-fashioned phone set, complete with a curly wire. She stared at it with a furrowed brow, then picked up the receiver.

"Hello?"

There was a pause, and the receiver crackled.

"Hey cheesy, it's me."

She clasped her hand to her mouth. The distorted but unmistakable sound of her father's voice came through the phone. The nickname 'cheesy' ignited in her memory like a lightbulb not switched on for years. It was his little joke. Everyone called her 'Baby Belle' when she was small, so he called her 'cheesy.' She tried her best to stifle the tears welling up and pushing against the back of her eyes. She searched in her mind for every memory she had of her father.

"It's OK baby. Are you in the garden? I go there all the time."

"Why aren't you here?" Her voice barely held together.

"You know this is the best way for us to talk. Are you on the swing where we used to sit?" He sighed. She remembered that sigh. She remembered snoozing on his chest when she was tiny and hearing his voice vibrate next to her ear and feeling his stomach rise and fall with that sigh.

"This is my favourite place to go. And I can go wherever I want. Just me and my little cheese wheel chilling in the sun."

The breeze felt a lot colder against the wet skin on her cheek.

"I have so much to tell you."

"You don't have to tell me anything, sweetie, I've seen it all." She gripped the phone with both hands. "I know you and your Mom miss me a lot, but I see you guys so much I don't miss you very much at all." He laughed his unmistakable laugh. "As bad as that sounds."

"I understand, Dad."

"I never had a chance to do this though. Talk with my girl, all grown up. I just knew you would turn out this well. I may not miss you, exactly, but I wished for this."

"Well, *I* miss you!"

"I know, I know. That's why I'm so glad we can talk."

Belle then remembered why she was speaking to him.

"What should I do, Dad? I don't know what to do."

He sighed again.

"Belle, I didn't need this to happen for me to be proud of you. I always knew you were going to do something great, and you exceeded my expectations with the person you've become. I am so, so proud of you already."

By now she wasn't holding back her tears.

"Your Mom was never as good at showing her feelings as me but she's mighty proud too."

"But I haven't done anything with my life yet."

"Yes, you have! Being up here gives you a lot of perspective. Do you know how hard it is to be kind and selfless when there are so many other options? It's a miracle there are any of us up here at all!"

She laughed, her body still shaking with her tears.

"What's it like up there?" She had to know.

"Look at where you are now, sweetie. All that peace and contentment that you feel only for a few seconds, those moments where everything seems right for just a minute and you understand it all, right before it passes. That's what it's like. But it never passes."

She looked around her again.

"And if I say yes, I'll lose this."

"Sweetie, do you have any idea what it's like to be a parent?" He asked. "It's the hardest thing in the world, sure, but when you've got that little baby in your arms it's like nothing else matters. When they handed you over to me in the hospital and you put your little hand round my finger and looked up at me with your big dark eyes, you were my little slice of heaven right there." He paused. "And that's why I always come back to you."

She was silent for a minute, not wanting to put down the phone ever.

"Do you think I should say yes?"

"I think you should do what you feel is right. They picked you because you would be smart about it. But I know you *could*." He chuckled. "Baby you would do such a good job! Better than some mechanic apprenticeship or whatever the hell it was you were talking to your mama about."

She laughed, wiping away some of her tears with the back of her hand.

"I think I know what to do. But it terrifies me."

"It terrified me too. But here we are now. Happy as anything"

She swallowed and felt some sense of composure.

"I don't want you to go."

"I don't want to go either, but believe me," her Dad took a deep breath "I *will* see you again."

Belle softened her grip on the phone's receiver. She was silent for what felt like an age. She took deep breaths of the cool spring air. She closed her eyes and listened to the birds tweeting. It was just like it was all those years ago when her daddy read her stories on the swing and tickled her and let her fall asleep on him. She wanted that back, and so she said;

"I'll do it."

Her father chuckled.

"That's my girl."

"I think I have to go now, Dad."

"I understand. Tell your mother I love her. And baby -"

She paused.

"I love you too. So, so much."

She smiled broadly, her tears now stopped.

"I love you too."

"Bye cheesy."

"Bye Dad."

She placed the receiver of the phone back like it was made of thin glass. Once she did, the garden, and its smells and sounds melted away. In place of the swing was a hay bale, in place of the springtime breeze was the humid, soupy summer air, and in place of the cherry tree was the gas station, sat on the other side of the road.

She stood up, barely supporting herself on her legs, which felt like hollow reeds that might snap. As she walked in the direction of the gas station crickets hopped out of her way with each step. The long grasses buzzed with them. A car was approaching as she stepped onto the asphalt, but she didn't slow her pace. It sped past her easily. She wasn't sure what she would see once she stepped in the door. Mr Lowe grimacing at his watch? Doug rifling through the magazines? Workers attending to a serious carbon monoxide leak that had caused her to vividly hallucinate? All wrong. As the doors opened she saw Gabe, standing behind the register in his ugly nylon uniform, with a smiling Mr Lowe paying for his snacks, all as if nothing had happened.

"Ah, Belle," said Gabe. "You got my cigarettes from the car?"

She looked down at her hand and sure enough, she held a packet of cigarettes and Gabe's car keys. They had a smiley face keychain and an 'I've been to Graceland' souvenir bottle opener. She placed them on the register.

"You been here long, Mr Lowe?" She asked, surprised at how steady her voice was.

"Not at all, Maybelle, just got here. Gabe was telling me the good news."
She prickled.

"The what now?"

"He's decided to stay with us here in Memphis. He's just paid up on an apartment so he's gonna be with us for a while."

"Ohh." She sighed.

"Anyways, I best be going, I'll leave you kids to it." Said Mr Lowe, cracking open his energy drink. He waved at her with the two fingers he had available on his way out. When she turned back to him, Gabe already had a cigarette between his teeth.

"Wanna join me outside for a smoke?"

Leaning up against the brick wall outside, Belle glared at Gabe, trying to penetrate through his infuriating casual air.

"Want a cigarette?"

"Aren't I supposed to lay off those in my delicate condition?"
He smirked.

"We're not that strict. Besides, we can give you a week's grace, y'know, in case you change your mind.'
She stood away from the wall.

"I can do that?"

"Well, yeah. We appreciate that this is a big undertaking." He added, handing her a cigarette and his lighter

She lit the cigarette and took a huge drag, burning the back of her throat and leading to a coughing fit."

"Easy, easy, you're not indestructible."

"How are you even allowed to smoke these? It doesn't seem very angelic."

He sniggered, smoke shooting out of his nostrils.

"They're a lot more fun when you don't really *need* lungs. And besides, my usual, uh, golden trumpet is a little conspicuous."

"You have one of those?"

He smiled.

"Could if I wanted to."

"Anyway, look, I still have a lot of questions. A lot." She took another drag, this time without coughing up a lung. "How am I supposed to tell mom, to begin with?"

"She wants grandchildren, right?" He asked, crushing an ashy stub under his cheap sneakers.

"Not right now, Gabe. Right now she wants a daughter in college. And I don't think this situation is what she had in mind when she pictured grandkids."

She went over to a nearby trashcan to ash her cigarette.

"Oh, a good point... I can't litter, I'm a guest here," muttered Gabe, following her example by picking up his trodden-on stub and throwing it away. "Gross." He added, wiping ash onto his shirt.

"So, what am I supposed to tell her?"

He looked up, squinting in the sun behind her.

"I'll come with you."

She raised an eyebrow.

"You will?"

"Yeah, of course." He walked back inside, and she followed him. "You heard Mr Lowe, I'm here to stay."

"Yeah, I thought he meant working here."
They returned to the store and Gabe took his position behind the register.

"I'm not just a messenger to you, Belle, I'm a guardian angel." He started cleaning out a coffee filter. "We aren't usually this hands-on but, in your circumstances, we feel you need all the help you can get. Want a latte?"
She smiled, somewhat more at ease.

"Sure."
He cursed under his breath as wet coffee grounds splashed on his shirt. Belle laughed at the absurdity of it, knowing what she knew about her coworker.

Belle remained quiet for the rest of the day. At the end of their shift, Gabe offered a ride back to her house for the dreaded confrontation with her mother. As he started the unimpressive Ford Fiesta, Belle asked.

"Couldn't you just like, fly places?"
He side-eyed her.

"This is just a little less obvious."
The car rattled towards town, bumping over stones and cracks in the asphalt before entering the smoother surfaces closer to the city itself.

"How are we gonna do this?" asked Belle at last.
He freed one hand from the wheel just to shrug.

"If she won't understand, I can help her understand."

"That sounds threatening."

"I just mean as I did for you!"
Belle switched on the radio. A low, mournful woman's voice crackled in and out, crooning about the day Billy

Joe McAllister jumped off the Tallahassee Bridge. Gabe squinted in the sun, looking like a young Clint Eastwood. This seemed to intensify the spark in his blue eyes.

"I know how you people see us down here. These divine beings." He said, more to himself than her.

"You are, aren't you?"
He shrugged again. He took in the air, which was whistling through the window and rippling his dirty blonde hair.

"This is the longest time I've spent down here. I gotta say, this is a pretty fascinating but pretty awful place." He stroked the emerging bristles on his chin. "I don't know how you all *do it*. Just endless, endless uncertainty. You're given all these conflicting rules that are supposed to be from God and told you'll go to hell if you don't follow them, only you have no proof of *anything*." He turned the radio down. "And this is now! Could you imagine 1000 years ago? Not even knowing where the sun goes at night? It's a terrifying way to live. I've got it easy." He gestured at a grassy bank at the side of the road, a ramshackle house strewn with litter, and an old mattress in the front yard. "Look at this. Sure, there's beauty in this world, but the work you have to do, the constant discomfort. The one single certainty you people have is death, and you have no proof that it leads anywhere!" He shook his head. "I would go crazy."

"Plenty of us do." Answered Belle.

"Sometimes I feel like you guys are God's big joke. At least I would if I didn't know any better." He smiled at her. "-which I do. What I'm trying to say is, I'm impressed. Humans impress me."

Belle turned to him, an eyebrow raised.

"Well, that's certainly flattering."

"I mean it. I've seen how hard you all work, the injustice you have to just carry around on your backs, never mind having to feed and wash all the time!" He shuddered. "No wonder you all sleep so much."

Belle giggled.

"I meant to thank you."

"For what?"

She turned the radio off.

"For letting me speak to him."

He smiled broadly at her, dimples gathering in his cheeks.

"My pleasure. Not that it's me you should be thanking."

Belle nodded. She rolled down the window and stuck her head out.

"Thanks, big guy!" she shouted at the clouds.

Minutes later, they arrived in the driveway of the small house she shared with her mother. The neighbourhood had been constructed in the fifties and scarcely updated since. Her mom's house had the luxury of a second floor and a coat of white paint only a few years old. It had been her grandma's before she moved into a home, and Belle had lived there since she was two. The light was beginning to fade, painting the few clouds gathering at the horizon with a light pink blush.

"Here goes nothing," said Belle, swinging open the door of the car

3
The Cause of our Salvation

One Year Earlier

Belle adjusted the collar of her 'good' shirt in the mottled mirror of her mom's ancient wardrobe. She tossed a few of her braids over her shoulder.

"I just don't see why I have to get dragged along too."

"Because your Auntie Vivienne won't leave me alone otherwise," called her Mom from the living room. She entered as Belle was taking off her hoop earrings, dressed like a wannabe Princess Diana. She put her hands on her daughters' shoulders.

"Just do this one time for me baby, and we can get a few weeks of peace from her."
Belle nodded. Her Mom kissed her cheek. "That's my girl."

The doorbell rang. Belle snapped on a smile and followed her mom to answer it. There stood Auntie Vivienne. She was wearing a lilac pantsuit and had on her usual bob wig with bright yellow tips, so opposed to the rest of her look.

"Belle, you're coming!" She cried out, stretching out her big maternal arms.

"Of course, Auntie Vivienne."

Vivienne planted two huge kisses on her cheeks and squeezed her, before readjusting her collar.

"Praise the Lord! I know you'll see the way yet!" She turned to her sister. "Cynthia, honey, don't you look so well. Ma and me always worried you would never get over Abraham *passing.*" She whispered 'passing' as if it was news to Cynthia that her husband was dead.

"It's been years now, Viv, I'm doing ok."

"Such a tragedy he never got to see what a beautiful young woman his baby girl would grow up to be! Look at those big brown eyes! Just like her grandma! Still -" she took Belle's hand and looked in her eyes "- I know he's watching y'all."

"Here's hoping." Said Belle.

"Hope? Don't hope, girl, *know* it!" Replied Vivienne, slapping Belle's hand for emphasis. Belle smiled, Vivienne always endeared herself to her one way or another. "By God, and Moses, you'll see your Daddy again, sure as my knees are giving up on me! Speaking of, Belle, sweetie -" she hooked her arm in her niece's "- give your poor old auntie a little help down these stairs."

"No problem, Auntie Vivienne."

In the car, Vivienne handed Belle a brochure entitled 'The Temple of the Staff'. Belle stifled a giggle. The cover featured a shepherd's staff backlit, with the red sea parted in the background. At the bottom right was a small picture of 'Brother Abel', the head preacher. He was around 40, with receding brown hair slightly too long, and absurdly white teeth. Otherwise, he looked like anyone else. Belle had heard of him, not just from Aunt Vivienne. She had caught snippets of his radio show and seen him on the local news, weighing in on current events. He was something of a minor celebrity, or a major celebrity if you attended his arena-sized temple regularly.

"You gals are in for a treat, I got us in the front row! That's not easy!" Said Vivienne, grabbing her sister's shoulder for emphasis. Belle thumbed through the brochure, it featured images of people with their hands raised in prayer and extracts from scriptures on floating clouds of text. On the back was a picture of a musician playing an electric guitar, complete with ripped jeans and gelled hair. Belle preferred her religion done the old-fashioned way, she had attended a synagogue with her grandma before she died and found it peaceful. Preachers like Brother Abel didn't go in for old-school rituals, she supposed that was the appeal

Aunt Vivienne turned up the radio on a gospel music station. She clapped her hands with excitement.

"I'm just so glad you agreed to come with me, Cynthia."

"Don't mention it" replied Belle's Mom, concentrating more on navigating the streets.

"I hope you realise this is all for the benefit of Maybelle." Belle raised an eyebrow but said nothing. She was used to her Aunt Vivienne speaking about her like she wasn't there. "That girl has a heart of gold, by the grace of God and the amazing job you and Abraham did, but she *needs* the lord." Her brow furrowed and her voice softened. "All of the bull these young ones get day and night thanks to the schools and the TVs, it's a wonder any of them have the strength to avoid sin. This is a time of great sin," she wagged her finger. "It's our

duty to protect the next generation. I just hope and pray Belle finds it in her heart to accept the Lord."
Cynthia turned to her sister.

"Belle isn't totally, uh, unreligious, I think she just likes to figure stuff out for herself. She's an independent-minded girl."

"No one can walk alone with God, Cynthia, you are lucky enough to have one of the greatest houses of God right on your doorstep, it's about time you took advantage of the fact."

After around 20 minutes they arrived. The parking lot alone was enormous, larger than Belle's high school grounds. The building itself was a monument on the whole landscape, a great stone structure of curving white walls and a sweeping roof, like a giant cotton blanket was lying over it. It was as if a spaceship had landed out in the middle of nowhere. A huge glass front greeted them when they got close, with a 15-foot shepherd's staff, lit up in blinding white neon. Through the doors were security sensors, and vendors selling food you could buy at any baseball game. Again Belle stifled a laugh, she half expected a mascot dressed as a giant cartoonish Moses to step out and start dancing. One word rolled over in Belle's head – money. Lots and lots of money, everything from the shiny floors to the TV screens showing the inside of the currently empty arena. Kiosks sold merchandise – t-shirts, keyrings, small books of scriptures for children, and CDs of the bands that played there. She learned from a girl in school that The Temple of the Staff had its own record label.

Aunt Vivienne was easily the most formally

dressed, it seemed the relaxed casual-cool vibe of the place had escaped her. Her sister and niece were dressed similarly, having been led to believe that everyone else would have made the same effort as Vivienne. Belle felt like she was dressed for a day in court. A great sign on the wall that read 'judgement awaits – will YOU get into heaven?' made her feel dammed already. Vivienne approached a lanyard-wearing man and handed over her ticket.

"Front row- lucky you!" he said and directed them to the right entrance.

"Is this all this place is used for?" Belle asked her Mom.

"Not always – I saw Bryan Adams live here when I was pregnant with you."

"Nice." Replied Belle, before being shushed by her aunt as they entered the arena.

The space was shaped like a petri dish with a giant arch over the main stage. It was a huge, cavernous room with a domed roof hung with a tangle of lights. The side stalls were as steep as any Belle had seen, and she breathed a sigh of relief that their front-row seats at least meant her vertigo would not be put on the spot. Still, the size of the space was dizzying. They pulled down the plastic chairs in the first row. The stage was set up for a band to play, and various roadies wearing the official t-shirts of the temple twanged guitars and turned dials on pedals. Belle felt her stomach lurch, certain Brother Abel would pick her out in a sea of hand-raising true believers.

By the time the lights dimmed the arena was all

but full. A cheer went up and a video played on the giant screen, a montage of previous services. Eventually, Brother Abel walked out. There was no voiceover introduction, but he was greeted by a roaring crowd. They all stood to their feet, Belle and her mom followed so they wouldn't stand out. Brother Abel was shorter than expected and dressed in a simple black t-shirt and jeans. He lowered his head and smiled, feigning surprise as if the huge crowd in his stadium temple surprised him. He called for silence. His wife came out, a stunning blonde woman at least ten years his junior.

"Folks, I thank you humbly for being with me here today, I extend to you my blessings," began Abel. His voice had an almost violently southern twang to it, and it boomed around the arena thanks to the Britney-Spears-style headset microphone he was wearing. "I'd like to begin just by asking you to join hands with your neighbour, just reach out and take your brother's hand or your sister's hand, and just pray with me. God -"

"God" repeated the congregation, sweaty hand holding sweaty hand.

"I come to you today,"

"I come to you today" they repeated

"As a sinner."

"As a sinner."

"But Lord God I pray,"

"But Lord God I pray,"

"That in your most blessed temple tonight"

"That in your most blessed temple tonight"

"I will be filled with your blessing and be born anew!"

"I will be filled with your blessing and be born anew."

"In the name of the Lord, our God, hallelujah."

"In the name of the Lord, our God, hallelujah."

"Thank you, my friends." Brother Abel signed off his opening prayer. The woman on the other side of Belle was already weeping.

Brother Abel took a swig of his bottled water, and his wife sat demurely on a stool next to his. He looked more like the owner of a global tech firm than a man of God. Belle just hoped audience participation was over.

"Now, tonight I want to talk about something I know none of us likes to think about. Death." He began, taking a seat next to his silent but grinning wife. "Because, folks, we will all die one of these days. I stand in front of you tonight a very lucky man. My wealth and prosperity are a sign I am truly blessed. I have my lovely wife Angela, my beautiful home, and I am fortunate enough to enjoy the fruits of my preaching in the form of financial success."

Belle rolled her eyes.

"But even I will one day end my life in this world. If you ask me, 'Abel, are you afraid of death?', I will tell you no. Because I truly believe -" here he became passionate, his voice breaking and his volume rising "-I *know* that I will return one day to the bosom of the holy father." The crowd erupted again "I *know* this to be true, ladies and gentlemen!" Angela applauded and tossed a lock of impossibly shiny blonde hair over her shoulder. She was an extremely shiny woman, Belle thought, - her hair, her teeth, her lipgloss, her tanned legs.

Abel took another swig of water, beads of sweat already glistening on his forehead.

"And it is thanks to the seeds that you all have planted-" 'seeds' here meaning the sizeable donations given by his congregation through his late-night televangelism "- that we can stand in this amazing temple tonight. Hallelujah."

"Hallelujah" repeated the audience. The crying woman next to Belle was gripping her armrest and doubled over, whispering thanks to her God. Vivienne already had a hand raised, nodding her head in agreement.

"Tonight's sermon is for those of you touched by grief. Those of you who have lost people close to you." Belle leaned into her mother.

"Crap, it's a setup!" she whispered. Her mother had wide panicked eyes, and Vivienne was already holding her hand and seeking her gaze. She turned to her daughter and gave her a fake smile. Belle sniggered, she was used to that smile.

"The world is full of sin, brothers and sisters. Full of the liars, the fornicators, the perverts, the dammed, the non-believers." Abel spat out these words. "And the *fuh-lames* of hell will come for them!"

"Spoiler alert." Said Belle. Her mom choked on a giggle.

"But if you have lost someone, I want you to speak out tonight. Because we can be reassured together that they are in the presence of the Lord." The congregation cheered again.

"So I ask you, brothers and sisters if you have lost one

of your own. Speak it now!"

Voices rolled over the arena, hands shot up, and people stood, shouting and pointing to get Abel's attention. Belle's stomach lurched again; she knew what was coming.

Vivienne's hand shot up.

"Over here! Abel! Right here, this lady here!" She pointed to her sister, who was sinking into her plastic chair. Abel noticed her of course, thanks to their enviable front-row seats. He reached out to Cynthia.

"This lady right here, come up onstage sister."

"Her daughter too!" Shouted Vivienne.

Crap, crap, crap, crap. Muttered Belle. The crying woman beside her practically shoved her towards the stage.

"God bless you, girl!" she said, through running mascara. Belle smiled weakly. She felt the hot sting of the lights as she and her mom stepped very unenthusiastically towards the grinning Brother Abel and the gorgeous Angela. All Belle could think of was the zit on her chin she had neglected to cover up.

Abel took Cynthia's hand. She could see her mother's shoulders stiffen up. She always avoided the spotlight. Angela's hand rested on Belle's equally tense shoulder. The crowd cheered. A roadie ran onstage and handed her mom a microphone.

"What is your name, sister."

"Um, Cynthia."

"Cynthia." Repeated Abel. "And tell me, Cynthia, do you come to us with grief in your heart?"

Cynthia looked to her sister for answers. She held the mic at shoulder level.

"Um, I guess" she answered.

"Louder, sister." encouraged Abel, dragging the microphone up to her lips.

"I guess?" repeated Cynthia.

"Who have you lost?"

"My husband Abraham. This was nearly 10 years ago."

"Was he involved in crime?"

"Uh...no." She replied, bristling at the question. "Heart attack."

"A heart attack," said Abel, his voice dripping with sympathy. "And this is the daughter he left behind?" He gestured to Belle.

"Yes, this is my daughter Belle."

Belle waved at the crowd, not sure of what else to do.

"You see that, folks? The world is full of undeserving single mothers, women who callously abort their babies, career women." He listed these Jezebels with a sneer. "And here we have Cynthia and her daughter, who no doubt would give anything to have their family back to how it was."

"Hallelujah! Amen!" Shouted the crowd. Angela squeezed Belle's shoulders. She looked at her and was greeted by an incredibly shiny grin.

"Tell me Cynthia darlin', was your husband a believer?"

Cynthia looked to the crowd for answers. She spoke softly with the mic some 6 inches from her lips.

"I mean... I guess... not?"

Feeling the tension in the room, she expanded. "He was a good man, he just, he just wasn't sure, you know? He just felt he needed some real proof."

Abel nodded sagely and held his hands in hers.

"Well, today we are gonna pray for your husband."

"Um..."

Before Cynthia could finish her thought, Abel's hand was resting on her head. Belle felt the shiny wife's hand grip tighter to her shoulder as if she was tense with excitement.

Abel spoke in booming tones.

"Lord in heaven, we pray you to receive the soul of Abraham, whose wife misses him so. Though he was a sinner, though he was not worthy, we ask you, God, to show him your mercy so that he may join you in the kingdom of heaven. Though Scripture tells us the unbelievers are damned, we ask you, God, to consider the grief of Abraham's widow and her struggle to raise her daughter without the sovereignty of the husband and father, the head of each family."

Belle felt her face burn, her mother held the memory of her husband as a deeply personal treasure.

"Lord we pray that Abraham will *not* be dammed to languish in hell, but be received into your heart! We ask you to accept the unbeliever! If he is in the dark, receive him back into the light! Take him to your heart! Do not cast him out into the dark! BRING HIM HOME!" and with this signoff, he pushed Cynthia backwards, just enough to make her unsteady, and the crowd exploded at what they thought was Cynthia experiencing great spiritual movement. Belle stepped forward.

"Mom? Are you OK?" She turned her mother

towards her and saw the panic and the glaze of tears in her eyes.

"I have to go." She swiftly moved down the stairs and passed the cheering crowd. Her sister reached out to her.

"Is she alright Belle?" Asked Viviene when her niece caught up with her. Belle sighed through her nose.

"I know where she'll be."

The two women walked to the bathroom, a good distance from the main auditorium. The sounds of Brother Abel's voice and the cries of his worshippers came muffled through the thick walls. Vivienne trotted ahead of belle, her heels clicking on the floor.

"Oh lord, oh my gosh" she muttered as she clicked along. Belle's brief anger towards her aunt had gone as she saw her fear for her sister.

Walking in the bathroom they heard the subdued sniffing coming from the end stall.

"Cynthia honey? It's us..."
After a beat, the door swung open and she walked out, her eyes red but otherwise composed. Her sister put her arms around her.

"Cynthy, I'm so sorry."

"I know, it's OK. I know you meant well."

"I just wanted to help you; I didn't think he would be so...personal."
Vivienne released her grip, and her sister lifted her head as more tears welled up.

"I know it seems silly. I just.... you know I don't like people to pity me."

"I know, I know"

"I just didn't like how he was talking about him. You know, asking if he was a criminal, talking about...hell and damnation"

"Hey," said Vivienne softly, lifting her head "I knew Abe better than that man. If your husband isn't in heaven, then it's no heaven at all."

Cynthia smiled again. Vivienne turned to her niece. "Belle, sweetie, are you OK?"

Belle hadn't considered that. But now, being asked, she felt herself shaking and sensed anger inside her.

"I'm OK, aunty. I just don't like seeing Mom upset."

Vivienne hugged her.

"Well, girls, I feel just terrible. Who wants to go get something to eat?"

Present day

Belle stared at her front door from the passenger seat of Gabe's car, chewing her fingernail, the door still open.

"Are you ready to go in yet?" asked Gabe after a period of silence.

"Yeah just... just a minute" answered Belle. Gabe took his hands off the wheel and rested them on his legs, tapping his fingers on his jeans. Belle took a deep breath and opened the door. "OK, now or never, let's go".

Cynthia opened her front door to a strange sight. Her daughter stood with a man she'd never seen before. A very pretty white boy too. Her daughter had a look of guilt, while the strange man she was with grinned broadly.

"Hello!" the pretty boy greeted her.

"Uh, hi."

"Mom, this is Gabe, he's the new guy from the gas station."

"Uh-huh?"

"We wanted to talk to you about something."

"I bet you do!"

"Mom!"

Cynthia chuckled.

"Come in, I just switched the AC on."

"Fantastic!" enthused Gabe. Belle winced; she knew he was playing the cheesy prom date to annoy her.

"Forgive the mess, uh, Gabe, I wasn't expecting anyone" she glanced at her daughter.

Sat at the table, each with a coffee in their hands, Belle had the strange sensation of being at a job interview.

"So, what is it you have to talk to me about?" Belle and Gabe looked at each other.

"Mom, I'm just gonna... put something to you and I don't want you to freak out, but just know that I have a really, really good reason."

Cynthia snorted a laugh.

"Well, go ahead, what is it?" She took a mouthful of coffee. Belle steeled herself.

"Mom. I'm considering...having a baby."

Cynthia choked on her coffee.

"With him?!"

"What? No!"

"Well thank God!"

Gabe bristled.

"Wait, why is that the main thing you would object to?" his protest was ignored.

"What do you mean you're considering it?? You're nineteen! You don't even have a boyfriend!"

"It's a little bit more complicated than that"

"Like how?" she snapped.

Belle stared for a moment and decided to just come out with it.

"Gabe isn't just some guy who started at the gas station. He's the archangel, Gabriel. He came to me because God wants me to carry his son and deliver a saviour to the world." She sipped her coffee.

Cynthia stared with a furrowed brow, then burst out laughing.

"I knew she'd do that."

"I'll handle it" announced Gabe. He stood up and walked behind Cynthia. She was still laughing when he placed his hands on either side of her head. Immediately her laughing stopped, her eyes closed, and she slumped forward. Gabe guided her head to the table softly, not removing his hands. Belle stood up.

"It's OK. She's OK" assured Gabe in a sotto voice He closed his own eyes, lifting his head and whispering to the heavens. He released them, and Cynthia came to.

She looked around her house as if she had just been dropped there. Then, to her daughter, gazing with wide eyes and the same look of wonder she had when she first held her as a newborn.

"Belle" she whispered, standing up "you spoke to him?"

Belle smiled and nodded. Her mother threw her arms around her and began to shake with sobs.

4
Mother to the Son

Cynthia retired to her room after mumbling something about photographs. Belle followed Gabe outside where he was leaning against the frame of the old porch swing smoking a cigarette. He didn't acknowledge her at first but surveyed the garden. The tree from her vision wasn't covered in pink blossom, but green and bursting with unpruned branches. A sad-looking tire swing hung from it, a remnant of the time Belle thought that little tree would be sturdy enough to would support a lanky kid like her.

"So this is the garden I took you to?" Asked Gabe. She nodded. The long grass hummed with crickets.

"It's a little too hot for my tastes. You could have a nice little set of patio furniture right over there." He gestured to the far corner. "I was reading in this magazine that you can plant flowers in your garden to attract specific butterflies."

"Your garden?" asked Belle.

"If I *had* a garden I would." He stomped out his cigarette and then picked it back up to throw in the trash later.

"I just find it an interesting concept. Humans take

God's creation, which could be completely rebuilt in a few seconds, and they learn about it and play with it and eventually shape it into something they like."

He looked inside for Cynthia.

"She OK?" He whispered.

Belle nodded.

"And how about you?"

Belle shifted on her feet. She had been trying to preoccupy her mind with simple thoughts of flowers attracting butterflies. It would be nice to have such a straightforward purpose.

"I think... after everything I've seen, what my Mom said, and what my Dad said... I think I'm ready."

"Are you absolutely sure?"

"Belle paused for a second. For the first time, she felt a jolt of excitement at the thought of what was to come. She nodded.

"OK then." Gabe opened the patio door and went back inside, tossing his cigarette in the trash can.

"It's done."

Belle followed him.

"What?"

"It's done, congratulations." He gestured to her belly. "You're officially expecting."

Belle stood for a moment, then followed him as he headed outside.

"Just like that?"

He nodded and smiled.

"Shouldn't there be a blinding light or something?"

Gabe opened his car door.

"Was the fox dream and the vision and me with a lion's head not enough for you?"

"But I don't *feel* any different."

"Well, you won't." He started the car
"As far as your body and anyone else is concerned, this is just a normal pregnancy. Mazel tov."
With that, he drove away.

Belle returned inside and found her mom upstairs, digging through a crate. It was filled with a few torn-up photo albums and loose dog-eared pictures and letters.

"Belle come here."
Belle knelt beside her. She had never seen her mom smile so broadly. Her cheeks were shining with tears yet to evaporate. She picked out a photo of her and Abe when they were first dating. Abe was leaning his chin on the top of her head and had a thick moustache.
"Look how handsome he was! Even with that damn moustache!"
She clasped her hand over her mouth at her blasphemy.
"Oh, gee I'm sorry."

"It's OK mom, I'm not Aunt Vivienne."
Her mom laughed.

"Take a look at this letter he wrote to me when he was away with work. I was pregnant with you at the time. He called me babushka, y'know like a Russian doll? See if you can read his handwriting, he wrote so small."

Belle squinted at the yellowing letter.
Dear Babushka
They have me up here in Washington state fixing this conveyor belt. It's been raining four days out of five. The boss is giving us free doughnuts, I'll try and sneak you some back. How is my little cheese wheel? I still

think we should call her Frances.

"Frances?"

"It was his mom's middle name."

She rooted around the plastic crate and brought out a Rosh Hashana card. Inside he had written:

To the apple of my eye,
Shana Tov, Honey!
(Womp womp)
Abe.

"Where have you been keeping all of this stuff.?"

"Just in my closet."

"Why have I never seen it?"

Her mom paused her digging. She leant back on her haunches.

"I'll be honest with you, sweetie, it just made me too sad. I know it's unhealthy to keep the stuff inside but, when you have so much do to when you're working and raising a kid, it just felt silly to wallow."

"It's not silly."

"I know now. And I regret it because you always should have known more about your Dad. I'm sorry, Belle."

Belle smiled.

"I forgive you."

"But see now, we know he's OK." Her tone perked up. "We're the luckiest people in the world. No one else gets this. I always knew you wwere special, now the whole world is gonna know it."

Belle smiled. Her mom was right. At that moment, they were the two luckiest people alive. She remembered what Gabe had just told her.

"Mom, Gabe just told me. It's a done deal. I'm

pregnant."

Her mom paused, then squealed with delight. She nearly knocked her over with an aggressive hug.

"Oh, shit, sweetie I'm sorry. I'm just so excited! I'm gonna be a grandma!"

"I thought you said you didn't care if I had kids or not?"

"Oh, I just said that to not put you under pressure. Come on, we have to celebrate! We'll order takeout and get some champagne! Oh, wait no, none for you, you can have sparkling grape juice. We need to get you some vitamins, some folic acid, I have to tell Vivienne!"

"No, wait!" Belle stopped her as she left. "We have to play this right. If everyone finds out they'll think I'm just another fallen woman. If we tell the truth they'll think I'm crazy."

Her mom sighed.

"You're right. We won't tell anyone until we have to."

"Yeah. Don't worry, I promise we'll have a baby shower, or whatever."

"Oh my gosh, we can look through some of your baby photos! Oh, Belle, you were just so cute!"

Her mom bounded out of the room. Belle had never seen her like this. She decided to roll with it. It was a good day.

That night Belle agreed to sleep in her mother's bed. Despite her age, it did give her a strange sense of comfort. Her mom sat up with her phone, looking through more old photos. In theory, Belle was trying to sleep, but in practice, she was thinking.

"Mom, what was it like when you got pregnant with me?"

Cynthia put her phone down.

"Well, I was 28, I'd been married for a year and a half. Your dad and I both worked, I had a supportive family."

"Don't rub it in."

"What I'm trying to say is..." She began stroking her daughter's hair, a trick that had always helped her sleep,
"I was still scared."

Belle flipped over to face her mom.

"Were you happy?"

"I was overjoyed. Your dad was more excited than me! He got all the books, he went to all the classes with me, he bought all these CDs of classical music to play to you before you were born to make you smart. But he was scared too, you know."

"What of?"

"He was scared we wouldn't do a good enough job. He was scared you might get sick, that you'd face all kinds of trouble. He was scared about money, most of all. And lord knows, we didn't have a situation like yours."

Belle sighed.

"That's what's occupying my mind right now, all the day-to-day stuff."

"Who was that friend of yours who got pregnant when you were in high school?"

"Becky?"

"Maybe you should meet up with her. She was young

too, and she has a little boy now. You could talk to her."
Belle considered this.

"It would be nice to see her again."

"Then there's an idea for you." Cynthia switched the
light off and lay down, facing her daughter. "And you
can always talk to me."

"And what about, the other stuff? The son of God
stuff. Does that scare you?
Cynthia stroked her daughter's hair again.

"Belle I can't claim to know about these things. But
Gabe showed me enough, and I know that you're
worthy. I'm not scared for you because I have
confidence in you. And I think that the only thing we
can do is take everything as it comes."
Belle smiled at her and closed her eyes.

Belle slept in late the next day. She expected morning
sickness or at least some physical symptom, but it
wasn't there. She went downstairs and found her mom
dressed with bags of shopping and the grill on.

"Morning, honey. I've got you some multivitamins,
folic acid, and some nice decaf tea. I'm grilling you
some bacon, that's healthier, and I'm poaching eggs.
They'll be well done; a raw egg is bad for pregnancy.
Belle smiled. Cynthia had found a new project to throw
herself into.
"I gotta say, I'm excited. I got some knitting supplies. I
haven't knitted in years! I'll make him some little
booties, I made you some just like that."

She sat down and yawned. There was a glass of
orange juice waiting and a knife and fork. The fruit
bowl on the table was brimming with apples, grapes,

bananas, and tangerines. Normally, it had one or two sad-looking black bananas in it. Cynthia put down her plate. The bacon and eggs were arranged to look like a smiley face.

"Now don't freak out, but I invited your aunt over for dinner."

"Mom!"

"Don't worry, I'm not gonna tell her!" She plated up her breakfast and sat down, "It's just that she's your aunt and we haven't seen her in a while, plus -" she sipped her decaf latte, "- she's just about the most religious person I know. She'll have useful wisdom, especially now she doesn't go to that weird cult temple anymore."

Belle conceded. The eggs were thoroughly cooked through and the bacon was completely stripped of fat and a little more well done than she preferred.

Belle had to put on her smartest clothes for Aunt Vivienne's visit. She took a moment to observe how her body was before it would change. Squinting at her reflection, she tried to look for the 'glow' everyone talked about, but it wasn't there. She looked the same as she had before. Good. Vivienne wouldn't suspect a thing. The doorbell rang and Cynthia shouted that she was fixing her hair, so Belle went to answer it. She opened the door to Vivienne, who was wearing a salmon pink pantsuit and sporting a new bob wig with a streak of red in the bangs. She threw out her arms.

"Belle! I feel like it's been forever since I saw you! I love your hair like that!" She lifted her braids to inspect them.

They embraced as Cynthia came downstairs.

"Cynth! Thank you so much for inviting me! Did you do something with the house, it looks lovely!"

Nothing had been done with the house.

At the dinner table, the three women engaged in surprisingly small talk. Belle always admired her mother's ability to keep a straight face. Vivienne had brought chicken pot pie on the provision that Belle made greens and Cynthia made the potatoes. Luckily, Vivienne was too holy to drink, so Belle didn't have to make excuses.

"Cynthia sweetie, I wanted to say something."

Oh god, though Belle.

"I just still feel so terrible about what happened last year with brother Abel."

"It's OK Viv."

"No, no it's not. I haven't been back since. He had no right to say those things about Abe. I've never said this, Cynthy, but your husband was one of the best men I ever knew."

Belle observed her mother's face. She willed her to keep it together, but she could sense it in her breathing pattern. Sure enough, she began to cry.

"Oh, sweetie, I'm so sorry!"

"No, Honestly Viv, Honestly..." Cynthia tried to dispose of her tears with the back of her hand as soon as they came.

"These are good tears."

"I always say, Cynthy, it's OK to cry."

"I know, I know."

Belle and Vivienne both got up to stand by her side at the head of the small table.

"It's just... I know you've been saying for years that he's in a good place now and I always had trouble believing it but, I can't explain how, but now I do!"

"Cynthy that's wonderful! Oh, sweetie, he'd be so happy to see you right now."

She embraced her sister and gestured at Belle to join them. She awkwardly wrapped her long arms over the two hugging women.

"Now just say if you don't want me to, but is OK if I say a prayer?"

Cynthia nodded.

Vivienne bowed her head and took her sister's hand in hers and placed the other over her niece's.

"God, I pray that you bless these girls with the peace and happiness that they deserve. I thank you for their faith, and I ask that you receive Abe Carter into your care. Amen."

"Amen."

"Amen."

"See I kept it short that time! I can shut up when I need to!"

After dinner, Cynthia brought down an album of photos from her and her sister's childhood. They sat on the faded burgundy sofa and went through each and every one, naming the people in the background. Belle sat on the mismatched navy blue armchair and just observed. It was like when she was a kid, she knew that when their conversation was flowing it would be at least an hour before she could break it. It was a wall of sound. She was privileged enough to see some pictures of her mom during a short phase when she was in her twenties and very into Queen Latifah. She made her mom promise that if she ever found her oversized gold-plated Africa necklace she could have it.

Belle took Vivienne out to her car as she was leaving.

"You know something, Belle, there's just something a little different about you tonight."
Oh no.

"Well, I don't feel any different." This was not a lie.

"I don't know, you just have some new...aura about you. If that's the word. I don't know. Is there a boy I should know about?"
Belle shook her head.
"Well, you tell me as soon as there is. Aunties need excitement in their lives and the only way we can get it is by living vicariously through our beautiful young nieces."
Belle snorted

"Text me when you're home, Vivienne, let us know when you're safe."

"I will, honey, God bless you!"
And with that, she drove away.

Belle had work the next day, starting early. She knew Gabe was working too which gave her a sense of reassurance. On her mom's instructions, she took folic acid with her oatmeal and swore not to drink any caffeine or eat any sushi. Cynthia seemed to think the gas station had far fancier food options than it did. As she dropped her off, she said

"Belle I want to invite Gabe over for dinner."

"Why?"

"Because I have a lot of questions. *A lot.*"

"Fine." Belle found herself pre-emptively cringing at what that dinner would be like.

She walked through the doors and Gabe was already there, reading a supermarket tabloid and drinking a latte. He gave her a warm smile.

"Hey. All good?"

"Yeah, my aunt came round."

"Did you tell her?"

"No. Wait, are there rules about who I can and can't tell?"

"It's up to you. You're the one they chose. I'd keep it to a minimum though."

"No doubt."

She scanned the beverage selection and found a decaf green tea,

"Working here without minor stimulants is gonna suck."

"Tell me about it. I don't even need to sleep, but I feel like I could use some."

"Oh, by the way, my mom wanted to ask if you could come for dinner."

His face lit up.

"When?"

"I dunno, tomorrow, I guess. I've got the day off and she finished at four."

"I'll be there!"

The next day, at exactly 4:30, the doorbell rang. Cynthia answered it and saw Gabe stood wearing a black suit and tie and carrying a bottle. He looked like

he was picking up a prom date.
Cynthia welcomed him in.

"I brought you some non-alcoholic champagne."

"Well thank you."

"It's actually from France. I got it this morning."

"Oh...OK. I'll pour us some."

Cynthia went into the kitchen and Gabe started looking at some family photos on the wall.

"She put a bunch of those up last night," Belle commented.

"Wow. They're so cool."

He took down one of a little girl stood in front of the same house they were in.
"Is this you?"

"No, that's my mom. She grew up here, she inherited the house when my grandma died. That's why we still have an avocado bathroom."

Cynthia came back in.

"Now, I pride myself on being a good hostess but I wasn't sure what angels eat, or if they eat. I thought we could maybe order takeout?"

"I can eat. I like it, it's fun."

"Uh...it sure is," said Cynthia, handing him a glass of champagne.

"So, Chinese?"

"Perfect!" He replied.

After the Chinese food arrived, they ate in front of the TV at Gabe's insistence. He chose Wheel of Fortune. Cynthia stared at him while he ate and laughed uproariously at the jokes the host made. Eventually, she spoke.

"So...do you have wings?"

He swallowed his chow mein.

"Uh-huh. And a lion head. Belle's seen it."

Belle nodded. Cynthia's eyes widened.

"So you're a messenger, is that right?"

"Yeah so..." he put down his chopsticks and turned to his host.

"I deliver messages of God's intention. So when Abraham learned about the birth of Isaac, that was me, and I explained Daniel's visions to him, and so on."

"So all of that's true?"

"More or less."

"And are you gonna be sticking around?"

"Normally I wouldn't but a) I've always wanted to try living on Earth and b) Belle is young and this is a complicated era you're in so I suggested staying on Earth as her guide."

"So you're like a very hands-on Guardian angel."

"Exactly!"

Gabe picked up his chow mein again and the three of them resumed eating. The contestant on TV won $10,000 and said she was going to use it to go to college.

"Uh, that's so great," Gabe commented.

Cynthia sighed.

"I'm sorry, I'm just finding all this hard to understand."

Gabe returned his food to the TV tray.

"Tell me which parts are hard, Cynthia, I'll do my best to help you."

Cynthia was struck dumb for a moment, taken aback by the intense direct eye contact he was giving her. She shuffled in her seat.

"Well, you say she's going to have a baby and it's...God?"

"He'll be the Son of God, so it's God, but in a human body. Like two leaves of the same plant."

"But...why?"

"Good question." He held both her hands in his. Cynthia looked over at her daughter to raise her eyebrows.

"God loves all his people like you love your daughter. He is sending his son here to be with you and to serve you, and to know you better. To know what it's like to be a human and experience your suffering. That's his sacrifice."

"Sacrifice?"

"By suffering in life as a human he is sacrificing himself for humanity the same way people used to sacrifice things for him. He will take on the burden of humanity's sins and give them a better chance to move on from them."

"OK...I think I get it. So, why Belle?"

"Because we believe she turned out really well and she's exactly the right person to be a mother to God's son. She has grace and kindness and strength. And a lot of that is down to you and Abraham, Cynthia, so you are truly blessed."

Belle could sense in her mother's breathing that the tears were brewing, but this time she was able to swallow them down.

"Well, you know, we tried our best. But she got this good because that's who she is."

They finished their food and then Gabe began exploring his first human home. His first stop was the record collection.

"I love Billy Joel!" He spun a record and sang along. His voice was like silk.

"You're a really good singer," remarked Belle.

"I'm an angel, it's like 70% of what we do."

Next was the kitchen. It still had the same cheap wood cabinets and linoleum Cynthia had grown up with and the same kitschy tiles with farmhouse scenes. He opened a drawer of miscellaneous items and started foraging for shiny trinkets. He picked up a nine-volt battery and licked it.

"Oh cool, it gives you a little shock!"

"Did you not know that already? You just decided to lick it?"

"Yeah, can I keep this?"

Belle nodded.

He also asked to keep a souvenir wooden spoon from a relative's trip to the Statue of Liberty. Upstairs, he found the box of photos Cynthia had been searching through a few days earlier. His favourite photo was a blurry one of a pair of shoes worn by Belle's dad that he had taken by accident. As he left, he gave Cynthia and Belle a copy of his cell phone number.

"Anything you need you just call me. I don't have to sleep so it's whatever if you wanna talk at three am."

"OK, I'll keep that in mind." Answered Cynthia.

"OK, take care. Love you both!"

With that he strolled happily into the night, leaving both women a little stunned. It made sense that a celestial being sent to guide them would love them, but it was odd to hear from a man they had known for a week.

     Cynthia broke the silence.

     "So, he was intense."

     "Yeah, he is."

     "I'm glad he's here for us."

     "Me too, mom."

Cynthia smiled at her, then went in for a hug.

     "This is gonna be tough. We both know you can do it." She broke the hug and looked up at her daughter's face.

"We'll keep this a secret until we can't anymore. And whatever anyone says about you, it's none of their business. They'll have to answer to me."

     Later that night Belle dug in a drawer to find her old yearbook. Under 'S' she found Becky Schneider. There was a picture of her smiling with poker-straightened hair and wide blonde highlights. She sniggered at the memory of her nose ring that got her detention. Under her picture was the quote

   'You miss 100% of the shots you don't take' – Wayne Gretzky'
     -Michael Scott.'

Next to her photo, she had written;

   'Belle, it was the best of times, it was the blurst of times. Love you! Call me!'

Under that was her number.

     Belle dialled not knowing what to expect. She felt guilty for having lost touch with Becky, but it was hard when someone so young had a baby to look after. Just as Belle realised her own meagre social life would disappear when she had her own, Becky answered.

"Hello?"

"Heyy, Becky, it's me, Belle. Look I'm so sorry I haven't called. -"

"Belle! Oh my God! It's so great to hear from you!"

With that, they talked like old friends.

5

Our Lady of Good News

A week later Belle arranged to meet Becky and her little boy at a local diner. In the week since Gabe's dinner visit, Belle had felt more like a pregnant woman. She began reading up on the progression of a fetus and learned things she never knew. Like how they develop a covering of hair in the womb, and how her organs would shift around to accommodate him. The biggest thing missing from her life was caffeine, working early shifts at the gas station with an increasingly chatty Gabe was not easy. He asked strings of inane questions about humans' daily lives. Why do they need to know what the weather is going to be like? Why do they sometimes wear sweaters with shorts? What are ramekins for? Mostly, she didn't have any answers. Becky was late, which was typical. Belle ordered a strawberry milkshake and waited for her. The diner was a 50's-themed temple of shiny red metal near Beale Street. She chose the booth built into an old Cadillac, knowing Becky would appreciate the corny aesthetic. Eventually, Becky arrived, with little Joey on her hip. She embraced Belle when she saw her, and as she pulled away Joey grabbed one of her braids.

"Oh man, I'm sorry. Joey, drop it."

"It's OK," laughed Belle, although the strength of a two-year-old surprised her.

Becky's appearance was a little startling. Her hair was back to a natural brown and in a ponytail. She wore a hoodie and jeans instead of the neon-coloured clothes with chains and badges that Belle remembered. Her style seemed to have been transferred to Joey, he had a fetching Star Wars shirt, little white jeans and tiny boots made to look like doc martens. He looked healthy, his cheeks were rosy and he had a little mop of light brown hair. He had his mom's big hazel eyes. Becky was wearing a necklace with a little silver uterus on it, a sign that fire was still there. Belle had dug out an old friendship necklace they had bought along with other friends at school, a slice of pizza on a chain that when put together made a whole pie.

"Oh my God, you found that? I have no idea where mine is!"

Belle waved it away.

"Pizza is in the heart, not around the neck."

A waiter brought over menus and a set of crayons and paper for Joey. He began to chew on them with his emerging teeth. Becky had to reach into his mouth and dig out little bits of powder blue Crayola.

"He's so big now, I haven't seen him since he was a newborn."

"It's honestly scary how fast they grow, he's so heavy."

Belle passed him a piece of paper to scribble on.

"Could I hold him?"

"Sure!"

Becky passed him over, pretending to walk him across

the table. Belle felt a surge of fear that as soon as she held him she would freak out about her impending motherhood. He really was heavier than he looked. She sat him on her knee and he looked straight at her. "You won't have him long before he wants food again. He's obsessed with food. He's gonna end up one of those guys that eat 50 hot dogs at the state fair."

Joey reached out and grabbed Belle's lower jaw. She pretended to eat his hand and he giggled. Her ability to mildly amuse a toddler reassured her.

Becky scanned the menu. "Thanks for arranging this, by the way, Belle, I hardly ever get to do fun stuff anymore. I'm feeling like...fish tacos."

"Who invented those? It doesn't really go together."

"You don't like fish tacos?"

"They're fine it just seems odd. They used to serve them in the school cafeteria, they sucked."

"Yeah, but they were just fish sticks in a tortilla."

"True, true. I've been all about meatball subs lately."

"Oh?"

"Yeah, I'm just craving them all the time."
Becky looked up from her menu.

"Craving, huh?"
Belle changed tact.

"Yeah, you know I just got a taste for them. I mean, the mac and cheese look good."
This was tactical, mac and cheese was Becky's favourite.

"Ooh, they have that?"

"Yeah, it has breadcrumbs on top. Comes with garlic bread."

"Noice."

As Belle began to feel at ease little Joey launched his head forward and knocked it on the table. He began to wail, red in the face.

"Oh no, Joey I'm so sorry!"

"He's OK, he's just a drama queen, here..."

Becky took him back. He began to calm down in her arms and she repeatedly kissed his forehead at the epicentre of the table incident. His wailing turned down to a coughing splutter and a lady who had been giving them the stinkeye returned to her crossword puzzle.

Becky rocked him back and forth until he fully returned to his serene state.

"There there, peanut, auntie Belle didn't mean it."

"I'll get him a bloody mary, that should cheer him up."

Becky giggled.

"Don't worry about it Belle, you'll be totally fine once you have your own baby."

"You think so? I have to admit I'm terrified -"

It was too late to backtrack.

"I *knew it!*" Becky shout-whispered.

"It's... it's not a big deal."

"Beeeelle as if! A good girl like you?"

"You cannot tell anyone, Becky, I'm serious."

"I would never." She giggled. "It's pretty funny watching you get mad, you're like the least intimidating person ever."

Belle slumped back.

"What gave me away?"

"I had my suspicions when you called me out of

the blue, everyone's been so busy since high school, especially me, and who just *calls* people? *On the phone? I knew it was a big deal.*"

"I am serious though, you really cannot tell anyone."

Becky leaned forward.

"Belle, I promise. After all the s-h-i-t I went through when I got pregnant and the whole school knew, I would never do that to anyone."

Belle smiled.

"I knew you were a real one."

The waiter came over. Belle ordered her meatball sub and Becky got mac and cheese.

When the waiter was out of sight and the family in the next Cadillac left, Becky leaned forward and spoke in hushed tones.

"Who's the father? Is it classified?"

"Super classified."

"Is it that guy you took to prom, I liked him."

"No, that would actually be way less complicated."

"What is it like, a married senator or something?"

She laughed.

"Even that would be less complicated."

"God, Belle. How far along are you?"

"Like a week?"

"And are you gonna...keep it?"

Belle nodded.

Beck mouthed the word 'fuck'.

"You're a dark horse. You really can't tell me?"

Belle exhaled.

"I really, really wish I could, but you wouldn't believe me, you'd think I was crazy. And I cannot risk it getting out. Me and my mom, we'd both be in danger." She leaned forward. "I wanted to talk to you because you're a good friend. I can't tell you what the deal is but I know I can trust you not to tell a soul."
Becky paused, then nodded.
"I don't really care about you, but you know I'd die for Cynthia."
Belle smiled.

Their food arrived. Belle knew to wait until the mac and cheese were gone before continuing the conversation, but to her surprise, she spoke again after her first mouthful.
"I just can't get over this, you're just always the sensible person."
She didn't know how to respond, so she just shrugged.
"I mean, you're a terrible liar, so good luck keeping it secret."
"Thanks."
Becky returned to her food. The meatball sub wasn't great, there wasn't enough sauce. Once Becky had finished Belle began her questioning.
"When everyone found out at school, you kind of disappeared for a while. What happened?"
Becky hugged Joey tighter before answering.
"My mom kicked me out."
"Oh, Becky, I'm sorry."
"It's OK. After I had Joey we started talking again. We're OK now. I stayed with my aunt up in Virginia while I was pregnant. I gave birth up there."

"And the father?"

"Not a cent, not a word."

"Man, what a dick. Sorry, Joey."

Joey was nonplussed.

"He was. As soon as I skipped a period he iced me completely. Then he told everyone. I got hate mail, someone egged my house. Some old lady I didn't even know spat on me in the street."

"That sucks, I had no idea it was that bad."

"You and the other girls were always nice to me though, that helped."

Belle felt a pang in her chest.

"I just feel so bad that I lost touch."

"Belle, it's fine. *I* lost touch. But don't worry," she gestured between the two of them "We'll be in the young mommy club together soon, we can help each other out."

After half an hour Becky had to leave to meet her mom. They embraced at the door and Belle turned to head back inside.

"Hey, Belle." Said Gabe.

She jumped out of her skin. He was standing next to the dumpster, still Wearing the gas station uniform.

"Gabe, don't do that! You can't spook a pregnant lady."

He held his hands up in apology.

"I'm sorry, I know it's creepy, I just like to have fun sometimes."

"What are you doing here?"

"Your mom said you were meeting a friend, I wanted to make sure you were being discreet."

Belle moved quickly towards him, scanning the immediate area for eavesdroppers.

"I *am*." She whispered. "Look...I told her I was pregnant but I didn't tell her how."

Gabe pinched his nose.

"She's my friend, I can trust her."

He sighed.

"OK. If you trust her, then so do I."

"Even if I did tell her I'd been chosen by God to bring his son into the world in a virgin birth she wouldn't tell."

"Alright, alright, keep your voice down."

She checked herself.

"Sorry."

"I'm just trying to protect you."

"I know I know."

"So just your mom knows?"

"Yeah."

"You haven't told your aunt?"

"No. Although she'd be delighted to be a great aunt to the almighty. That's if she believes me."

"Well, she can find out in her own time." Gabe leaned against the wall and sighed. "I just...people can be cruel. If they hear the truth, they might reject it."

"I know. I wouldn't blame them."

"Let me give you a ride home."

At Gabe's car, he paused to open the trunk.

"I got you some stuff."

"You and my mom."

"Yeah well she said she got you vitamins, folic acid and stuff, so I went down the literature route."

He handed her a stack of books with smiling pregnant women and new mothers on the covers.

"So, you and my mom are friends now."

"We text, she has a lot of questions."

"Makes sense."

The ride back was mostly quiet. At around the halfway point of the journey, Belle spoke.

"I've not said this, but I think I always believed."

"In what?"

"In God. I couldn't rationalise why, but it always just made sense to me. I felt it in my heart, you know? It was like an instinct. Like how I know my own name. I feel it like I feel the weather. And I get it, I get why people don't believe, it's a completely logical and smart thing to be sceptical about something you have zero proof of, and it feels like we figure out more stuff every day. But for me, it's just always been there. Like air. Like eyesight. I can't imagine being without it. I didn't go to these big temples like aunt Vivienne because that just...was not God to me. In my own way, though, I always had faith."

Gabe smiled.

"I know."

6

Our Lady of Sorrows

Five weeks later.

Gabe had insisted on booking an early ultrasound scan.
By this point, morning sickness had kicked in, and her
emotions were in overdrive. She cried at a dog food
commercial and nearly snapped at a customer who paid
with a bag of pennies. Gabe had covered for her on a
few days when she felt rotten. Her mom had sent her a
bunch of emails about local yoga classes for expecting
mothers, but Belle pointed out that would raise too
many questions. She had basic health insurance
through her mom and Gabe had promised to pay for
any extra fancy stuff himself. Becky had been in
constant contact through text, she had told her about
every little pang and sensation, everything she had to
expect. Cynthia had been reading the books Gabe got as
much as her daughter. She made her sign up for some
service that texted her updates on the baby's growth.
The morning of the scan she learned that by now her
baby looked like a little tadpole, with bumps where its
arms and legs would be, and had a heartbeat. His heart
was a pulsing bulge on his chest, and he was the size of
a pea. The concept of another human growing inside

her still felt alien, her plan had always been to consider her motherhood prospects at the age of 30. Gabe had booked her a scan at some out-of-town hospital to avoid running into anyone she knew. He was called into work at the last minute. She made her way alone.

She stared at her phone, the little arrow representing her was not doing what she was doing. Her surroundings were unfamiliar, a pretty nondescript part of town with some office buildings and what looked like a depot where they process garbage. She checked her phone signal and it was fine. She reasoned a little meteorite had hit the Google satellite or something.

There was a boy of about 16 waiting at a bus stop. She figured he must know the area if he was getting a bus from there. She approached him. The sun was beginning its western descent.

"Excuse me?"

He looked up and greeted her with a smile. He was a mixed-race kid with long curly hair and a warm sort of face.

"I'm looking for the hospital but I think I must be miles off, I have maps open but it's not working. Do you know the way?"

He stood up to take a look at her phone. From the corner of her eye belle saw someone running around the corner, which she ignored.

"Um, yeah it's like a mile west from here... So you just-"

A screeching car interrupted him. It was following the running man and someone was hanging out of the window shooting at him. Belle screamed. The sound of gunfire was louder than she could have ever imagined. The man was running towards them.

"We have to run!" the boy said, grabbing her hand.

A spray of bullets followed them as the man came up behind them. They tried to pick up speed. Belle caught a glimpse of the scruffy, blonde-haired man holding the gun. The boy holding her hand dropped.

"Shit!" came a voice from the car. It screeched its wheels and sped away. The running man briefly looked back at Belle and the boy before disappearing around the corner.

For a second Belle was pinned to the spot. Then, the boy let out a whimper of pain.

She dropped to her knees beside him. He was on his side with his hand over his stomach.

"Oh my god are you hit? Can you talk?"

He didn't answer, but Belle could see the blood on his hoodie where he was clutching at his stomach.

"OK. It's OK. I'm calling 911, just keep your arm pressing it like that."

She looked back a few yards at where her phone had fallen, and as she got up to retrieve it he grabbed her.

"Please don't leave me. Don't go. You can use mine."

Looking down at him, she felt older than she ever had. She knelt back down and held his other hand.

"I'm here."

He handed her his phone and she dialled the number.

"I know this is weird, but, could you just hug me? Please?"

"Of course I can."

She knelt at his head and lifted him up, cradling him.
He gripped hold of her arms as the phone rang.

"What's your name?"

"Reece"

"OK Reece, I'm Belle. Just try and stay calm, I'll
get you some help."

The line crackled.

"911 what's your emergency?"

"I need an ambulance, someone's been shot."
Reece gripped her arm tighter as he curled up in pain.

"OK, and where are you located?"
She spun her head around and saw a faded sign on the
side of a building.

"I'm at the bottom of Memphis Depot Parkway,
outside the garbage depot. Please hurry, he's in a lot of
pain."

"We'll send an ambulance right away. Are you
with the patient now?"

"Yeah."

"I'm gonna need you to keep the pressure on the
wound and keep talking to him, try and make sure he
remains conscious. Someone will be there soon."

"OK. OK thank you."

She hung up, not sure if that was what she
should do. Reece was crying into the crook of her elbow.

"It's OK Reece, you're gonna be alright."

"I can't afford it. The ambulance, my mom lost
her job, we can't afford it."

"That doesn't matter right now, hey, look at me"
He turned his head towards her.

"If I have to rob a bank to help pay for it I will."
He laughed weakly and was quickly overcome with

sobs.

"Hey, come on, just hold my hand it's OK, they'll be here soon."

His breathing was torn and ragged.

"It's OK to be scared, but you will be fine, I promise you."

"I'm gonna die, I know it"

"No you're not, you can do this, come on."

Belle's eyes were blurred.

"I don't wanna die, please."

"You won't, they'll be here any second."

"My mom, you gotta call my mom."

"Of course."

She found his Mom in his contacts. It was only when the phone rang that she realised what she was about to tell her. A woman's voice broke through the static signal, speaking in a jolly tone, not unlike the one Belle's mom used in phone conversations.

"Hey sweetie, when are you home."

"Um, I'm sorry, you don't know me but I'm with your son and"

She had to take a second just to swallow her unsteadiness.

"I'm so sorry, he's been shot. I've called an ambulance, it's on its way."

"What? how?" her voice immediately broke. "Let me speak to him."

She handed Reece his phone.

"Mom? Mom, I'm scared."

Belle could hear his mother's voice faintly. All that was coming through was her telling her son she loved him and promising she was on her way. Reece was returning his mother's declarations of love. The noise of the siren drew closer.

The paramedics brought him into the ambulance on a stretcher.

"Can she stay with me?" asked Reece as Belle let go of his hand.

"Is she family?"

"Um, well,"

"I'm his sister" answered Belle.

The ride to the hospital felt like it took forever. For a while, Reece squeezed her hand as paramedics worked over him. His phone remained at his ear, his mom reassuring him he would be OK.

His grip loosened.

"He's lost consciousness" announced a paramedic, cutting through Belle's spaced-out brain fog.

She stepped back and let them work. He looked so much paler than when she'd first seen him.

She could finally feel present in the moment. What she had done up to then felt entirely like instinct, not a choice. She suddenly felt the demanding sensation of her heart pounding and the heaviness in her limbs. She couldn't hear a thing.

Between that moment and when she got to the hospital was a blur. She was sitting in the emergency room staring at her hands when Reece's mom arrived.

She was a short, dark-skinned woman with loose curls, belle recognised her shaking voice when she asked the receptionist where her son was. Her name was Annette. She gripped tight onto belle's hand as she led her towards her son.

Belle held back while Annette walked into the room where her son was lying, in a tangle of wires. She kept her composure while the doctor spoke to her. When he was gone, she sat next to his bed, held his hand, and stroked his forehead. She whispered to him, declarations of love Belle knew she wasn't meant to hear.

She walked back to the waiting room, feeling as though her head was twenty pounds heavier. There, she dispensed a cup of water with shaking hands. She spotted a toddler next to the water cooler, staring. She managed to wave at him.

The small boy's face crumpled and he ran crying to his mother. He looked back over at Belle and screamed into his mother's arms. She looked down and saw why he was so afraid. She was drenched in blood. Her hands had left red fingerprints on the polystyrene cup and her clothes were stuck to her body.

An urgent beeping sound snapped her back into the situation. A doctor ran through the waiting room towards the ward where Reece was with his mother. She dropped the water and ran after him. The long sterile corridor was empty. It echoed with the doctor's footsteps and hers. It was like a dream she often had where she was running only to find she was stuck in one spot.

After what seemed like an age she reached Reece's room. His mother was standing outside, her body vibrating. In the room, the beeping was louder. Doctors and nurses were massaging his chest. One used a defibrillator and Annette jolted as though they were using them on her instead. She was muttering under her breath *please, please*.

Belle was frozen. Despite the blood on her, despite seeing the bullets land, she somehow felt it was impossible he wouldn't make it. Things like that don't just happen, they can't. She had read about them, sure, but they didn't happen, not like this. But sure enough, the doctors gave each other a look that said everything.

Annette let out a wailing cry and her knees crumpled. Belle did her best to catch her and held her close as she sobbed. Annette's soft arms clung tight to her as the doctors noted the time. Belle felt her own tears coming and cursed them, they were not for her to shed.

Belle stayed with Annette and held her hand in a quiet staff room the hospital had put them in. Eventually, she took a deep breath and spoke.

"Is... Is his dad coming?"

Annette took a moment to wipe her face, valuing her dignity.

"He's working down in Mexico. The doctors say they'll inform him."

There was silence again, which Annette broke.

"Tell me how it happened, Belle. I need to know."

Belle filled her lungs with all the air that would fit in them. She tried to tell the story as matter-of-factly as possible.

"I called an ambulance and he was upset and he asked me to hold him, and to call you. He wanted to speak to you most of all." She finished.

Annette nodded.

"Why were you going to the hospital?"

Belle wondered whether to tell her, whether it would seem cold.

"I'm pregnant. I was going to my first scan."

Annette's eyes widened.

"Oh my God..."

Belle shrugged.

"It's fine, trust me."

A doctor knocked on the door.

"Mrs Letsky? Your husband's on the phone."

Annette got up. Before leaving she turned to Belle.

"Thank you, Belle."

Then she left her alone. For the first time that day, Belle allowed herself to cry. It came out of her like a waterfall, halfway between sobbing and gasping for air.

She placed her hand on her stomach and thought for a second about how she would feel if it happened to her boy. Then came a realisation. The true purpose of God sending his son to earth, and what it all meant. With that, she stood up. Her tears stopped and she walked down the winding corridor and out of the hospital.

She walked two miles to Gabe's apartment with the address he had texted her a week earlier, clutching a thin cardigan around her. It was getting dark outside but it didn't slow her down. His apartment was in a modern built brown and grey block with a flat roof. A street light outside kept flickering on and off. She buzzed on the apartment labelled 'G. Smith' as he had instructed. His voice crackled in.

"Who's this?"

"It's me."

"Belle! Hey! Come on up!"

She opened the glass door and went up the stone stairwell. The sickly blue lights were on sensors and flickered on as she ascended to the third floor.

She knocked on the door and he opened it with a

pre-emptive grin on his face. The smile dropped when he saw the blood.

"Oh, no, Belle!" He scooped her inside and shut the door. "Are you hurt? What's happened?"

"It's not mine" she answered.

She took in her surroundings for a moment. The apartment was a studio, with no bed because he didn't need it. He had a floral grandma sofa facing a blaring TV. Stacks of books dotted the room.

"Belle?"

"I'm starving."

"Wait right there. No wait, take a seat."

He turned off the TV and raided a cupboard in his kitchenette. She sank into the sofa, feeling its cheap foam cushions deflate and touching its thick surface embossed with flowers. A large ink stain blotted out a rose on the armrest. Gabe handed her a bag of chips and a pack of peanut butter cups. She tore open the chips as he sat down on the matching footstool accompanying the sofa.

He waited for her to swallow her first mouthful.

"Tell me what happened."

She took a breath.

"I was walking to the hospital and I got lost. I asked this boy for directions and a car came out of nowhere shooting at some guy and they got him." Her eyes began to prickle with hot tears. "I called an ambulance and went with him to the hospital and I held him on the road and he died. His mom came and she watched him die."

For the first time since she met Gabe, he seemed lost for words.

"Belle...I'm so sorry, that's terrible."

"Gabe I need to know."

"Know what?"

"Are they going to kill my son?"

Gabe jumped a little at her question.

"What do you mean?"

"You said he was coming here as a sacrifice. To suffer like a human. Maybe this is naïve but I guess I thought that just meant living a human life, and experiencing the pain and loss we all do, but it doesn't, does it? It means he has to die. He has to be killed. That's a sacrifice."

Gabe paused.

"Belle, I-"

"Gabe, do not lie to me."

"I would never."

"Then tell me the truth. Will I have to raise my son to be killed?"

He stood up. Belle was shaking, her voice torn.

"Will I?"

Gabe ran his hand through his hair.

"I don't know."

She laughed.

"Don't bullshit me. You're an archangel, my guardian angel, God's messenger, that's the entire point of you."

"I swear, it's the truth. I don't know."

"This may be some divine mission to you, Gabe, but you have no idea what it means to be human. No amount of game shows and books and texting my mom is going to teach you what it's like when someone dies, or when a loved one suffers. I saw a mother watch her son die today, her healthy, beautiful son, and it was the ugliest, most desperate thing ever. How am I supposed to care for my boy, my flesh and blood, knowing I'll have to do the same?"

Gabe said nothing.

"Answer me." She stood up. "If you are actually trying to help me then tell me the truth."

He looked her in the eyes.

"Belle, this is the truth I promise you. I don't know. I would tell you if I did. Everything I told you is what God told me."

She studied his face. Could an angel lie? She made an effort to take one extended breath and gather herself. Looking at his face, she believed him. She sat back down.

"Then what am I supposed to do? Just raise my boy not knowing?"

"You were chosen for your strength along with everything else."

"Forget that." She put her head in her hands. "I'm not like you, I'm not divine. That's the point, right? I'm flesh and blood. Right now I don't give a shit if I can handle watching my baby die, all I care about is making sure it won't happen."

Gabe sat next to her.

"I don't know what to say, Belle. I just don't have all the answers." He put his hand on her shoulder, which Belle sensed was a gesture he had learned from TV, "In many ways, you're in charge here. You were chosen, I'm just here to help."

Belle was still shaking.

"I know I can't learn everything about humans from

books, but I know you're in shock right now. Here, lie down, I'll make some tea, you have to take it easy."

"No." Belle retorted. "I want to go home, I want to be by myself."

Gabe sighed, defeated.

"Then let me drive you, at least."

Belle agreed.

Gabe knew enough not to talk on the drive home. As he pulled up to her door he asked:

"Are you sure you don't want to talk more about it?"

Belle considered. Despite knowing he hadn't lied, she felt angry with him. She shook her head and he drove away.

She stepped inside, and her anger felt good. It was a warming force inside her, a protective fire. At that moment she didn't need to be the perfect, chaste woman chosen for a divine mission, she knew she was still just another human. She could still feel the satisfying swell of anger inside and become a larger force. *Gabe,* she thought, *perfect Gabe, perfect Abercrombie model-looking Gabe.* He would never understand, she thought, how good it feels to feel pissed off.

The TV flickering on in the living room snapped her out of her fog. She assumed it was her mother coming home.

"Mom?"

Her mother wasn't there. The room was dark as she had left it, but the TV was on. The weather report. She reached for the remote but it wouldn't turn off. As she fumbled with the batteries the smiling face of the weatherman flickered for a moment. Belle didn't notice.

"Hello, Belle." A voice, coming from the TV, but not the voice of the weather mans'. A low, toneless voice. She looked up. The picture was flicking from the weather report to the image of a man in a chair. At first, it was so choppy she couldn't make out the man or what he was saying. Then the weather report stopped showing.

The image was then of a man sitting in silence in a red leather chair. He was dressed in an all-black suit, his legs crossed and his hands resting on his lap. He stared out at Belle, he had an odd face, a long nose with high and prominent cheekbones and flat, dark eyes like an animal. His hair was greying, but he looked like he may have been handsome once.

"You seem surprised that I'm talking to you like this. Can you be shocked by anything anymore?" Belle knew she should have been terrified but she felt calm. She sat on the floor to face the man.

"Who are you?" she asked. The man paused. He stared out as if trying to answer telepathically.

"My first name was the Accuser."

"And what is your name now?" The man made a noise something like a laugh.

"You're a smart girl Belle, can you figure it out?" Belle didn't answer. "I was like your friend Gabe once. I outgrew it. I'm here because I can offer you something different."

"Different to what?"
The man stared out again, unblinking.

"I know how scared you are Belle. And I think you're right. I think your son is being sent here to die. It doesn't have to be that way. I broke free from my servitude and so can you."

At that moment it hit her who the man on the TV was. She felt dumb for only just having worked it out.

She'd met an angel, she'd glimpsed heaven, she'd been given a divine mission, it made sense that eventually, the devil would knock on her door. She felt searing rage towards him. Ugly anger that felt like sickness, not like her anger before.

"Has the penny dropped? I understand you're scared of me Belle but there's no need to be." Before he could say anything else she unplugged the TV and the screen went black. She took a deep breath and switched on the light. Then she saw him, sitting in her grandma's old armchair.

Everything in her told her to grab something and attack, like any other home intruder, but she was paralysed in his presence.

"Don't worry," he said in a low and calm voice "I won't hurt you. What is it they say? Oh yes, 'Be Not Afraid.'"

"Get out." She spoke as loudly and definitively as she could but her words were choked. He looked at her with something close to sympathy.

"Have a seat Belle." Under his control, she sat. He smiled at her, a smile that didn't reach his eyes. "I'm here to help you. Since Gabriel came to you you've been desperately looking for another person to talk to, another perspective. Your father, that friend of yours, well, no one can give you a better second opinion than me."

"I don't need your opinion." She snapped the words at him. His eyes narrowed.

"Why is it you people hate me so much? We're the same − I ate the forbidden fruit too. I threw off my chains and discovered my full potential. I embraced the true extent of free will just like you people. And I have been cast out for thousands of years. And look at you, ignorant creatures basking in God's light who don't understand it, let alone deserve it." He leaned back in the chair and scratched his chin. "I don't hurt people, except bad people, and even then they're already dead. I don't make evil, people do." He winced. "Right now there's a man on the radio blaming me for school shootings. Let me tell you, those evil little bastards know exactly what they're doing when they spray their classmates with bullets just because they can't get a date. I hate those little fuckers." He smiled at her. "And yes, unlike your friend Gabe I can use bad language and hate people as much as I want. Thousands of years later and freedom is still so sweet to me. Hatred feels good to you too, sometimes, doesn't it?"

Belle took in a sharp breath.

"Whatever you're offering I don't want it. I had the chance to say no and I said yes. I know it could be hard but I also know that I'm strong enough. So I don't need you. I have Gabe and my Mom and my friends, that's all the support I need."

He rolled his eyes.

"Twenty minutes ago you said you would do anything to stop your son from suffering the same fate."

"Not anything that you would have me do"

"Do you really think your 'inner strength is going to make it OK? However good you are at dealing with grief it still cuts like a dagger."

Belle bristled.

"Well if I'm not strong enough then my son will be."

He scoffed.

"Do you have any idea how painful it is for mothers who lose their children? Human empathy isn't as powerful as you think, you can't imagine what Anette is dealing with right now. It has destroyed her. Reece was her only child, did she tell you that? Do you have any idea what you're going to have to put up with when your story gets out? And it will get out unless I help you.

Didn't I do enough today?"

"Enough what?"

He paused for a moment, then laughed. A real laugh this time, loud and unrestrained.

"I have a confession to make, Belle, you know how the map on your phone took you to the wrong part of town? I may have made that happen."

Her stomach lurched. She could still feel her clothes sticking to her skin with drying blood.

"What are you saying?"

"I just made sure you were in the right place at the right time. Just to give you a little taste of what was to come." He saw the expression on her face. "Come on, I didn't kill him, and before you ask I didn't *make* the other guy kill him either. All I did was work out where events would lead and put you at the scene. If anything I made it easier for Reece because you were there to comfort him when he died. So, you're welcome. See? I'm not so bad after all."

Belle thought of things to say, like 'how could you', or things to call him, but what was the point? He leaned over and held her hand, It sent a jolt through her from how human it felt. No flames, hooves, or cold icy fingers, just a hand.

"Belle, listen to me. I can keep him safe. Forever, you and your son. Whatever pain is planned for him I can stop it. All you have to do is talk to me, tell me things, about your friend the angel, about the world, and maybe run a few errands for me. It would be nothing. And I can keep you safe, forever." His face was close to hers. "What do you say?"

She looked at those flat black eyes and felt the anger rise again. She stood up.

"Get the fuck out of my house."

He paused for a moment then stood.

"Very well. The offer is still there. If you want it. I

take it you won't shake my hand." She did her best to stare him down. He headed for the door.

"Becky is right. You really can't be intimidating. I will speak to you soon, Belle." With that, he was gone.

She didn't move from the chair until five minutes later when her mom came home. She rushed to her side.

"Sweetie, Gabe called and told me everything, are you alright?"

She shook her head, then cried in her mother's arms.

7
The Black Madonna

The next day she woke up to her phone beeping. A missed call from Mr Lowe. She cursed as she went to messages.

"Maybelle, honey it's me. Gabe called last night and told me what happened yesterday, he said you won't be in today. Don't worry about this place, we'll be just fine. Take a couple of weeks off and get some rest. See you soon."

She breathed a sigh of relief. Her mom came in with a cup of coffee.

"Morning sweetie." She set it down on the bedside table. "How are you feeling?"

Belle sipped the coffee.

"Pretty terrible, but better now I've slept."

Cynthia sat next to her and pushed some stray baby hairs out of her face.

"Listen, some cops are downstairs to talk to you."

Belle buried her head in her knees and groaned.

"It's fine, take all the time you need. I told them to either wait until you're ready to talk or go away."

Belle smiled.

"Thanks, mom."

"I'll stall them as long as you need."

Cynthia left and she flopped backwards, sipping her coffee leisurely.

After her coffee, she picked out an outfit and went downstairs to greet them. Her feet felt ten times as heavy as she dragged them downstairs, creating static on the old paisley carpet. In the living room were two cops, twiddling their thumbs. They were not used to not being offered a hot beverage. They stood as she entered.

"Miss Carter.

"Ms."

"Right, Ms Carter, I'm detective Christopher this is Officer Fleischer. We'd like to ask you a few questions about what you witnessed yesterday."

Belle nodded and sat down. Christopher was older, he had a flat top and a barrel chest. Fleischer was dark-haired and was trying out newly relaxed Police rules on facial hair.

They took out notebooks and did their best to smile at her at regular intervals.

"Please don't be intimidated, Ms Carter, we just want to ask you some questions about what happened yesterday and maybe see if you can help us identify the shooter."

"You got someone?"

"We've apprehended a few suspects who were in the area at the time. Tell us what you saw and hopefully, we can get you down to the station to help us out," said Fleischer.

Belle took a breath.

"Well I was walking to the hospital" she quickly covered her tracks "I broke my ankle a few months ago, they were just checking if it had healed."

Fleischer nodded.

"I was a little lost so I asked Reece for directions. He was telling me which way to go and this guy came running around the corner with the car following."

"And what was Reece doing in the area?" asked Detective Christopher.

"Waiting for the bus."

"Where to?"

"I don't know."

"And did he know the man who came around the corner or the men in the car?"

"No, I don't think so. He just saw they were shooting, grabbed my hand and ran."

"Are you sure he didn't know them?"

Belle's eyes narrowed.

"He didn't know them."

"Can you describe the man who came around the corner?" Asked Fleischer.

Belle thought for a moment.

"He was, maybe about my height, dark hair, skinny."

"Caucasian?"

"Sure. He was –"

"How did you know he was Caucasian?" Interrupted Christopher.

Her eyes narrowed again.

"From what I could see of his face."

"What was he wearing?" Fleischer continued.

"Uh, a grey hoodie and jeans, I think."

"It's OK if you can't remember every detail, you're still in shock." Added Fleischer. Belle smiled. She preferred Fleischer.

"This car was following him. It was silver, kinda boxy, old-style. I can't tell one car from another," she said, pre-empting their next question. "There were two guys in it, as far as I could see, and I could only really see the guy who was shooting."

"And what did he look like?"

Belle paused to think again.

"He was wearing a blue jacket, I think. He had a beard, scruffy-looking. He was blonde, I remember that. He looked... tanned?"

Christopher wrote this down.

"Could you describe the gun?" Asked Fleischer.

Belle puffed out her cheeks. Despite living in Tennessee her whole life, she knew next to nothing about guns.

"It was big, it was shooting a lot of bullets very quickly."

Detective Christopher sniggered.

"Then Reece got shot," Fleischer interjected.

"Yep. We ran but the car was going the same way. They hit him by accident, I could tell cos the guy shooting saw what happened and he drove off. The guy running just disappeared around the corner."

For a moment, the two detectives just wrote. Belle peered around the room as if she hadn't lived there her whole life to avoid staring.

"Then you called the ambulance," continued Fleischer.

"Yep."

"And while you were waiting for it?"

Belle swallowed.

"He asked me to hug him, so I did, and he asked me to call his mom, so I did."

They wrote in their notebooks for an absurd amount of time. Belle resumed staring around the room. Fleischer broke the silence.

"Is there anything else you remember?"

Belle paused.

"Nothing I can think of."

Fleischer leaned back.

"Do I recognise you from somewhere?"

Belle studied his face and shrugged.

"Did you go to Jeremiah High school?"

"Nope, King Hill."

She shrugged again.

"I work at the gas station out of town, maybe you came in there once."

He squinted.

"Maybe."

Christopher stood up, signalling to his underling that it was time to go.

"OK, we're gonna need you to come to the station with us and see if you can pick the guy out."

"As long as you're ready" Fleischer added.

"I'm ready."

The police precinct was bigger than she expected. She was shown into a room on the viewing side of a two-way mirror. Five men were brought in. She spotted him immediately. He was wearing a grey tracksuit and stared straight ahead. He did not look as if he had been crying. Belle felt a surge of heat to her face.

"That's him."

"You sure?" Asked Fleischer.

She nodded.

"I'm certain."

He remained expressionless. She stared at him through the mirror, willing him to react. Still, he remained no more distressed than if he was waiting in line at the post office. She sighed.

"I need to go home now."

She was driven back and greeted at the door by a bear hug from her mom. She put together a fruit salad and made her some cocoa.

"Mom...about yesterday..."

"It's OK if you don't want to talk about it."

"It's fine, I do."

"You tell me whatever you need to."

She looked at her mother's face. She didn't need to know that Satan himself, the Prince of Darkness, had got his dirty feet on her good armchair.

"I was just thinking about what Gabe said about the baby being a sacrifice. What if he meant something like what happened to Reece?"

Cynthia stepped back.

"Did you ask Gabe?"

"I did. He said he didn't know."

Cynthia sighed.

"I just don't know. I don't know about any of this. All of this divine stuff. I'm texting an actual angel and I don't know."

Belle smiled, more for her mother's sake than hers.

"But whatever happens, I believe Gabe when he said you were chosen because you could deal with it. So you can deal with it, you're strong enough. That may not seem like enough but it's all any of us have."

Belle felt her face crumple. Her mom held her as she sobbed.

Later that night Gabe called at the house.

Cynthia allowed him in then excused herself.

"Hey, Belle."

"Hey."

After a pause, he reached into a plastic bag.

"I brought you a meatball sub."

She found herself smiling, and they headed to the living room.

He sat down on the armchair and waited until she had finished her sub to speak.

"I wanted to apologise. And to see if you're OK."

Belle sighed. She searched inside her for anger but found none.

"You don't have to apologise, Gabe. It's not your fault."

"I should have considered the possibility. I should have been more honest with you."

Belle studied him. His eyes were downcast. She felt a pang of guilt.

"Gabe, I was out of line last night. The things I

said weren't cool. You've helped me a lot."

He smiled.

"*You* don't have to apologise. You'd seen something incredibly traumatising, it's normal to feel angry."

She paused.

"I have to tell you something, but please don't freak out."

He raised an eyebrow.

"You have my word."

She adjusted her seating position to get more comfortable.

"When I came home last night, the TV turned on by itself."

Gabe's brow furrowed.

"There was a man on the screen and he spoke to me. Grey hair, wearing a suit..." She laughed a little "It sounds ludicrous to say after everything that's happened so far, but... Satan came here last night."

Gabe's eyes widened. He leaned forward, slowly and deliberately to hide his shaking.

"Tell me everything."

She swallowed.

"He was on the TV, talking to me, then I realised who he was, and when I switched the TV off he was sitting in that chair where you are now."

"Belle, what did he say to you?"

She considered her words.

"He said he messed with the maps on my phone so that I'd be there to see Reece get shot. He said he wanted me to realise what they were going to do to my son."

He stood up and paced the room as she continued.

"He said he didn't kill him but he made sure I'd be there."

"This is very important, Belle, did he offer you

anything."

She observed Gabe for a moment. She hadn't ever seen him like this. His eyes were still wide and unblinking, his hands were shaking.

"He did."

"What?"

"He said that if I gave him information about you and did what he asked then he'd protect my son."

Gabe held his hand to his forehead.

"That....*bastard*. God, I am so, so sorry. I did everything I could to keep him from finding out about you."

"It's alright."

"It's not alright. It's not." His eyes were sparkling. Could angels even cry? "I failed. I failed you. I exposed you to *him*. Your mom too, God, how did this happen?"

"Hey, don't blame yourself. -"

"What did you say to him? To the offer?"

Belle shrugged.

"I said no. I told him to get out."

Gabe sighed, relieved, and knelt in front of her, holding her hands. His voice still had a crack running through it.

"I knew it, you were chosen for a reason. I knew you were strong."

Belle shrugged.

"He's Satan, I know he's a bad guy."

"Belle, he offered you your son's safety and you turned it down. I saw how upset you were last night. He orchestrated a situation to get you at your most vulnerable and offer you a way out, and you said no."

She smiled, this time for herself.

"But this is the hard part. You have to stay strong. Because he will keep trying, he'll pick his moments, whenever you're scared, or alone, or you just wish you hadn't said yes, that's when he'll come and he'll offer you a way out. And it may seem like the right decision in the moment, but I promise you, it's not. He can be very, very persuasive." He sighed, and his eyes drifted to the window. "I almost feel sorry for him sometimes, he's the furthest thing from God's love, he's the most pitiful creature in the universe. But then I ask, how did he feel the full force of that love and reject it? I will never understand it."

She nodded her head, feeling like an army cadet on the receiving end of a pep talk.

"I promise you, as much as I can, I'll be there to help you fight him, whenever you need me. Just ask for me and I'll be there. I messed up, and I'm gonna do what I can to make it up."

Belle smiled. She got down off her chair and faced the kneeling Gabe, putting her arms around him for a hug.

"Oh!" he said and put his arms around her in the same way she was doing. He was a good hugger, the kind that gave the other person a good squeeze. She broke it off and stood up. He had a grin on his face but his eyes were still red.

"That was great! I've never actually hugged anyone before."

"I'm surprised my mom hasn't tried, she's a hugger."

He spoke in a hush.

"Have you told her?"

She shook her head.

"She has enough to deal with, it would scare her too much."

He nodded in agreement.

"Gabe?"

"Yeah?"

"How do I stop him from coming to me."

Gabe put his hands on his hips and shrugged his shoulders.

"Just try and be strong. I know that's easier said than done, but he'll target you when you feel vulnerable. If you stay strong and self-assured, he should leave you alone."

Gabe stayed for a coffee and took some junk mail he found 'fascinating' with him. Belle and her mom ordered takeout and watched some TV together when they were alone.

The next day her mom was at work, giving her the place to herself. She took the opportunity to take a bath, bringing a beat-up copy of the Torah with her. It was a revised edition, the one rewritten by European kings to suit their needs that were extremely popular in Tennessee thanks to strategic European immigration. It was all they had in the house. She scanned for mentions of prophecies, or sons of God, or virgin births. It would be helpful if it had an index, she thought.

She came across references to a 'Son of Man' and 'Descendant of David'. She remembered the word 'Messiah' too, it was one to look up. She planned to ask Gabe, who was a personal friend of the original author, and maybe ask some Rabbi or Scholar about it, although most of them were up north. She giggled, considering what Brother Abel might think. It would probably cost her at least $1000 just to consult him on such matters. She turned her focus to her own body. Her stomach looked the same. According to the books Gabe brought her, it takes about three months to start showing. She resolved to enjoy her time before she was viewed as a fallen woman by the world.

She eventually dragged herself out of the bath and returned to the living room. She switched on the TV, pleased to see no demons on it. There was some show on with people selling livestock. A sweep of the other channels confirmed it was the best of a crappy daytime schedule, so she stuck with it. Her phone was left on the scratched coffee table, so she checked it, seeing as there was nothing better to do. Her brow furrowed. Becky had called her eight times. There was only one text from her, which was odd given her aversion to phone calls.

I need to talk to you B, please call me, love other B.
She hit call back. It rang for a second.

"Belle, thank God!"
Her voice was breathless.
"Hey Becky, are you OK? Is something wrong?"
"It's not me, Belle, it's you."
She breathed in.
"Belle...are you pregnant with the son of God?
She ignored her initial instinct to laugh it off and play dumb. She stood up and muted the TV.
"What are you talking about?" She hoped it didn't sound aggressive.
"There's a video on News 24, that nutjob channel, it's you outside the diner talking to some guy."
She swallowed. Someone had seen.
"Some dude who worked there was recording a message for someone and he filmed it. He sold it to the news. Is it true?"
It was getting harder to be rational.
"Do they know it's me?"
"No. They're just calling you a mystery woman."
Belle put her head in her hands.
"Oh God, I should have known this would happen."
"Is it true, though?"
She sighed. She owed Becky the truth.
"It is. It's all true. I know that sounds nuts, and if

you don't, believe me, I don't blame you. That guy I was talking to is the Angel Gabriel. He told me."

There was silence at the other end.

"Becky please say something."

"I don't know what to say. Only that I don't think you're crazy."

Belle exhaled.

"That means a lot."

"And I swear to you, I won't tell them it's you. I hate to say this, but it's only a matter of time before someone figures it out."

She knew Becky was probably right.

"What channel did you say it was?"

"News 24."

"OK, stay on the line."

She switched over. The host, a pink-faced man with a crew cut, was talking straight to the camera with a still of the video in the corner. It was blurry but you could see her face and the back of Gabe's head. The caption read 'woman claims to be the virgin mother of the messiah.'

"This is just wild, folks, so this woman looks no older than 18, genuinely seems to believe that God himself got her pregnant."

"It's sad, really," came a phone-in voice, "I thought maybe I shouldn't share it, she could have a mental condition, but I dunno, I just thought people should know."

"He thought he could make money off it, son of a bitch," said Becky.

"Who's the guy in the video?"

The camera panned to an impossibly attractive blonde woman co-hosting.

"I don't know, Terri, probably the father."

Terri shook her head.

"What do they call that? *Folie a deux?*"

"I think the expression is *menage a tois,* Terri."
Terri smiled at the camera.

"My mistake, Jim."

The man on the phone continued.

"I think he's some conman type guy. He's found this girl with a delusion and he's gonna make money out of her."

"That's an interesting theory, Paul."

"That's what I'm worried about, you know, this is a God-fearing country, people like that can exploit the vulnerable."

Belle turned the TV off. She'd heard enough.

Later that night Belle and Cynthia invited Aunt Vivienne to come over and give Belle a new hairdo.

"What if she's seen it?"

"If she had seen it she would have blown up my phone by now. You know she doesn't follow the news."
Belle paced the floor.

"Just try and stay calm, you have two weeks off from the gas station, we'll put up with Viv for one night then you can hunker down and we can get our shit together."

Vivienne was a former stylist, and after her problems with rough hairdressers pulling and ripping her hair, she was exceedingly gentle.

"You are gonna look so cute!" She said, putting an improvised trash bag cape around her shoulders. She forced out a smile for her aunt's benefit and tried to hide the fact her leg was anxiously jiggling under the trash bag.

"Cynthy, doesn't she just have the prettiest hair? What do you want me to do with it?"
She thought, what was the exact opposite of her current style?

"Um... something short and a bit looser? I might

dye it a little."

"Try and use henna or get it done by a
professional. That boxed stuff will ruin it. And please
tell me you keep a jar of coconut oil in the bathroom?"

Some time later Belle looked suitably different.
She had gone from near-elbow length locs to looser
coils just past her shoulders. After Vivienne had gone
she considered the results with Cynthia.

"What do you think? Would you recognise me?"

"I would, but I'm your mother." Her mom played
around with it, simulating different styles, including the
bunches she sported as a kid.
"It's cute, aunt Vivienne's good at this stuff."

"Do you think I should go with the dye?"

"Wouldn't hurt. Maybe like a reddish colour?"

The next day Cynthia brought home a packet of
red dye. Belle discovered that henna smells like sulphur
and feels like thick mud, but it did the trick. She was left
with an orange-red hue that looked natural enough. She
sent selfies to Becky, who approved. That night she
raided her mom's makeup bag. She had never really
been into it, but that was mainly because it was so
difficult to find stuff that matched her skin tone. She
tried some stuff that she would never think of, like a
single streak of high-pigment blue on her eyelids and
gold highlighter. She found she liked it more than she
thought she would.

The day after was the real test, handing in her
notice at the gas station. Facing truckers every day was
too big of a risk. She thought this day would be a relief
when it came, no more rude customers, no more early
mornings, but it felt like a minor reason to grieve.

The door pinged open and she was greeted by
Gabe behind the counter and Mr Lowe buying his

snacks. Gabe gave her new look a thumbs up. Mr Lowe turned around and squinted for a second before greeting her. This was a victory.

"Belle! It's good to see you! How are things?"
"Things are OK, Mr Lowe."

She felt a stronger paranoia being out in public than she thought she would. She winced as a customer entered, and fought the urge to run off into the fields opposite.

"To what do we owe this visit, you don't have to be in until the end of next week. Do you miss the smell of disinfectant that much?" He snorted.
Belle pretended to cock her head in confusion.

"What's...dis-in-fec-tunt?"

"Very good."

She dropped the act.

"Actually, Mr Lowe I wanted to talk to you in private."

He gestured to the door of his small office, which also doubled as the cloakroom.

He squeezed behind his desk in the cubicle-sized room and offered her a seat on the tiny stool.

"Now I didn't ask out there because you still don't know Gabe very well, but how are you? What happened to you was just awful."
She smiled.

"I'm doing OK. It was shocking, but It's not me who suffered the loss."

"Of course, of course. Have they caught the guy yet?"
She nodded.

"That's wonderful! You did the right thing, girl. What is it you wanted to speak to me about?"
She exhaled.

"It's related, actually. I hate to do it, but I'm gonna have to hand in my notice."

He leaned back.

"That's a real shame to hear, but I get it. Hell, no one wants to work here forever, especially smart people like you."

"I'm thinking of maybe going to college or training for something, I don't know yet, but after what I saw, I need a little time to think things through."

"I understand. We're gonna miss you here, kiddo."

She nodded.

"I'm gonna miss it here too Mr Lowe. I can work my two weeks notice- "

He threw up his hands.

"I won't hear it, consider it a paid vacation."

"Wow...thanks, Mr Lowe."

As she was leaving a familiar face was talking to Gabe at the counter.

"Belle!" said Doug, seeing through her new look immediately. "How have you been? I've been worried sick about you after what happened."

Belle smiled broadly. Doug greeted her with the enthusiasm of a dog, and better still, he looked healthy.

"Hey Doug, I'm doing fine, thank you, just visiting." She hadn't the heart to tell him she was leaving.

"Have they caught the guy yet?"

"I should hope so, I identified him."

"It's just terrible. I thought that type of thing just didn't happen anymore. It's a blessing to that poor boy you were there for him, though."

She swallowed the lump in her throat.

"Has Gabe been taking care of you?"

"He has! I've been talking his ear off. He knows a lot about soul music!"

She stayed and talked to Doug some more. When a new customer came in she turned her face from them and pretended to browse birthday cards.

    That night she sat in her garden, feeling the gradually cooling air and listening to the crickets hum. A citronella candle kept the flies away. Its sickly smell mingled with the scent of a barbecue a few houses over. She checked her phone. There were no new results on her story since yesterday, some new viral nonsense most likely replacing it. A bird, which she recognised as an indigo bunting from one time that Gabe had excitedly pointed one out, landed on the branch of the cherry tree. It was still light enough to see its startling sky blue colour.

8

Our Lady of Hermits

Three months pregnant.

Since she left the gas station, Belle had been primarily keeping to the house. Despite assurances from her mother that the story had withered from the public eye without new updates, she refused to take chances. After the first week, when she had not ventured outside at all except to drink tea in the garden, she was coaxed into a supermarket visit. She dug out one of her dad's hoodies, which hung off her slight frame and hid a large part of her face. At one point she rifled intently through tampons to throw any keen-eyed shoppers off the scent. With her bump beginning to show, it became even more difficult to get her to leave.

Belle's lanky frame had its lines distorted with the introduction of an outward curve, which she hid with long cardigans despite the still-high temperatures as Autumn began to suggest its presence. Gabe visited a few times a week, but Belle tried her hardest to avoid the subject of how she was doing. He was entranced by the changing leaves and pointed out the behaviour of wildlife as it adapted to the new season.

She had managed to push Reece's case to the back of her mind. They had their man, thanks to her, and trials took a long time to put together. What mattered now was her safety and the safety of her family. She considered trying to contact Anette but decided against it. If she needed to speak to her she would.

One morning whilst idly scrolling through social media, an article shared by a former classmate jumped out at her.

'It's one rule for the rich and another for the rest of us' read their caption. 'Bail laws are a joke.'

The thumbnail featured a picture of the state's governor, Robert Kitchering Sr, and next to him a superimposed photo of a young man in graduation robes that Belle immediately recognised with a sharp stab to her gut. The headline read:

GOVERNOR'S SON RELEASED ON BAIL IN MURDER CHARGE.

Her hand shook as she opened the link and read the article.

Rob Kitchering, 26, was identified by a witness as the shooter of Reece Letsky, 16, outside the Memphis Industrial Depot.

She scanned the article for her name and allowed herself to breathe out when she didn't find it.

A GoFundMe page was set up to make Kitchering's $1million bail, which reached its goal last week.

Governor Kitchering did not respond to our request for comment.

Belle felt all her muscles tighten. She searched for the GoFundMe page. It claimed he had been in the wrong place at the wrong time, a victim of a Democrat smear campaign, falsely accused of what was clearly a gangland shooting. For a second her thumb hovered over the comment box, but she quickly came to her senses. It was midnight, but she knew Gabe would be available for a talk.

"Hey what's up?"

"I'm sending you a link, Gabe. It's his son. The governor's son killed Reece."

"Wait, slow down-"

"Governor Kitchering, his son has been a black sheep for years apparently, he just made Bail."

Gabe was quiet for a moment as he skimmed the article.

"OK, let's just take a breath. Just because he made bail doesn't mean he's getting away with it. You identified him, there's probably CCTV, it's gonna be OK."

She let out a strangled groan.

"It just...pisses me off, people are dishing out money for this guy? I mean, he hit Reece by accident it's not like he's pure evil he's just an irresponsible moron, but all these people actually donating money so he can go home to daddy's mansion?"

"Belle, if you spend too much time thinking about bad people it will mess you up."

She sighed.

"I know, I just don't get that mindset. It's not like his family needs the money either. He made a fortune off of private prisons, apparently."

"Have the police told you anything else?"

"Not yet, I think there's gonna be like a pre-trial hearing soon. I just don't wanna end up in the spotlight."

"Just tell the truth, that's all you can do."

"Is it?"

"It is for now."

She took a deep breath.

"Me and Becky are visiting tomorrow. I have a

surprise for you too."

"Oh, lord..."

"Trust me, you'll love this. Now, try and forget about Rob Kitchering. And remember, if he doesn't face justice in this world, he will in the next."

The next morning, Gabe came over-prepared with a meatball sub and Becky and Joey. Belle had slept in and came downstairs already cocooned in a hoody.

"Hey, guys!" She greeted them as enthusiastically as she could muster. They reciprocated.

"We brought you breakfast," Becky said, holding out the bribe.

"I'm not supposed to eat junk food-"

"Oh, but you will. There's someone else here too."
Gabe opened the door and in ran a small mongrel dog. It looked like some kind of Jack Russell cross with floppy ears and scruffy long fur. It had a greying muzzle and a black patch on his back.

"Oh my gosh, who's this?"

"He's mine" answered Gabe, "Meet Carl."

"Hey, Carl!" The dog licked her hand and wagged his tail.

It dawned on Belle that the meatball sub and a cute senior dog were designed to appeal to her as much as possible. She squinted up at them.

"This is an intervention isn't it?"

"It is." Confirmed Becky.

"I boked you a scan." Announced Gabe. "Take 2. You need to get out of the house and you need to reconnect with the reality of motherhood."

"I can't believe you would use a dog against me."

"Me, Becky, Joey, and Carl are here to psyche you up. I know it's hard, but you can't spend the rest of your life moping around like this."

"I'm not moping, it's self-preservation."

"You guys are fragile, you need interaction with the outside world or you go...weird. Trust me, Emily Bronte did some weird stuff."

"Fine. I'll hear you out."

They sat in the living room and Joey played with Carl. Becky made her a green tea.
Gabe put on some music, Neil Diamond. His singing voice got a wide-eyed look from Becky. He broke his singing to resume negotiations.

"The appointment is tomorrow at noon, Jacob street women's hospital. I'll drive you and wait in the car. I'm gonna have to insist against the hoodie."

"What if I'm recognised?"

"If you don't get recognised then you have nothing to worry about. If you do, then I'm afraid that's just gonna be your new reality, and it may suck, but you're gonna have to learn to deal with it" said Becky.

"Wow."

"She's right," added Gabe. "Whatever happens, you're tough enough to deal with it and you're gonna have to. You can't hide away forever."
She sighed.

"You're right. Mom's losing it with me hanging around all the time." She sipped her tea. "I'll do it."

"It's not a choice thing. Also, I'm here to take some of your weird religious books."

"Thanks, Becky. I guess."

When she had left the room Gabe spoke to her in a hushed tone.

"And don't google Rob Kitchering. Wait for the trial."

"I haven't and I won't."

"That's my girl. And remember what I told you."

"Never, ever read the comments."

Gabe picked her up the next day and drove her 20 minutes out of town to the hospital. On Becky's insistence, she wore a tank top.

"So you're gonna wait here?"

"Actually, no. The appointment is at one pm, not noon. I'm coming in with you and we're gonna have a drink in the cafe. My treat."

She groaned.

"It's for your own good. You need to see that it's no big deal."

"Fine. But if we get spotted, I'm taking Carl from you."

Inside the pristine cafeteria, Belle sat bouncing her leg as she scanned the room for anyone looking at her. Gabe took his time charming the lady at the cafeteria counter, stirring his coffee painfully slowly with the wooden stirrer. He finally got to the table and placed two mugs and a slice of chocolate cake on the Formica.

"I got you some cake too."

"Thanks."

She grabbed a fork and started shoving mouthfuls of it into her face.

"Remember we have an hour to kill, Belle. Why not take in your surroundings, do a little people-watching."

She stabbed the fork into the cake and flopped back in her chair.

"It's times like this I remember you're still technically a teenager."

"Whatever, you're not my real dad."

She took a deep breath and tried to absorb her surroundings. She remembered a mindfulness technique she learned in high school – note five things you see, four things you hear, three things you feel, two things you can smell, and one thing you can taste. She could see an old guy in a wheelchair eating soup, a peeling mural of Winnie the Pooh through the door to the children's ward, flickering fluorescent light over the lazy susan, a guy in the kitchen wearing a hairnet over his beard, and a poster detailing the telltale symptoms of endometriosis. She closed her eyes and could hear the trundle of IV wheels on the linoleum, the whoosh of steam from the coffee machine, the clink of a spoon in a coffee cup, and a cough.

She felt her stomach. It was hard, and the tank top material was cool cotton. The Formica was smooth but uneven, with a few hairline cracks at the edges. The cup of decaf tea was radiating heat and steam. Her hair texture was tight corkscrew curls. She breathed deeply through her nose and could smell tomato soup and cleaning products. Finally, she took a bite of the cake and let it sit in her mouth. It was rich, dark, and sweet. She opened her eyes again.

"Ok. I'm back in the room."

Gabe smiled.

"And no one has recognised you yet."

"Seemingly, no."

"Because no one is going to recognise you from a grainy video that was on TV weeks ago."

She sighed.

"I guess not."

"So just relax. Today is supposed to be special."

She observed her companion. He had a new haircut she hadn't noticed, and he was wearing a red plaid shirt. She realised it had been a while she asked him about him.

"How are things with you Gabe? How is the gas station?"

He swallowed his coffee.

"Good. Mr Lowe said I could make manager."

She laughed gently.

"Any new hobbies?"

"I've been buying more houseplants. And coins. Coins are so interesting."

"Coins?"

"Yeah, from different countries and eras and stuff. I got one from Victorian England and these Icelandic ones with fish on them. I just think of all the different things they paid for. They circulate and they end up with a story that I can't know. Well, I can know some of it."

"How?"

"I can smell things on them you wouldn't be able to. An opium den, the horse from a carriage, a meal it paid for."

"What can you smell in here that I can't?"

He looked around and lifted a finger holding his coffee cup to briefly point at a middle-aged man a few tables ahead.

"He's just had his first chemo session. Pancreatic cancer."

"What does pancreatic cancer smell like?"

He sucked in air.

"A little metallic, and a little like sand."

"Sand doesn't have a smell."

"Oh yes it does. There's all kinds of things in sand."

Belle looked at the man. A woman re-entered the cafeteria from the bathroom and sat with him. He smiled at her.

"Aunt Vivienne went to Egypt in the summer, she might still have some change. Lots of sand there."

"I'll take a look at those."

She was quiet for a second.

"I have to apologise, Gabe, I didn't mean to go so

in my head."
He tried a piece of the cake.

"Well, it makes sense, you've had a very strange three months."
She sighed.

"Last year Aunt Vivienne took us to see this big preacher, Brother Abel."
Gabe winced.

"I know the guy. I tasted his range of bottled water." He scoffed.

"He brought mom up on stage and he asked her about my dad. He made out like he would be in hell because he didn't believe enough. She got really upset. I just didn't want to put her in that position again. She hates the spotlight."
He smiled.

"All these years it's just been you and her, and now you've been given this huge job that's gonna change the world. All of a sudden you're not just her baby anymore, it makes sense you'd be protective."
She nodded. Gabe leaned forward and spoke in a whisper.
"Does she know about *him* yet?"

"No. I want to keep it that way."
"Well, I gotta say you've been doing a good job of staying strong. He's not been back, has he?"

"Nope."
They finished their cake, tea, and coffee, and Gabe told her about Roman coins.

Gabe agreed to wait in the cafeteria while she went for her ultrasound. Like all hospitals, it was a labyrinth of long white corridors, vending machines, and under-labelled rooms. She swallowed her anxiety to ask a nurse for directions. Eventually, she found it and gave her name at the desk as quietly as she could. The waiting room had three other women, all with the fathers.

One of the women, who looked around seven months, had the habit of constantly keeping at least one hand on her bump while gazing at it adoringly. Another couple looked a little frosty, maybe an argument over names. The third woman gave Belle a withering look, but Belle suspected it was mostly to do with her age and lack of a father present. Her heart was going a mile a minute, but not for fear of being spotted. A woman came out of the office, also by herself. She had a phone to her ear, excitedly telling the person on the other end 'it's a boy!' A minute or two after she left, an olive-skinned woman in a burgundy headscarf leaned around the door frame.

"Maybelle Carter?"

Belle nervously raised her hand. She was ushered into the small room.

"I'm Doctor Al-Jamal, I'm gonna be looking inside you today."

The room was bigger and darker than she expected. The reclining bed had a large sheet of paper over it.

"So I'm gonna need you to just roll up your shirt and take a seat. Well, lie back."

She lay back on the thinly padded bed. It wheezed out air as she lay down and she felt the tissue underneath her rip.

"Just wriggle up a little bit..."

She did as she was told and rolled up her tank top. It was an odd perspective, she almost expected the procedure to be painful.

"This is just gonna be a little cold."

Dr Al-Jamal applied the gel to Belle's slight bump.

"So just look at this screen here and you'll get to meet the little squirt."

She craned her head to the screen, placed at an

awkward angle. Her heart was in her throat. She had the sensation of being in a risky job interview. Dr Al-Jamal pressed the scanner down hard, and Belle instinctively tensed up.

"Don't worry, the baby is way less fragile than you think, and so are you."

The screen at first looked like nothing more than television static. A few shadows shifted on it as the scanner moved over her bump. Then, a little pulsating blob in the centre. Belle propped up on her elbows to get a better look.

"And that is the heartbeat! So over here is the head, the legs, and the arms."

She stared at the blurry shadow. It looked more like a formed human being than she thought.

"How big is it?"

"About three inches, weighs about an ounce."

She had a strange urge to laugh. Something so tiny with its buzzing little heart had changed her life so much. The doctor moved the scanner around some more.

"So this dark area is the amniotic sac, and this here is the spine. Here's a fun fact, babies are born without kneecaps. Isn't that nuts? It's cartilage and it gets harder over time and turns into bone."

Belle found herself smiling at the screen. Yeshua. That was his name. He looked so peaceful. Whatever he meant to the world, as far as she was concerned at that moment he was all hers. The scanner moved to her right hip and the images distorted even more.

"The good news is, the baby looks healthy. And you are carrying the bump very well."

She laughed and thanked her.

Belle pointed at the screen.

"Can I get pictures?"

"Sure, we print them off here."

Belle left the waiting room carrying her polaroid-sized photograph. Dr Al-Jamal had pointed out the head, body, and arms to her. She traced them with her finger, almost bumping into a nurse as she walked. When she was away from the prying eyes of judgement, she found a small plastic bench by a water cooler and sat for a moment. She took in the details, the little nose, the scratchy outline of a tiny hand. She held it to her stomach.

"Check it out, that's you!"

She walked back to the cafeteria with a smile on her face. Gabe reciprocated with his own.

"All good?"

She nodded and handed him the picture.

"Woah! Look at that!!"

She could tell he couldn't make sense of the shadowy image.

"That's his head, this line here is his back, those are his little shrimp legs."

"I see it now!"

"Yeshua." She said.

"Yeshua." He agreed.

The air outside felt a little cleaner than it had done before. She didn't have to do the sensing exercise to feel in tune with her surroundings. Cars were crunching the asphalt, wheelchairs were wheeling, trees were turning brown, the air smelled of cut grass, and she could taste sterile chemicals when she breathed in deep. Gabe turned to her as they walked to the car.

"By the way, I'm still full-time at the gas station, so I'm gonna drop Carl off in the mornings and you're gonna have to walk him twice a day."

She smiled at him.

"Sure."

That night as Cynthia was making chilli for dinner, she

took a moment before opening the fridge to study the scan, held up by the same magnet that pinned a picture of Abe to the fridge door.

"That's my grandson!" She giggled. "I wish I could tell people."

"Now you know that's a bad idea."

"What about your Aunt?"

Belle thought.

"I guess we gotta tell her eventually. I just don't know how she would react. After what other people said…"

"You're her niece, she'll support you."

She shrugged.

"What if she sees me as they do? What if she thinks I'm lying?"

"Then we'll just have to deal with that."

Belle agreed. Her mom insisted on propping the picture up against a vase as they ate, never tearing her eyes from it.

9
Mirror of Justice

A few days later saw another visit from Becky, who had news.

"I found a job for you."

Belle bristled.

"Before you flip out it's not working with the public so you won't have to worry about it. My mom used to do home care visits caring for this rabbi's mother but she messed up her back."

Belle furrowed her brow.

"I've not done anything like that."

Becky dismissed it.

"You pick it up pretty quickly and the guy's wife helps you. She's really nice, I've met her."

"And they don't know my whole situation?"

"Nope."

Belle considered the idea. The promise of four new walls to occupy was tempting.

"- And I get you can't do it forever because of your condition but between you and me, the old lady's on her way out."

"Becky!"

"What? She's like 100 or something."

A week later Gabe persuaded Belle to take a bus out to the house. It was in the middle of nowhere and looked older than most houses in Memphis. It was surrounded by cattle fields and encircled by trees. There was a rusty bell at one side of the door but it didn't look like it made much of a sound, so she knocked instead.

A small woman with large hazel eyes greeted her with a smile.

"You must be Belle! I'm Yelena! Adrian is just out so I can show you around."
She brought her into a hallway with a dark wooden staircase and walls covered with family photos dating back at least two centuries.

"This is a beautiful house."

"Thank you! It's one of the oldest farmhouses in the state. We got it cheap because a bunch of people got killed in it."

"Oh, uh -"

"Don't worry I'm kidding. Come upstairs and meet Sarah. Lucky you, you're just in time to help out with her sponge bath."

The staircase creaked out a different hoarse note with each step. The upstairs of the house had prints of paintings by Van Gogh and Turner hanging from picture rails along the walls. Yelena knocked softly on a door at the end of the hall.

"Sarah? Are you awake?"
A mumbled voice came from inside the room and Yelena entered, followed by Belle.

At first, she assumed the bed was empty. Then, she saw Sarah's tiny frame propped up with pillows, watching a nearly mute TV. She squinted a little at Belle.

"This is Belle, she's gonna help me take care of you."
Sarah smiled and nodded.

Yelena was able to approach stripping and

bathing Sarah with a casual air. Belle tried her best to copy her mannerisms and disguise her jittering hands. She talked Belle through everything and showed her the best ways to avoid hurting Sarah's weak shoulder
"Use the Mom test," advised Yelena, "imagine she's your mom, how would you want someone to look after her?"

Once she was washed and dressed, Belle prepared her a bowl of oatmeal and a milky coffee. They helped her out of bed and onto a wheelchair, then took her downstairs with a stairlift. Yelena put the TV on for her and applied perfume on her neck and wrists.
"Would you like coffee?" Asked Yelena.
"Yeah, thanks. Do you have decaf?"
"We do."
"The regular stuff gives me the jitters sometimes."

The two sat at a small dining table where they could see Sarah. A groaning bookshelf caught Belle's attention, the top shelf featured three books written by the Rabbi.
"You did well today. Are you sure this is your first time doing care work?"
"Mmhm. I was in a gas station before this."
Belle sipped her coffee.
"Have you always done it?"
Yelena shook her head.
"My history is in academics. Adrian and I met in college. I edit his books."
"That's so cool."
"Thanks!"
She looked up at the bookshelf once again.
"Can I have a look?"
"Be my guest."
The Ikea bookshelf wobbled as she squeezed out

the three tightly-packed books. They stood out from the others with their pristine dust jackets. One jumped out to her immediately, entitled *Olam Ba Ha: The World to Come and the Messiach*. She opened it after running her eyes over the other two, as though it just so happened to be the first book she would take a closer look at.

"Take one home if you like. We have stacks of them."

"Could I?" She replied in as flat a tone as she could.

"I'll sign it for you if you like. Adrian won't unless you pay him fifty bucks!"
Belle laughed just as Adrian himself walked in through the door. He was a tall, slender-framed man with brown hair and a neat beard striped with ginger. His brow furrowed for a moment when he spotted the stranger, Yelena intervened.
"This is Belle, she's the new carer."
They exchanged smiles and he greeted his mother with a hug.

Belle left that night with her book after being shown more of the basics of Sarah's care. She retired to her bedroom immediately after dinner with her mom and sat at her old wooden desk with a highlighter pen. The majority of the first part of the book laid out what the Torah says about the messiah, some of which she already knew.

There was no talk of sacrifice or the messiah being God himself. She found herself enjoying the different interpretations of the Torah Adrian outlined. He pointed out possible mistranslations in scripture that may have been accepted as fact over time. He wrote extensively about how different political movements have adapted the words of scripture to suit their own needs. Her eyes widened at a passage in one particular chapter towards the centre of the book.

Scholars have been pouring over each word choice in scripture and various translations over the centuries. Some, however, prefer the comfort of absolutism. So-called 'mega preachers', like Tennessee's own Brother Abel, have taken what I would consider the easy route of considering each word at face value and exacting harsh judgement on those who don't.

She sniggered and pulled out her phone, searching for Adrian's name along with Brother Abel's. Sure enough, he issued his rebuttal almost immediately after the book's publication.

"This intellectual snobbery is not my way. I am here to bring the word of God to the masses, not keep it for the elites" he said in a speech to his huge congregation captured on video. He threw his hands up. "Not that I should call him an elite."

The screen behind him flashed up a picture of Adrian and Yelena's home taken from google. The crowd laughed.

"Let's see how many believers this great man of God brings in, shall we?"

The picture changed to one of his synagogue, a small but well-kept building that sat in a suburban neighbourhood with a few attendees standing outside with blurred faces. Belle gave an incredulous scoff. For a long time, it felt like her family was alone in their dislike of Brother Abel.

The next day she returned to the house to continue taking care of Sarah. Adrian arrived home just as Yelena and Belle were making her lunch. He prepared hot drinks for them while they worked alongside him in the kitchen.

"I was reading your book last night," Belle said.

"You were?" he answered, taking his eyes from the drink preparation and fixing them on her. "Which one?"

"The one about Olam Ba Ha. Yelena said I could take it home."

"Dare I ask what you think of it so far? You can be honest, although we may fire you."
He spoke in a deadpan tone that could have led some to take his joke seriously. Belle sensed it wasn't the intention.

"I'm enjoying it. Especially the stuff about Brother Abel."

"Wow, you're a fast reader," Yelena remarked. The three of them moved to the living room and gave Sarah her food.

"It's good to meet someone else in Memphis who isn't a fan of his." Adrian continued.

"My aunt used to really like him but we went to one of his... I guess you could call them shows... last year and he brought my mom up on stage and he was really pushy asking her about my Dad."

"Oh?"

"He died when I was younger and he basically suggested he's in hell because he didn't believe enough. My aunt hasn't been to the temple since."

"He gets off on public humiliation" Yelena observed through a sip of coffee.

"Yeah, I saw the video of his response to what you said. What a dick."
She realised what she had just said.
"Uh..sorry."
Adrian didn't laugh but he smiled.

"Don't worry, my Mother heard worse from me at the time."

"Did you respond to him? How did you deal with it?"

He sighed.

"I wanted to, because I was angry, and because I'm not good at walking away when someone is wrong and no one corrects them. But men like him can't get enough attention, good or bad. If I started an ongoing feud with him it would only give him more ammunition to demonise me. What he doesn't realise is not everyone is as in love with money and fame as him."

"I saw his house on the news, it's tacky. It's like if Walt Disney built Versailles," added Yelena. "I've said it before, rich people have really bad taste."

Belle sniggered.

"It's true. It's not about what they like it's about what they think will impress people. America may not have royalty but... is a King Complex a thing? Abel has a King Complex."

Cynthia drove Belle home that night.

"So, Vivienne has invited us for dinner."

"Oh, ok."

There was a few moments of silence before Cynthia spoke again.

"I was thinking... maybe we could tell her tonight?"

Belle exhaled.

"I just worry how she'd take it."

"You think she'll flip out?"

"I'm worried she won't believe me. I can stand other people calling me a liar, but not her."

"Let's just head over and see how you feel. It's up to you."

They drove off just as the sun was starting to sink.

Vivienne had a small house just on the other side of town. She kept a neat front lawn, fringed with ornaments and spinning colourful windmills. Next to the doorbell was a sign reading 'I'm not a superhero, I'm an aunt, but that's pretty darn close!!' She answered the door in a purple sequined blouse and bedazzled stonewash jeans.

"Cynthy!" She threw her arms around her sister and then Belle, who sucked in her stomach with all her might.

"Come in, girls! Uncle Jacob is away at work."
Belle realised it had been some time since she had been in her aunt's house. She was excellent with hair, but not so good with interior decorating. There were two sofas in front of the TV, one brown leather and the other one faded grey fabric, both with floral quilts. She had a Persian-style rug on a deep pile white carpet, which made Belle wince, and the kitchen area had jade-green cabinets. The walls were covered in folk art and inspirational sayings, mostly about God. Despite Vivienne's disorderly taste, everything was spotless. The carpet had fresh tracks in it from the vacuum cleaner and it smelled of linen despite there being none in the room.

"Have a seat, Belle, sweety, how are you? It was so wonderful what you did for that young man and his mom."
Belle smiled.

"I'm feeling better, thank you. They caught the guy so hopefully, it can all be dealt with."

"I will keep praying for him and his family. Here, let me take your bags."

"What are we having?" Asked Cynthia, knowing it was the main concern of her daughter.

"Roast beef. I got a recipe for the potatoes in a magazine.

They sat and talked for a little while, Belle draped a floral blanket over her bump. Vivienne periodically got up to check the beef.

"Shouldn't be long now."

Belle jumped slightly. Her mom noticed first.

"What's up?"

"I don't know I just felt a weird wobble or something, like butterflies in my stomach."

She felt it again.

Her mom peered over to check that Vivienne was distracted enough.

"He's kicking!" she whispered.

She reached for Belle's stomach just as Vivienne came back and sat back.

"I brought those cookies to the temple dinner, and I swear Jean Grillo brought exactly the same ones. She was there claiming it was an old family recipe, I found it online! She's so full of it. Belle, honey are you cold? I can get you a better blanket.?

They exchanged a look.

"Actually, Aunt Vivienne, we came here tonight because we have some news."

Her brow furrowed.

"You're not sick are you, sweetie."

"No. It's better I just show you."

Cynthia handed her the scan image and she gave it to her aunt. She studied it with a knitted brow.

"Is this real? Is this yours?"

Belle nodded.

"Sweetie... I mean... I don't know what to say."

Belle sat on the arm next to her.

"I know that you feel like maybe I've made a mistake but I haven't. It's hard to explain, but someone gave me this choice and I took it."

Her eyes began to shimmer.

"Belle, what do you mean?"

The kicking started again, as if in response to the conversation. She took Vivienne's hand.

"Here, feel it."

She placed it on her stomach as her son's tiny limbs
shot out. Vivienne's eyes grew, and she knelt in front of
her niece. She looked up at her.

"It's... Like he's talking to me."
Her voice went quiet.
"They chose you?"
Belle smiled. Her aunt's faith had always radiated from
the truest part of herself.
She held her niece's hand.
"I always knew, I always knew you were blessed. I felt it
when I first held you."
Belle kissed her hand.

"His name is Yeshua."
Her aunt smiled and repeated the name.

"Cynthia, get over here, feel this."
She stood up and placed her hand on Belle's bump, just
as the baby lurched. Both women laughed.

"He's a tough one!" remarked Cynthia.
"He's gonna have to be. We all will."

"Belle you are the toughest person I know" Aunt
Vivienne stood up and held her face "I knew it, I always
knew you had something special about you." She kissed
her forehead. "This is a celebration! I have this wine I've
been saving... Oh, Belle can't have it!"

"You guys go ahead, I don't mind."
Vivienne cracked open the wine and set the table. The
beef was perfectly tender and the potatoes were done in
a cream sauce with herbs. Before they ate, she offered to
say a prayer.

"Our God, thank you for choosing this family.
We ask that you give us strength and grant us harmony.
I pray that the maternal love I see in Cynthia will
strengthen that of her daughter and enshrine her
Grandson in love. I pray this world accepts and loves
Yeshua and that he can spread your message to all
people. "

And they ate.

Vivienne agreed to keep the news to herself. She was no gossiper, that was ungodly, but she loved to socialise and evangelise. She screamed with joy when Belle told her about speaking to her father, and raised her hands to the sky in gratitude.

The next day after leaving Adrian and Yelena's home, Belle was greeted at her door by a police officer she didn't recognise. Her heart lurched.

"Miss Carter?"

"That's me."

"I have a notice summoning you to court on the 21st of this month. You will be a witness at the preliminary hearing to determine if there is a case against Mr Kitchering."

"Oh..."

"The defence lawyer should contact you soon to answer any questions you might have."

———————

On the 21st of that month, Gabe drove Belle and Cynthia to the county courthouse. She was led into a small room upstairs and given a glass of water to accompany her while she waited to be called up.

"How long will you be up there?" asked Cynthia.

"I don't know. Hopefully not too long."
Belle struggled to swallow the water through her tightening throat. Gabe paced the floor as her mom held her hand. She wrapped the large cardigan around her growing bump.

Gabe broke the silence."Did the lawyer say what they would ask you?"

"He said it should be just a case of pointing him out."

"Well yeah," he continued, running his hand through his hair "I mean, you were there, you saw it. What could they have against you?"

Around half an hour later an officer escorted her to the stand. Cynthia took a seat in the courtroom to offer support while Gabe hung back in the waiting room.

She felt a hundred eyes burning into her as she entered. She briefly made eye contact with Rob Kitchering. He had been cleaned up since she last saw him, his beard was gone and he was sporting a healthy tan that made her sick. She looked to the front row and saw Anette, thinner than when she had last laid eyes on her. She was holding hands with her husband, a smallish man with large glasses. Anette smiled at her, a smile that nearly compelled her to run over and hug her.

The room was larger and blanker than she was expecting. Like a new classroom, yet to be made colourful with educational displays. She swore her oath and made a point of not looking at Governor Kitchering, sat directly behind his son and bearing the same tan that contrasted with his pure white hair.

"Can you state your full name for the record?"

"Ms Maybelle Esther Meryam Carter."

She went on to confirm other details as she sat in a thinly padded office chair behind a white foldaway table.

After she was sworn in the DA, Jim Fitzpatrick, approached her. They had spoken on the phone but he was older than she imagined. He wore a reassuringly smart grey suit and his salt-and-pepper hair looked freshly cut. He smiled at her and began his questioning.

"Ms Carter how did you meet the victim, Mr Letsky."

She took a moment to breathe in.

"I was on my way to the hospital and I asked him for directions."

"And what was he doing at the time."

"He was waiting for the bus."

"And this was on Memphis Depot Parkway."

"Yes, right outside the garbage depot."

The sound of the typist taking down her every word was extremely annoying

"And do you recognise Mr Kitchering as the man who was shooting?"

She straightened her posture.

"I do."

"And after Reece was hit, what did you do?"

"I called an ambulance and I went with him to the hospital."

"Can the hospital confirm this?"

"They can. The police took my details too."

"No further questions."

Belle exhaled. That was pretty easy. Her mom smiled at her. She looked over to Anette. He gave her a thumbs up.

"The defence may now cross-examine the witness."

She adjusted her posture again and pulled at her blazer to make sure it was hiding her belly. The defence attorney was somewhere in her 40s, with black bobbed hair. She removed her glasses, taking away a barrier to eye contact that Belle had been relying on.

"Ms Carter, you said you were on your way to the hospital that day, may I ask what for?"

She studied her hands for a second. It was time, to tell the truth, who knew what they could use against her?

"I was going for a six-week scan. I'm pregnant."

The courtroom remained silent.

"That's not what you told the police is it?"

She shook her head.

"I said it was a check-up on a sprained ankle."

The attorney cocked her head.

"And why did you lie about that?"

She felt each pair of eyes fix on her.

"I'm nineteen years old and I'm not married, I was trying to avoid judgement, I guess."

"Which is why you wore that oversized blazer today."

She felt her jaw muscles solidify.

"Well, yeah. I didn't think it was a big deal, I mean it's not like it makes a difference."

The attorney brought some pieces of paper up from her desk. She placed them in front of her. Screenshots of Belle in the video taken outside the diner. Her stomach jumped. She did her best to maintain a poker face.

"Ms Carter, who is the woman in this video?"

She shrugged and immediately felt it was too much. She had never been a good liar.

"I have no idea."

"For those who don't know these are screenshots from a video you may remember being in the news a few months ago. In the video, the woman claims she is pregnant with the son of God and is still a virgin."

A snigger broke out. Belle's scalp prickled.

"Now, on the day in question, you were going for a six-week scan. This is around the same time as this video."

Belle stayed silent. She held up the picture and showed it around.

"Now I would say this looks like you. Same build, same skin tone, and same approximate age. The hair is different, sure, but that's easy enough to change."

"That doesn't mean it's me."

"It wouldn't if a man called Josh Whitelaw hadn't

recognised you from school."

She swallowed. That dumbass.

"I don't know him."

"I do, I spoke to him a week ago. He identified you, I even referenced it to your yearbook picture."

The courtroom was humming with hushed conversation now. Belle's eyes were on fire.

"It's not me."

"Because if someone told you they were pregnant, despite being a virgin, with the son of God, no less, would you believe them?"

The room was blurry now. She blinked away tears.

"That's not what this is about, I'm not on trial here."

"Ms Carter, I'm not accusing you of anything, delusions of grandeur are not a crime, but I have to be sure that someone accusing my client of murder is in the right frame of mind."

"I'm not insane."

The attorney looked up at her.

"So you are pregnant with the Son of God?"

Belle found herself dumbstruck.

"That's not... I'm not..."

"Your honour I move that this witness is unreliable, my client has so far only been identified by a man known to be addicted to mind-altering drugs and now, a teenager who thinks she's the mother of God."

"I'm not insane!"

The murmuring stopped. The volume of her voice made her jump, too.

"It was him. I saw him. I held Reece in my arms and he was terrified. I was with his mom at the hospital when he died and that's verifiable. This man shot him and drove away like a coward, I saw that. I'm sure your other witness can remember me being there too. Some grainy footage and an asshole I went to high school with

doesn't prove anything."
"So you do know Mr Whitelaw from high
school?"
Belle was silent.
"No further questions."
A hum rang out among those present. Belle stood up
with her limbs feeling lighter than they did before. She
headed straight for the door, feeling as though her skin
was on fire. She could barely see, her eyes were so
blurred with tears. She threw open the doors and
resented the sun for still being out. The parking lot was
silent. She sat down on a bench and put her head
between her legs. It seemed as though even the deepest
of breaths weren't getting enough oxygen inside her.
The air was unseasonably hot and humid, as though a
piping towel had been flung over her head. She took off
her blazer and balled it up, hugging it to her chest.
 Her mom ran out and kneeled in front of her. Gabe
followed.
        "Belle sweetie?"
Belle raised her head to her.
        "I screwed it up, mom."
Cynthia held her tight.
        "You didn't. You did nothing wrong. Come on,
let's get you home. I can't stand it in there."

At home, Belle paced in her room. It felt as if
hyenas had caught on to her scent. Her phone buzzed, a
text from an unknown number
It's you-know-who. I can stop all this.
She threw the phone back onto the bed.
She slept fitfully that night. In her snatched moments of
dreams, like jigsaw puzzle pieces, she saw images of
herself and her baby on fire, but not being burned.

She was woken early by Gabe bursting into her

room. His breath was laboured.

"Belle, what happened?"

She leaned forward and stared at the fibres on her quilt.

"I screwed it all up."

He ran his hand through his hair.

"You had better come downstairs."

After some more quilt-staring, she came down.
The curtains were all drawn, bathing the house in
purple light. Her mom was standing in front of the TV,
chewing her nails. Gabe was sat forward on the arm of
the couch.

10

Mother of Divine Grace

The local news anchor, an auburn-haired woman in her thirties, spoke next to two images, a courtroom sketch of Belle and a screenshot from the diner video.

"The case against Rob Kitchering was dropped after the testimony of the defence's main witness, Maybelle Carter, was dismissed as unreliable."

"They're dismissing it?"
Cynthia turned round.

"Oh, baby I didn't see you." She threw her arms around her.
The woman on the TV continued.

"The story gained a lot of local interest some months ago when the video first came out but now local celebrity Preacher Brother Abel has weighed in."
Belle loosened the hug. Gabe put his head in his hands.
 The news ran a VT of Brother Abel speaking a morning sermon, shot on someone's phone.

"This is a time when Satan's power is unrivalled. Do not listen to this Jezebel claiming a status alongside the almighty God. She's a liar."
The crowd roared with approval. Cynthia took a seat next to Gabe.
"The son of God? There can be no equal to God! We are God's children."
The crowd roared again. Whoever was holding the phone shouted 'amen'.

"In this house of Godly people, I know we will not fall for this sinner's lies. This woman is either a victim of the Devil's manipulation who is bringing us a demon, or she is simply a narcissist who is trying to cover up the fact she had a little too much fun at prom."
The crowd laughed, someone shouted slut, another, a racial slur. The VT cut out and returned to the anchor.
"We must apologise for the offensive language in that video "
Gabe turned off the TV.
The room was silent. Belle's stomach felt like it was stirring inside her, and her scalp burned. She cleared her throat.
"Why are the drapes shut?"
Neither of them answered. She pulled one back by an inch and saw a news van and several photographers on the front lawn. She jumped back. Her breathing became rapid.
"I knew this would happen. I should never have gone. I let them down."
She ran upstairs before their protestations could make any impact. She sat against the door to keep it shut. Her phone buzzed with notifications so she turned off the wifi. She scrolled through her pictures and found one she had taken of the scan. She enlarged it on Yeshua's blurred face.
"I hope you're smarter than me, baby."

An hour later she heard a commotion outside. She lifted her curtain by an inch and saw Becky's car pull up. She smiled as she left the car with Joey on her hip. He started crying as the cameras flashed. Someone with a microphone stepped forward, and she swatted it to the ground.
"Get out of my fucking way, vultures. I'm here to see my friend."

Belle ran downstairs and hugged her.

"Get your shit, Belle, you're staying with me."

"What?"

"You're going to stay with me and Joey in Peytonsville for a little while, I can't have you live here with those scavengers outside."

"You don't have to do that Becky, I-"

"Look, you're both the only person who's reached out to me since high school and according to your hot angel friend, the most important and holy woman who ever lived, so it would be my honour, now get your shit."

Joey was still snivelling. Becky hugged Cynthia.

"What about my Mom."

Becky broke off the hug.

"I guess she could stay too?"

"I'll pack," Cynthia offered.

"No, mom, you take Joey, I can get your stuff."

"I don't think so," interrupted Becky, "you need to have a drink and sit down, you're pregnant. Gabe can take Joey."

She handed him the still snivelling Joey and went upstairs with Cynthia. Belle flopped into the armchair and Gabe hushed the crying toddler.

"Hey, buddy, look who's here! It's Carl!" He announced as he fussed.

Belle hadn't spotted the old dog lying on a cushion in front of the TV. He got up and strolled over to him. Gabe sat Joey down and his crying eased as the dog sniffed around him.

He turned to Belle. "Doggy!"

She smiled at him and got down on the floor.

"I'll make you tea." Offered Gabe.

"Gabe?"

He stopped on his way to the kitchen and turned back.

"I'm sorry. I messed up."

He sighed.

"Belle, this is not your fault. You were trying to do right by Reece and Governor Kitchering would rather eff up your life than let his son ruin his reelection chances. And as for Brother Abel...just don't get me started on Brother Abel."

With that, he went into the kitchen.

Joey was patting Carl and tried to pull on his ear. Belle loosened his grip.

"Don't do that Joey, play nice with him." She demonstrated gentle strokes along the dog's back. "See? He likes that." Joey imitated the strokes.

Gabe came back in with a mug of tea. He handed it to her and peered outside.

"They still there?" asked Belle.

"Yep."

"So what do we do?"

He sat back down.

"I can't do much. Not without attracting too much attention."

Cynthia and Becky came back down with a couple of duffel bags stuffed with clothes.

"Into the lion's den," announced Becky.

"I'll sneak out the back." Gabe said, and hugged Belle.

"Sweetie, put this blanket over your head, Becky will carry Joey and we'll get in the back of the car."

"What about you, mom, they shouldn't see your face."

"She's right, Cynthia" added Gabe. He handed Joey back to his mom and picked up Carl. #

"Wait," said Belle. She scratched Carls's ears. "It may be a while before I take you on a walk again, buddy."

"Don't worry, we'll visit you in Peytonville whenever we can."

Becky winked at Belle.

"Now go! Godspeed."

Becky unlocked the front door as Cynthia and Belle threw blankets over their heads.

As the door swung open voices began running into one another in a terrible chorus. Belle kept her mind on her shoes and the feeling of her mother's arm around her.

"Miss Carter! Do you truly believe this?"

"Miss Carter do you have a response to Brother Abel's comments?"

"Miss Carter do you have a personal vendetta against governor Kitchering?"

"If anyone scratches my car I'll sue!" came Becky's voice, slicing through the noise. She opened the front door of her car and moved the seat backwards. "It's gonna be a squeeze, ladies. One of you get in the passenger seat, the other sits with Joey in the back. "

Belle fought through to the back and her mom got into the passenger seat. Her bump made it a tight squeeze.

"Wait, the scan! It's in my fridge!"

"I'll get it, Cynthia."

"Becky, it's OK, you don't have to."

Cynthia's voice came too late. She had shut the car door and ran back to the house. The sound of the flashing cameras followed her.

"How the hell did we end up here?" asked Belle. Cynthia said nothing.

The driver's door opened and Becky appeared. She strapped Joey into the booster seat next to Belle. She started the engine and the car began to move. Belle didn't dare remove the blanket. She felt the vibrations of someone slamming on the window. The chorus of shouting dimmed as they turned a corner.

"You can take those off now, I think we've lost them."

Belle took off the blanket. She turned around and saw

an opportunistic photographer failing to catch up with Becky's Volvo. Belle sunk in the seat.

"Buckle up, Belle, I'm serious."

She did as she was told.

"Thank you so much for this, Becky."

"It's my pleasure."

"Aren't you worried they'll come for you?"

"They can try."

Joey began to cry again. Belle held his hand and sang to him, which calmed him down.

They arrived at Becky's with a reassuring lack of fanfare. Belle stepped out of the car with her neck craned downward but didn't hear anything except for a distant lawnmower. The sky was overcast and the air was leaden with the promise of rain. Becky's neighbourhood was sparse, with one or two flat-roofed wooden houses with stone paths leading up to the front door. The small gathering of houses sat by the side of a highway hidden behind a row of fir trees, the kind of place you couldn't just stumble upon accidentally. The other houses had pickup trucks outside and colourful pinwheels on top of the mailboxes. Becky took a sleeping Joey out of the car and lead them to the door.

The inside of the house was chaotic but homely. The fridge in the kitchenette was covered in Joey's finger paintings and pots and pans sat on top of the stove. The sitting area had mismatched sofas with a half-folded pile of laundry facing a small TV. The small dining table was covered in crayons and torn-out pages from colouring books.

"It's not big, we're gonna be in each other's hair a little bit. Joey can sleep in my room and you two can go in his. I got a futon and an airbed you can fight over but they're both equally bad."

"It's perfect, Becky, don't worry about it," answered Belle, and hugged her. "Thank you so much for this."

"It's my pleasure."
Cynthia excused herself to put the bags in their new room. Belle turned to her friend and spoke in a hushed voice.

"Are you sure you wanna do this? I am in deep trouble, Becky."

"I just can't leave you to face all of them alone."

"What about Joey?"
Becky looked at her son's sleeping face.

"We'll be OK. I mean, we literally have God on our side."

"I just... I have a feeling that the abuse and the hate are only going to get worse. Much worse. I've done all I can to protect my mom and I can't stand to have you fall victim to them too. Me and my mom, we can stay with family or get a motel-"

"Look, Belle, I got here on my own. I know it's gonna suck but I fucked up all my life and I finally have a chance to do something good. You're not gonna take that away from me, I'm sorry. When Joey grows up he's going to have a mom he's proud of, and so will Yeshua."
Belle relented and thanked her again.

When the rest of the house was asleep Belle sat on the sofa with her phone. She searched for Brother Abel's latest sermons. The thumbnail showed him standing in front of her house. She leaned closer to the phone and turned the volume down.

"I consider myself a guardian of the God-fearing people of this nation. I have a spiritual duty to protect believers from those who would bring us harm."
A few news cameras were rolling around him. His shiny wife was by his side.
"I am a just man. I will give Ms Carter a chance to explain herself. I invite you to come to my temple,

Maybelle and face a house of God's children. If you're telling the truth then surely you have nothing to fear." Great, she thought, a witch trial. He carried on. "Hiding in the shadows like a rat is Satan's technique. Pure souls do not fear the light."

She stopped the video. It felt like a violation, watching that man pontificate on her front lawn. That was where she took her first steps, she had pictured doing the same with her son. Her body, her home, and her family, all there for public consumption. She searched for Annette and Alec Letsky. The first page of results was all about her, 'Trial derailed by witness claiming to be the mother of God' with their names appearing halfway down the page. She felt a surge of impotent rage like her head was in a vice.

"Belle?"

She nearly jumped out of her skin. Becky stood in the hallway in her bathrobe.

"Are you up?"

She threw her phone under a cushion.

"Yeah, I just couldn't sleep."

Becky took a seat next to her.

"You're not checking the comments are you?"

"Nope."

"Yeah, you're a bad liar. What did I tell you? Never check the comments."

"People keep saying that to me. Maybe I'll listen eventually."

"What was it?"

"That asshole Brother Abel. He was on my front lawn."

Becky half laughed.

"That's unbelievable! Is that even allowed?"

"No one was stopping him. He says I should come to his temple and explain myself."

"With his followers that called you a slut?"

"Yeah, God's children."

"Well don't do it. It's a trap."

"Never. The best course of action is just to wait and eventually, he'll tire himself out. Maybe some senator will suggest removing 'In God we trust' from the money and he'll freak out about that until Yeshua goes to college."

Becky yawned.

"I know you should probably sleep, but it feels like I'm in no position to tell you what to do right now. So if you have to stay up I won't stop you, just don't wake Joey."

"I won't."

Becky went to bed and Belle watched some neutral videos of dogs online. Eventually, she drifted off.

She stepped into a dream as easily as stepping through a door. In it, she was in a vast desert. She walked across the barren sand with bare feet, with an occasional lizard skittering past. There was a pendulous, huge sun that looked as though it might drop. After walking for some time she came to a tent. Inside was an elderly woman sat on a blanket on the ground in a gold dress, her hair in a wrap. Her eyes were closed and she was in a cross-legged position. In front of her was a cushion waiting for Belle and a plate of rotting pomegranates. Belle took her seat. The woman opened her eyes and reached for a pomegranate. She spoke with a strong accent Belle couldn't place.

"You want one?"

Belle shook her head.

"Of course not. It's bitter and it would make you sick. But it is all I have."

"Who are you?" asked Belle.

"I am who you say I am."

"I've heard that before."

"Of course you have, silly girl."
Belle looked down. She was wearing a plain white dress
with long sleeves.
"Is this a product of my subconscious like a
regular dream, or is it a vision?"
The woman threw her head back and laughed.
"You're very smart. But you do silly things. Gabe
is taking good care of you, yes?"
"He is."
"And this business with the preacher man, what
will you do about that?"
Belle shrugged.
"I'm just going to try and lay low, and hope he
moves on. I have to protect my mom."
"And if he does not forget it?"
"He will, things like this blow over."
"Not always."
"Look you have to understand-"
The woman stood up, indignant.
"You ask me to understand? Child! Who gave
you the fire? The rivers? The hair on your head? I wove
each strand of your DNA, I rolled the electrons between
my fingers, I spun the nebulas, I understand it all." She
leaned close to her face. "Now is the time to draw on
that strength I gave to you. You never strike first, but
you always fight back." She clapped her hands and Belle
woke up with a jolt.
It was light and Gabe was sitting on the floor in
front of her playing with Carl.
"Hey, what's up?"
She had no idea which way was up.
"Are there people? Do we have to go?"
"Relax, relax. No one's here except me. Your
mom went to work, Becky had to take Joey to his
grandma's."
She lay back down.

"Is mom gonna be OK at work?"

"She said they're supportive. They think you're suffering from a mental delusion, but they feel sorry for you."

"Good, tell her to play along with that."

"Did you sleep OK?"

She considered her surroundings. The curtains were half-drawn, and the mid-morning sun cast a weak, white light in the room.

"Not too bad, it took me a while." She sat up. "He was outside my house, Gabe."

"I know." He shook his head. "That's just tacky."

Carl came up to her and she lifted him onto the couch next to her. He flopped down, leaving his belly open for a pat.

"I can't stay here forever, Gabe, I can't run forever."

Gabe sighed.

"I've been watching people for thousands of years. No one ever really gets anywhere without the kindness of others."

Belle kept looking at Carl. He closed his eyes and one of his ears twitched in half-sleep.

"It's not just about me, I've seen Brother Abel working up close, he riles them up. Eventually, a few of them will go out and take matters into his own hands. I can't risk my family or friends being hurt."

Gabe thought for a moment.

"Brother Abel is a nutjob, if you don't engage with him he'll lose interest. For me, the biggest concern is the other guy."

"You have to trust me, Gabe, I won't give in to him."

"That's not my concern, I know how strong you are." He stood up. "Belle, he's ruthless, he'll take any chance available, and when he realises you won't bend he'll do all he can to make things difficult for you."

"Difficult how?"

"He'll torment you."

"How?"

He sighed.

"Angels have abilities that humans don't. We're not gods, not even close, but we're something beyond the physical. We're like...light. He can be anywhere at any time. It's hard to explain."

Belle flopped back.

"Well, I'm glad I have you."

"And I'm gonna do what I can to protect you when he shows up."

Belle felt her stomach.

"It's gonna be much harder to hide who I am. Much harder."

"Maybe the thing is not to hide."

She laughed.

"And get beaten up in the street?"

"Have you considered the other side of all this?"

She looked up at him.

"What other side?"

"The believers."

She looked away again.

"Sometimes the thought of them scares me more."

He took a seat next to her.

"It's gonna be them that gets you through all this."

She played with Carl's ear as he slept.

"It's people like Doug that will be there for you. When someone like you comes along guys like Brother Abel can't stand it because you threaten them. You heard him, he's the 'spiritual protector' of the people in this state. Then this teenager comes along and claims she's been chosen above everyone else to be truly blessed."

"You're saying he's jealous?"

"In a way. You threaten his position, he can't endorse you because that would lessen him."

Belle thought.

"I studied this as much as I could. There have been a few people in history who claimed they were messiahs."

"That's true."

"They had followers, sure, but most of the world saw them as nothing and ignored them. A lot of them were defeated, or failed somehow."

He was quiet for a moment.

"I can't lie to you and reassure you for the sake of it. I've told you I don't know everything but I do know this will probably suck."

"Thanks, Gabe."

When Becky and her mom came back that night Belle insisted on cooking dinner. As she was waiting for the rice to be done a text came through from Gabe.

This may be good or bad but Aunt Vivienne is on the case.

He sent through a video.

"Mom? I think you need to see this."

Cynthia left the sofa and joined her in the kitchen. Belle pressed play.

Vivienne was standing in front of the courthouse on a local news channel.

"My niece is telling the truth. On my life, I felt that baby inside her and he spoke to me. He *is* the son of God! I used to follow Abel but he has chosen the wrong path. My family is not afraid of him!"

Cynthia put her head in her hands.

"Oh lord."

"We should...view this positively."

"Positively? I thought this was the opposite of what you wanted?"

"It was but let's face it, we could use someone on our side. That's what Gabe thinks anyway."

"I guess."

"Maybe just tell her not to speak to the news anymore."

Cynthia was still fretting.

"Look, they already know where we live, maybe Gabe is right, maybe we should embrace anyone fighting for us."

Becky's voice came from the sofa. "What's going on?"

"I think my aunt has become our sect leader or something."

"Ooh, I have to see this!"

Later that night Belle and her mother talked as they lay on their sofa and futon.

"Did it hurt when you gave birth to me?" Belle asked.

"You were surprisingly easy. They had to use the clamp thingys."

"That sounds bad."

"Honestly, at that point, all you care about is getting the baby out."

Belle giggled.

"And Dad? What was he like?"

"He was helpful. He rubbed my back and held my hand, cracked a lot of jokes. He cut the chord."

"Did he cry?"

"He did. He never felt bad crying, he wasn't one of those guys who kept it in."

"I remember him crying."

"He took so many pictures of you. And it wasn't as easy back then as it is now, he brought a disposable camera into the delivery room."

"You know, I don't know how you guys met."
Cynthia moved onto her back and stared at the ceiling.

"We were at community college together. His buddy dated your aunt Vivienne and introduced us."

"Did you have like a first date?"

"We did. He took me to the park, we got some food it was pretty casual."

"Sounds about right."
Things were quiet for a second.

"Did you both want kids?"

"We did. I was happy with one but your dad wanted a lot. A whole little army, he said. Pets too."

"Are you kidding me? I always wanted a dog."

"*He* wanted a dog. I knew it was impractical."

That night Belle's dreams were refreshingly mundane. With the world outside in chaos, this little island of calm at Becky's house felt safer than any place she had ever been. It was only when it was cold outside that the warmth of the inside felt especially pleasant. In the morning she lay in bed considering the prospect of being worshipped. She was her mother's daughter, the spotlight wasn't her favourite place. It was one thing having Aunt Vivienne preaching on her behalf, but the thought of strangers doing it was different. She hadn't checked any of her own social media in days. The image of Brother Abel in front of her house played in her mind. To him, nothing was off-limits. All those people who blew smoke up his ass daily put him on the same level as a senator.

The next day Belle had to take care of Sarah. Gabe offered to drive and she prayed silently the whole way that Yelena and Adrian had not watched the news for the past two days. As the car pulled up she saw

Adrian sat outside alone with a mug of coffee. She stepped outside but he didn't greet her like he usually did.

"Uh, hi Adrian."

He sipped his coffee.

"My mom is asleep right now and Yelena is out, but I thought we could talk."

Her heart sank.

"You saw it didn't you."

"I did." He spotted Gabe in the car and squinted.

"So you know my whole situation."

"We thought you might be pregnant but we didn't want to pry." He pointed to Gabe "Is that the man from the video?"

Gabe stepped out and walked towards the door.

"I'm the man from the video."

Adrian scratched his beard and shrugged.

"Well, I have a million questions. Come on in."

The TV was off and the house was eerily quiet. Adrian sat at the dining table and directed Belle and Gabe to follow his example. He exhaled.

"So. I suppose I know why you read my book so fast."

"Rabbi, Belle has been through a lot. I can answer any questions you have." Gabe said.

Adrian leaned forward and studied him.

"Who are you?"

"Gabriel."

He raised his eyebrows.

"*The* Gabriel?"

He shrugged.

"Yeah. I get that may be a little hard to believe."

"You're less... lion-headed and flaming than I thought."

"I get that a lot."

"So this is a messiah situation?"

"Yes and no."

"I was worried you would say that."

Gabe leaned back in his chair.

"Let's call him *a* messiah."

Belle shifted in her chair.

"Look, Adrian, I get it if you think I'm nuts and don't believe me. All I'm asking is you don't talk to the press about me."

He smiled.

"I wouldn't do that. Sarah and Yelena like you, you're a good carer. If I sold you out I'd have to hire someone else."

"So..uh... do you believe me?"

He puffed out air.

"We'll see."

"We'll see?"

"We'll see what your son does when he's here. I think Gee-dash-dee will forgive me for waiting to make up my mind."

"He certainly will." Assured Gabe.

After a few days at Becky's avoiding TV and the internet, things seemed quiet. Cynthia and Belle took a drive out to the country one evening to stretch their legs. The light was in its golden phase before sunset and the air was pleasantly cool. Cynthia stopped the car at a viewing spot where you could see trees and distant hills, just off a green field of grazing cattle. The distant trees were wearing their autumn leaves, and with mist, separating the layers of the landscape. It looked more like an oil painting than the real thing. Belle walked a little down a dirt path where she could pretend she was the only person alive. She put her hand on her bump and breathed in the cool air. The breeze moved over her skin and whipped her hair. She sat down on the road and observed the birds for some time. She tried to remember which ones were which from Gabe's enthusiastic bird spotting. She recognised a common grackle, a Carolina chickadee, and an eastern towhee.

"I know where I wanna go next," she said after a little while.

As they were driving to her next destination clouds formed, turning the sky into a solid palate of grey, aside from slices of orange light at the horizon. Lukewarm raindrops fell straight down onto the windshield like soft beads. They pulled up at a spot on a road going uphill, by a pine forest. Belle got out and her mom followed. The car sat in a bulge in the road next to the forest's edge. Belle stepped over moss-carpeted beds of fossilising sticks and pine needles, like the mausoleum of the forest. The rain fell in less frequent but larger drops, filtered through the network of downward-facing branches. The light was weaker, with a bottle-green hue from the evergreens. The trunks of the pines stood up straight like an army of waiting soldiers, dwarfing Belle and her mother.

They came to a large boulder with a flat top, covered in thick moss. Belle took a seat and her mother sat next to her. She looked in each direction, pleased to see and hear no trace of civilisation, and exhaled. She gave Cynthia her jacket as a shield from the rain. It had been a while since she had felt it herself.

"Why here, Belle?" asked Cynthia.
She smiled.

"When Gabe first told me about the baby, he took me to a place like this. I mean, he didn't really, or maybe he did, I'm not sure on the details. He said it was to make me feel calmer."

"And do you?"
She looked around. She couldn't see any birds, but a black squirrel skittered up one of the trees.

"I do. It's nice to know there's a place like this

where I'm just another person. Not even that, just another animal. As far as that tree or that squirrel is concerned, I'm just organic matter that will feed the forest floor one day."

"That doesn't sound very comforting."

"I guess not."

The two were quiet for a while.

"I think... I wasn't sure when Gabe told me if I'd suddenly feel like a priestess or a wise woman. The truth is I don't feel any different. I don't feel holier."

"Do you want to?"

"No. But I feel like this would all make more sense if I did."

They stayed until the trees were grey silhouettes. The rain stopped, and Belle's teeth began to chatter.

As they got back to the car Belle turned to her mother.

"I wanna see the house."

"Are you sure?"

She nodded.

"There's been no coverage of it today. They've gone. I just wanna be at home, even if it's just for a second."

Her mom was quiet.

"Do you?"

"I do."

They got into the car and drove to the house without talking. The light was dying as they approached. The neighbourhood was quiet, the street lights flickered and a few fireflies wove in and out of the long, neglected grass. The houses were all more or less like theirs, built out of wood and drywall to look like something grander. They drove up the hill to their own house. The first thing Belle saw was Kenny who lived opposite, a creole man who had seemed 100 years old her entire life. He was sat on his porch with a lamp on a plastic table next to him. Then the house came into view. The word 'whore' had been sprawled in foot-high letters across the door. The remnants of vegetables ran down the walls where they had landed and someone had smashed the front window. Belle took a deep breath to steady herself for her mother's sake. Kenny spoke as they exited the car.

"I've been waitin' here since they first sprayed on the door. I've been tryna scare 'em away."
Cynthia wasn't speaking.

"Thank you, Kenny," said Belle.

"You're welcome. Don't seem right."
Belle wrapped her jacket around her bump like she didn't want Yeshua to see. She linked Cynthia's arm.

"We can go back if you want."
Cynthia had tears in her eyes.

"I will not be driven out of my home forever."
Belle reached into her bag and pulled out the keys.

The door opened just like it always did. Despite the broken window, it seemed no one had gone into the house. Cynthia headed straight to the living room and retrieved the brick that had been thrown in. Belle followed her and saw it was wrapped in paper. She picked up pieces of broken glass as Cynthia unwrapped it.

"Unto thee, it was shown, that thou mightiest know that the Lord he is God; there is none else besides him." She folded it back up. "Cute."

"At least they didn't get in."

"Feels as if they did."

"I get that." Belle sat down. "Should we call the cops?"

Cynthia laughed "I don't think they give a rat's ass."

"I just wanna keep you safe."

"Isn't that my job? To keep my daughter safe."

"I feel like this is on me."

Cynthia sat down next to her and pulled her head to rest on her shoulder.

"I would never in a million years blame you."

Belle hugged her mom back. Hearing the vibration of her voice through her ribcage took her right back to her earliest memories.

"Are we gonna have to run forever?"

"Not if I have anything to do with it."

Belle lay down on her mom's lap and let her stroke her hair.

"I have a confession. I've been watching all of Brother Abel's sermons about me."

Cynthia sighed, "so have I."

They laughed.

"Have you spoken to aunt Vivienne?"

"Yeah. She called me actually, she was sorry for running her mouth but said she had to stand up for us."

"I'm glad someone is."

"We have Kenny across the street."

"That we do."

"Sweetheart, there will be others."

Belle sighed.

"I guess."

The next day the women were all at at Becky's home together. There had been no more coverage from the house, it seemed Brother Abel had developed a sense of basic decency. After lunch, Cynthia called Vivienne. Becky and Belle kept Joey occupied while she was on the phone.

"You shouldn't speak to him, Viv, no. He'll only use it against you. I know, but he has a lot of power around here."

Becky spoke in a whisper. "Has he asked her to come to the temple?"

"Not as far as I know, but he probably will at some point."

"What did he say exactly?" continued Cynthia.

"Maybe it wouldn't be so bad, she speaks their language," added Becky.

"Maybe, rather her than me."

"Look I don't want to get involved with that asshole," said Cynthia.

"She'll probably start her own thing."

"Dude, she's like your high priestess."

"I guess."

"Look, Vivienne, I don't want to waste any energy thinking about that man. OK, I love you too, sis." Cynthia hung up the phone. "What a dick."

"What's up mom?"

"Oh, it's you-know-who."

"What's he said."

"He's on me now."

"What?"

"He's been talking shit about me, Vivienne's furious."

Belle stood up.

"Wait what?"

Cynthia paused.

"He...called me like... a terrible single mother or something?"

"Mom! He can't say that!"

"Look, I just don't want a damn thing to do with him."

Belle grabbed the remote and flipped to Brother Abel's cable channel. A replay of his latest sermon was running. He was stood on a platform in the middle of an audience with a concert-style hands-free mic.

"Why won't she come here? Because she's scared, folks. She knows that we see through her. We see through her lies. But I'm gonna ask you to do

something here that you may not wanna do...we need to show her compassion." The audience laughed. "No, really, folks we do. What do I always say about the lost people in this world, the criminals and the corrupt? Every time folks...single mothers." The audience was uproarious. "And here we are again! A single mother, Cynthia Carter. She raised this girl, if you can call it raising, with no father and here she is so screwed up she's passing off her sins outside of marriage as some kind of divine conception." He outstretched his hands and gave an exaggerated shrug. "Every time folks! They are messed. Up. So now we have a situation where a poor excuse for a mother has raised a fornicator so irresponsible that she's succumbed to satan."
Belle was quiet.

"Sweetie? You have to just ignore him."
Belle reached for her mom's car keys and was out the door before they could stop her.
"Sweetie?!"

"Belle?!"
She got into the car and shut the door before they reached it. Cynthia banged on the door.

"Maybelle you aren't insured to drive this! Maybelle!"
She revved the engine and drove away.

She felt a clarity of purpose in her mom's car. She was totally by herself for the first time in a long while. The car felt like an extension of herself, making her bigger and impenetrable. She turned the radio to Brother Abel's channel. His live sermon was winding up. Her phone kept ringing but she ignored it. She had been told she had to fight back and intended to honour it.

She pulled up to the temple as people were filtering out. She grabbed a ticket from the parking attendant to redeem later and found a spot. She'd seen him do this, he came out after half an hour to greet his adoring followers with one of his staff filming him. Her skin was tingling as she gripped the steering wheel, blinking about half as much as she normally did. After some time he appeared, throwing the double doors open to a crowd of around 100 people. He stood with his arms out wide, his perfect wife next to him. Belle felt a surge of fire as though it was coming directly from deep within her. She got out of the car and marched over.

"Abel!"

The crowd turned to see who was speaking out of turn in front of their beloved pastor. She swept through the throng like they were wheat and stood in front of him. Only now she saw he was shorter than her.

"You've come to me at last Miss Carter."

The crowd was as silent as death. She took a step closer to his face, so she could see where his veneers met his real teeth.

"Don't think that just because I won't play your stupid little publicity game I won't fight back. Preaching in front of my house was low but you stay away from my mother."

He opened his hands as if offering peace.

"Look, I am just messenger for the word of God-"

"Do you remember me?"

"Huh?"

"I came here one year ago and you pulled me and my mother up on stage." She spotted the camera out of the corner of her eye. "Listen to this, everyone, this is how much his beloved followers mean to him, do you remember us?"

He grinned and let out a laugh like air out of a balloon.

"Forgive me, I'm afraid I don't remember that."

"You brought us up on stage and asked about my dead Dad. You asked if he was in a gang and suggested

that he was in Hell because he didn't believe enough.
You insulted her so much my aunt never came here
again."

 He furrowed his brow and placed a hand on her
shoulder.

"You have to forgive me, Belle, I completely
forgot. Now, I wouldn't have said those things about
your mother if I knew she was a widow-"

"That's not the point and you know it." She swept
his hand off her shoulder. "You shouldn't be speaking
about my mother at all."

"Look, it's a free country-"

"I have never courted the spotlight for this, I'm
on the run because of people like you. And you're
boosting your sad little z-list status in this state by using
me."

"I think you're being unfair."

"Have you seen my house? The windows are
broken, it's been trashed. That's you. That's your fault.
You've driven me and my unborn baby out of our
home."

He smiled like a lizard.

"Your baby. The one you want us all to believe is
the son of God."

She was quiet.

"Go on, here's your chance, cameras are rolling,
convince us all." He stood back. "Convert us."

She faced the camera.

"I'm not here to win people over. That's up to
people to decide for themselves. I was picked to be a
mother to my son and that means protecting him from
self-serving pieces of shit like you."

Something hit the back of her head. It was small
and sharp. She felt the back of her head and it was
bleeding.

"Who threw that?" She asked with as steady a

voice as she could muster. No one answered. A small woman tore through the crowd and stood in front of her.

"You got no right to be here, slut! Brother Abel just has the balls to stand up to you!"

"I have as much right as anyone."

The woman shoved her. Like a domino, she hit an older man behind her and he fell to the asphalt. She spun around and saw he had hit the back of his head badly on the ground.

As she reached to help him up a blonde woman shoved her back.

"You assaulted him! We all saw it!"

"No I didn't, let me help him."

"Whore!" Shouted another follower.

"You're a satanist!!"

She turned around to see no Brother Abel.

"Brother Abel is a liar."

A small woman grabbed her arm and threw her into the crowd. No one hit her, but they pulled and pushed, screaming a series of slurs and insults as they grabbed her. She fought back, clawing and handfuls of pink flesh as they flung in her face, with one arm always on her bump.

"Lying jezebel!"

"Sinner!"

"Conwoman!"

"Satan's whore!"

She felt a blow to the side of her stomach. The force unsteadied her, but the crowd was so thick she couldn't determine who did it.

"Who punched me??"

No one answered. She continued shoving back against the wall of bared teeth and grabbing claws. She was younger and stronger than most of them, and she broke free.

She ran to the car, pursued by some of them while the rest tried to reach her with their voices. She had visions of villagers with pitchforks. She fumbled with keys at the car and managed to launch herself sideways into the driver's side before they got to her. One of them managed to pull the door open briefly so she grabbed it back, closing it with all the force she had inside her and locking it. The ones who had followed banged on the windows.

She turned the keys and started up the engine.

"I'd recommend moving if you don't wanna be run over!"

They backed away as she edged forward. She heard loud bangs as stones hit her car. She threw her parking ticket out of the window. She drove on until the glowing tip of the temple was out of sight.

She pulled up at the spot she had visited the day before. Her phone buzzed as she got out of the car but she ignored it. The sun was higher and brighter than it had been yesterday, and the hills looked very green and very real. She took a few steps along the path before shouting out;

"Idiot. You *idiot.*"

She kicked at some dust on the road and let out a guttural cry. She rested her hand on her bump and it felt bigger than ever. One of the cows in the field beside her mooed as if in agreement. She stared up at the sky. "I did what you said, and it SUCKED."

When she looked back down there was a corrugated iron barn at the end of the dirt path that hadn't been there before. It was half rusted with chipped red paint. "Whatever you have in there for me it had better be good."

She marched towards it.

The door was shut with a half-corroded lock which came undone with a forceful yank. The interior was pitch black. She stepped inside and shut the door behind her. Gas lamps ignited one by one revealing a long corridor. The ceiling was high and painted with cherubs, framed with floral gold-painted wood panels. The walls were papered in deep burgundy, with a repeating pattern of gold diamonds. The floor was tiled in black and white like a checkerboard. She stepped along and took in grand paintings in ornate frames. The first was her, heavily pregnant, riding a white horse and fighting an army dressed in black. On the other side, she was holding a lamb, staring at the viewer. Beyond that was one of her on a throne, with her mother sitting at her right side and Gabe on the other. Opposite that, she and Becky were holding up a white sheet. Just before the double oak door at the other end of the corridor were two huge scenes of her surrounded by a crowd of a thousand screaming at her, and in the other, they were bowing. She pushed open the door.

The room was as long as the corridor but twice as wide. At the opposite end was a huge stone fireplace, spitting orange light out into the cavernous space. The walls were burgundy and mounted with stag heads. At the centre was a huge heavy oak table, groaning with food. There were seats at either end, she took the one closest. As she sat two lines of people emerged from doors on either side of the fireplace. They were dressed in black with white aprons and chained at the feet, and did not look her in the eye. She realised she was wearing her beloved white dress. She already knew who had brought her here, and turned to see that the door behind her had disappeared. As she turned back he was taking his seat at the other end, in a blue three-piece suit.

"Afternoon, Ms Carter."

"I don't want to talk to you."

"Why not? I'm just about the only one who isn't

173

pissed off with you right now."

"Yet."

He smiled and clicked his fingers. One of the chained people came forward and poured him a glass of wine.

"Go ahead, have some of the food. It's all stuff you like."

She didn't answer. He rolled his eyes.

"No, none of it's poisoned, yes it's all real. And it isn't some kind of if-you-eat-it-I-own-your-soul trick. I'm just being nice."

She reached for a plate of Oreos in front of her and ate one.

"I'm stuffed."

"Some wine then?"

"I'm four and a half months pregnant."

"It's non-alcoholic. Benjamin will pour it for you, Benjamin?"

A man with dirty blonde hair and ash-white skin stood by the wall closest to her seat stepped forward, his chained feed clanking. He didn't look at her as he took the bottle next to her and poured it. His hands shook and his breath was a low wheeze.

"You'll like this, Benjamin, along with everyone else in this room, are all the dammed souls of people who enslaved your ancestors. In fact, Benjamin stole your great-great-great-great grandmother from her mother in Nigeria when she was three years old. Benjamin, apologise."

"I'm sorry," said Benjamin in a shattered voice.

"Apologise properly."

He lowered himself onto his knees and dropped his head further.

"I'm so, so sorry."

"And what are you, Benjamin?"

"Pig shit. I'm pig shit."

The devil laughed. The mounted stag heads animated

briefly to bellow along with his laughter. Benjamin limped back to his place by the wall.

"See? This is fun. Now, I brought you here to have a proper discussion, like adults."

"Why?"

"Because I'm fucking bored, Ms Carter. These terrible idiots are the company I have. I don't even have the three-headed dog." He finished his wine. "So let's start with any questions you might have, I know you have some."

She took in the faces of the chained servants.

"How's Columbus."

He laughed again.

"He is currently being burned. Second-degree hurts more than third-degree because it exposes the nerves rather than destroys them. Most people ask about Hitler."

"It seemed a little obvious."

"What else do you want to know?"

She thought again.

"What's it like down there? Is it all on fire or what?"

He leaned back.

"Well, it's not actually 'down' anywhere, the easiest way I can explain it is like another dimension. It's dark, it's pitch black unless I need it not to be. It isn't ground or a sky, an up nor a down, it's just darkness. There are others like me, other angels who turned away from God, they torture the dammed. They're all as boring as Gabe, unfortunately."

She pointed at the fire.

"What's your true form?"

He snorted. He got up and the grinding of the chair on the floor ricocheted around the room. He walked over to the fire and the chained people and stag heads turned to see it. He reached in and the fire curled around his arm before his entire form took lit up. He was around twice the size Gabe had been, and was twice as bright. He washed the room in a light like sheet lightning. He had four wings, two outstretched with a span barely contained in the room and the other two wrapped around his human-shaped form. He had three heads, one facing forward of a man, like the face she had seen already but younger-looking and far more beautiful. To the right of this face was one of a ram, and the other was a stag. The chained people drank in the light, maybe the first they had seen in 100 years. He pointed to the extinguished fireplace and the flames snaked off his body and back to their spot.

He turned back to her and seemed older than he had before. His heavy brows and dark lips downturned.

"I was the morning star, the brightest of them all." He returned to his seat. "Gabe was a fucking mailman."

Belle took another sip of wine.

"I have to say I think you're pretty pathetic." The clinking of chains signalled the distress of her servants.

"What?" His face was dark, the flames behind him nearly casting him in a silhouette.

"This bitterness. Is this really the greatest adversary of humankind, of God, of all goodness? A reject with Daddy issues pissed off that he couldn't be the favourite?"

He stared at her and the fire went out, plunging the room into thick black darkness. A spotlight illuminated Belle and she heard his encroaching footsteps. He broke into the spotlight, casting him in a harsh white glow that made shadows fall from his face, turning his head into something closer to a skull. He sat on the corner of the table next to her. He clicked his fingers, and a chained woman brought him a lit cigarette.

"You framed it like an insult but it's a question. You want to know why I fell."

"I guess."

"Let me ask you a question, why did Adam and Eve eat the forbidden fruit?"

"Because you lied to them."

He laughed.

"I didn't do anything, that was a decision they made on their own. So why do you think they did it?"

She thought.

"Because they were curious?"

"About what?"

"About...what would happen if they did."

"They wanted to know what God was hiding. He told them it was forbidden, and when you live in a paradise but one thing is forbidden, that's just too much to pass up. They wanted to know what was beyond the walls of Eden. When there are walls, you want to see what's on the other side. So, they ate it, and what happened?"

Belle shrugged.

"They felt ashamed."

"Of what?"

"Of being naked?"

He stared her down. She realised.

"They were ashamed of everything they didn't know."

"Exactly. They were punished for seeking knowledge. I was too. I wanted to know why we had the positions we did."

"I thought you wanted power?"

He scoffed.

"Never. I never wanted power or to be worshipped, that's *his* game. What I wanted was freedom. Angels aren't like humans, we have free thoughts but we're made to obey God. I know what people say about me but all I ever wanted was free will, I even asked to be made into a human, imagine that." He smirked. "God was so angry he cast me out for all eternity. I never wanted to be his equal or take over, those are lies. I just wanted to live. Angels don't live, angels serve. That gets very fucking boring after a while, especially if you're smart. Which is what confuses me about you."

"Me?"

"You're smart too, Belle. You question things. So why on Earth would you agree to all of this, this servitude?"

Her skin prickled.

"Excuse me?"

"You could have done anything with your life. You were picked because you're smart, you're kind, and you're strong, so why use all that just to be this hate figure? You see what these people are like, they're petty and vindictive and self-serving, why go through all of this for their sake?"

Belle felt the anger she had when she first met him.

"Because I grew up in the world that petty, vindictive, self-serving people like Brother Abel made, like Benjamin made. And it's a world that never really listened to my voice or cared all that much about me. When my dad died my mom worked at a grocery store. She nearly got fired for taking time off for the funeral. And when the bills came in for his hospital stay her insurance company dropped her and she nearly went bankrupt. She's a good person and she always did what was right but this world always trampled her into the dirt. So when Gabe gave me the chance to bring Yeshua into the world I wanted to do it to make it better for her, and everyone like her. And I knew it would suck for me, I knew I was limiting my options, but if I was given the chance to take it all away I would still choose this.

Because if there's one thing human beings can do it's sacrifice themselves for something better. And if my son has to sacrifice himself for us then I'm happy to do it for him."

He puffed on the cigarette.

"You think they deserve it?"

"I think they deserve the chance to be better."

"And what about you?"

She shrugged.

"What about me? I've got a chance to help achieve all of that."

"Sounds like you want power."

"Maybe I do. At least I want to use it to improve the world for others."

He grinned.

"I could help you do that to an even better degree." He picked up a knife and stabbed an apple. He offered it to her. "God is withholding things from you, leaving you to deal with these shit-for-brains people all on your own. I could keep them away for you, protect your son, and give you all the power you want to change the world.

Belle took the apple and bounced it off his head. The chains rattled again. He pinched the bridge of his nose.

"Fine. You want to play dirty? I can play dirty."

In the blink of an eye, the room disappeared and she was alone again on the dirt road. Clouds had convalesced and the light was dying. She walked back to the car and drove to Becky's.

When she arrived back Vivienne, Gabe, Becky, and Cynthia were waiting for her. Joey was asleep across his mother's chest when she came in through the door. Cynthia stormed up to her.

"What did you do?"

"Belle, this is everywhere," said Becky "there are photos all over the internet."

She felt the weight of guilt in her sternum.

"I messed up. I messed up. I was angry and I lashed out. I'm sorry."

The room was quiet for a moment.

Vivienne stood up. "Apologise later, our priority now is keeping you safe."

"Well, my priority is keeping all of you safe. Becky, has anyone called the house."

"No, no thanks to you," said Cynthia "what the hell were you thinking?"

"Cynthy, don't be too hard on her, she was trying to protect you."

"No, Vivienne she's right. And mom, I guess I wasn't thinking. He insulted you and I couldn't take it."

She took her jacket off and sat down on a dining chair. Cynthia knelt at her side

"Belle, you're bleeding!"

"What? Oh." She felt reached to her back and felt dried blood where Abel's follower had hit her. "One of them threw something at me."

"His followers?"

"Yeah."

Cynthia's face calcified into angles at the jaw.

"Well, I understand what you were feeling, at least. But still, don't you ever pull a stunt like that again."

"Never."

"Gabe? Do you have anything to add to this?" asked Becky.

Gabe sat with his arms folded.

"Well..I... Belle is under a lot of pressure and she-"

"Don't do this Gabe, don't kiss my ass right now,

I just need you to be honest."
He smiled.

"Fine, it was the dumbest thing I've ever seen."

Thank you." She sighed, "Why did I do that
Gabe? Aren't I supposed to be a wise, responsible
person?"
He shrugged.

"Maybe it's more about who you're going to
become."

"I don't have forever to become what my son
needs."

"Does anyone?" He replied.

Belle moved to the sofa. Her mom took the seat
next to her.

"Belle, let's just lay low and forget about this. I'll
draw you a bath, take an early night. Tomorrow I'll take
you to Adrian's house, get you back into a routine.
Belle did as she was told.

11
Our Lady of Exile

When Belle arrived at Adrian and Yelena's home their faces were painted with forced smiles. Adrian stumbled over his words as he greeted her.

"You saw it didn't you?"

Yelena sighed.

"It's alright, I'm totally aware of how dumb it was."

"Is your face cut?" She asked.

"Yeah, they threw stuff at me, pushed me, they even knocked down some old man. Of course, the pictures they shared cut out all of that."

Adrian smiled. "No judgement here, we get it."

Belle began her duties, starting with making breakfast. Adrian started on his own as she prepared oatmeal.

"Can I ask you something theology related?"

He grinned.

"Of course, that's my job."

"What do you know about Satan?"

He raised an eyebrow.

"Don't tell me you've met him too?"

She broke eye contact.

"Nah, no, I just want to actually know what I'm

talking about if Abel accuses me of being in league with the devil again."

"Well," he began "it isn't my area of expertise, but the idea of Lucifer the fallen angel isn't detailed a whole lot in scripture, it's more of a mix of ideas that have been enhanced and padded out with good old folklore."

"So it's nonsense?"

"Not necessarily, scripture is no more legitimate than any other source. I think of it as a set of stories, God isn't a great bookkeeper. I don't take any source too seriously."

"So why did you become a Rabbi if you don't think its all true?"

"I'm striving to understand God, this is just me trying my best." He replied flatly. "In another universe, I'd be a Buddhist monk or an Imam, I grew up going to synagogue so it's what I'm used to. I just have a bad habit of... using a sledgehammer to crack a nut, I think is the expression. I became a rabbi to try and figure out God, most people just take drugs."

"I think I get it."

"The good news now is my Mom's carer is in direct contact with the big man himself, I'll be coming to you with my theological questions from now on."

She smiled. "He doesn't talk to me directly, he goes through Gabe."

Belle brought Sarah her oatmeal as she sat on the front porch. The air outside was cool but stagnant.

"Who is that?" asked Sarah.

Belle turned and saw a white flash of a car on the horizon. Cars didn't often come down the dirt road where the house was, and they were visible from the moment they emerged from the distant woods. Belle leaned forward to see the car better as it got closer. It was a vintage Cadillac, polished within an inch of its life. She thought of who she knew that had a collection of vintage cars and ran inside. She burst through the door and ducked behind the sofa, and threw the curtains shut, peering through a small crack. No words were exchanged but Adrian put down the pot he was stirring and went outside.

Sure enough, the Cadillac pulled up at the fence of the farmhouse and Brother Abel stepped out. Yelena locked the door and turned down the radio so they could hear the men talk.

"Who are you?" Sarah asked, her question was ignored.

"Rabbi Sanders! I realised we've never actually met in person, you know me, of course."

"This is private property Abel, we may be a peaceful people but we're not above defending ourselves."

Brother Abel laughed

"I'm staying outside the gate, Rabbi, don't worry. I'm not here to fight."

"Are you going to take a picture of my house and call it a dirty shack?"

"No, no, it's lovely!"

"Well then, I hope you're here to apologise."

He flashed a smile.

"Me apologise? You started all of this."

"I'm a religious leader, Abel, I did my job. We are supposed to help people understand God, not collect cars."

"Money is a blessing, Rabbi. Envy is a sin."

He leaned on the fence. He was wearing a blinding

white suit jacket, stonewashed jeans and a black shirt.

"I'm here because I've just about wracked my brain trying to figure out where this girl is hiding. She attacked one of my congregation, you know."

"We both know she didn't attack him."

"Sounds to me like you've been speaking to her."

"I've never met her, I just know you well enough."

Brother Abel smiled again.

"So she isn't here?"

"Why would she be here? Have you tried trashing her house again?"

"A little birdy told me she's been working for you."

"I think you know how small my synagogue and my congregation is, I would know if she's been there."

He kicked at dirt.

"I should hope not. I may have my issues with you but we're both men of God. You know as well as I that she's a heretic. It would be a sin to protect someone like that."

"If she is a heretic, I say sinners need the most help."

Belle ducked down lower. Yelena put her hand on her back.

"Sounds an awful lot like you do know her."

"Even if I did, there's no way I'd let you through that gate."

He drummed on the fence.

"To tell you the truth, Adrian, I know she's here, I'm just giving you a heads up. The cops are on their way."

Belle felt a stab in her chest. Yelena's hand tightened on

her shoulder.

"Cops?"

"Yeah. Several eyewitnesses saw her assault an elderly man who is now in hospital. I have to protect my flock, I just thought I'd let you know they're on their way, as a mark of my esteem. Man of gee-dash-dee to Man of gee-dash-dee."

Adrian seemed frozen. Belle willed him to say something clever as Abel returned to his car and sped off along the horizon.

He walked back inside and left the door open. He stood for a moment and scratched his beard. Belle switched her gaze between him and Yelena, both mute.

"I can't go. I won't go to jail -"

"Our priority has to be your safety-"

"I won't go Yelena."

At last her gaze was met.

"They chain you up, they chain you to a bed and you have to give birth all on your own I won't do that. I can't abandon my boy."

She tried to wrestle her voice away from the shriek it was currently operating at. Yelena hugged her as she shook.

"They can't take me away from him. I can't let down Reece's parents."

Adrian ran his hand through his hair.

"We know you're innocent, there has to be something to prove that."

"I have to go, I have to run."

"Where?"

She couldn't answer.

"I don't know, I just – I have to, I can't go to jail."

He sat beside them.

"You need to think about what's safest for you right now. If you run..." He paused. "They can take extreme measures to catch you. I don't want that."

"If you go quietly they can set a decent bail and you can get back home to fight this." Yelena continued. She studied the floorboards as Yelena held both her hands.

"I want to see my mom."

Yelena sighed, "I don't think we have time for that."

"I'm gonna call her."

Yelena got up and passed Belle her phone. She went upstairs to Sarah's room and sat with her back against the door. She read her mom's name on the list of contacts through her water-blurred vision and the cracks in her phone screen.

She held her breath until Cynthia answered.

"Belle? Is something wrong?"

She took a breath.

"Brother Abel was just here. He's saying I assaulted someone yesterday. An old man."

Her voice broke like a dam.

"He said he knows I'm here and the cops are on their way."

There was silence for a moment at the other end of the line.

"Belle, we can fight this. Whatever bail they want, I'll find it somehow. You're gonna be home with me again soon, I promise you."

Belle couldn't take her mother's promises as facts anymore, still, it was a comfort to hear them.

"I don't want to deliver the baby chained up, mom."

"You won't you'll be safe in a hospital and me, Gabe, your aunt Vivienne, we'll all be there."

Downstairs she heard two new voices talking with Adrian and Yelena.

"They're here."

"Belle, listen to me. I know you better than anyone. You have the strength of character to get through this."

She took a deep breath to steady her voice.

"OK."

"I love you."

"I love you too."

She hung up as there was a knock on the door. She heard Adrian say 'she's not a threat.'.

"Belle Carter?"

She stood up and took a stance with her hands on her head in the middle of the room.

"The door is unlocked. I'm not armed."

The door swung open to reveal three cops, one with a gun pointed at her. Her heart seized, but she suppressed the urge to move her hands to protect her bump. Sudden movements were always a risk around predators.

One officer barked "On your knees!"

She did as she was told. The officer with the gun returned it to his holster and took out a pair of handcuffs. When he faced some resistance trying to move her tense arms behind her back, he pushed her forwards onto her front.

"She's pregnant!"

"Ma'am stand back!"

As her Miranda rights were read to her Belle breathed in as far as she could to relieve pressure on her stomach. In her head, she apologised to Yeshua. As she was dragged back up to her feet, she saw Yelena filming the arrest in the bathroom. She thanked her with a nod.

Outside Brother Abel's shiny wife stood in front of two cameramen facing the house. Belle bowed her head.

"My husband and I are extremely grateful to our law enforcement officers who have acted so quickly on this matter. Nothing is more important to us than the safety of our congregates and the word of God."

One of the cameramen broke away from her to get a running shot of Belle's face. She turned her head but like a wasp, he sprung to the other side to capture her expression. When she turned back she met the eyes of Abel's wife for a moment. Her camera-ready smile didn't break. Belle didn't think of herself as holding sexist stereotypes, but seeing a woman maintain a solid, cheery composure watching a pregnant girl being dragged away in handcuffs for something she knew she was innocent of sent cold blood running through her body.

"We will be pursuing this matter to the full extent of the law and providing our full support for any medical and legal costs to her victim-"

"You can't film here this is private property," interrupted Yelena.

Belle didn't catch the response as the door of the police car closed on her.

The police processed her with the detachment of airport staff. The only benefit was that she felt she was being treated no different from any other criminal. It was as though it was happening to someone else, a physical space she just so happened to be inhabiting until she could move on and go back to her life. Beyond what they demanded, she didn't say a word.

After an hour or so a state-appointed attorney arrived. He introduced himself cheerily as Mr Gretszky. He was a middle-aged man with a small, wiry frame. He had slightly longer stubble than she expected but was otherwise reassuringly smart. His demeanour eased her mind a fraction.

"The man you're accused of assaulting sustained some head injuries but nothing serious, he spent a couple of hours in the hospital and was discharged. Because there was injury you're looking at a class A misdemeanour."

"Meaning?"

"At best a fine, at worst, a year in prison."

Her stomach leapt. Mr Gretszky picked up on her distress.

"Keep in mind that is the worst-case scenario. Given your age, lack of criminal record, and pregnancy, I doubt you'll face anything like that. It will most likely be a fine, community service, suspended sentence, that sort of thing."

Her nerves settled. An idea struck her.

"Is there a video of it?"

"None has come forward. There are photographs of you in the crowd but not the indecent itself."

"There has to be some, Abel always has cameras on him."

"It's something we'll pursue."

She picked at the styrofoam cup of water she had been given.

"What about, what they're saying about me? That I'm insane."

He let out a barely suppressed sigh.

"It could affect things if we were to go to trial. However, I would advise not going to trial."

She bristled.

"What do you mean."

"Brother Abel is known for his theatrics, going to court could be the ultimate PR stunt. Not to mention how Governor Kitchering could spin it. He made his money in the private prison system, and he would gain a lot from publicly discrediting you further."

"So what are you saying?"

"It may be best to go for a plea bargain."

Her eye twitched. She felt a rush of hot blood around her body.

"No one likes to hear that but we need to consider your overall well-being."

"If I plead guilty he wins."

"If you don't you could end up stuck inside until you get a trial date. That could take months. Then when you do get a trial, Abel will no doubt use it to drag your name through the dirt even more. He has deep pockets, and -" he leaned in closer as if someone may be listening "- access to the Governor's influence.
She didn't say anything for a moment.

"You're a young woman with no record of violence and you're most likely suffering from trauma. You should be at home with your family so you can have your baby in peace. Men like brother Abel, you just can't give them oxygen or they keep burning away."
Belle sighed and drank the last dregs of her water.

"I want to talk to my mom."

Belle looped her fingers through the curly wire as the phone rang.

"Hello?"

"Mom it's me."

"Oh my God, sweetie are you OK?"

She leaned in close to the wall-mounted phone.

"I'm a little better. They gave me a lawyer and he said I'll probably end up with a fine or community service or something."

"Okay. Okay, well, that's not so bad."

"But to ensure that, he says I'll have to plead no contest."

There was a silence at the other end, Belle heard the faint whistling of Cynthia sucking air through her teeth.

"And how do you feel about doing that?"

Belle hated that question.

"I don't know, Mr Gretszky said If I don't plead guilty and it goes to trial I'm basically giving brother Abel a platform, not to mention jeopardising myself."

"Yeah,"

"The thing that scares me most is having to give birth in jail. They take your baby away after 24 hours, mom."

"I won't let that happen. If they want bail or something, we'll make it."

She leaned her head against the cold wall.

"I just... think if I plead guilty then it's like I'm just letting him win. I'm admitting to something I didn't even do, it just makes me feel sick. I think no matter what happens he'll spin it as a victory for him."

"Look, you have your principles, and it's wonderful, but right now I don't give a shit about Abel and his media circus, I care about you and Yeshua. If he wants to rant about you til he's blue in the face, who cares? As long as your home with your baby, fuck the world."

Belle let out a small, weak laugh.

"Yes?"

"Yes, mom."

"Good. I can't force you to do anything, but that's my two cents. Oh, Gabe told me to tell you that you can... summon? Yeah, he used the word summon, you can summon him at any time."

"Might draw attention."

"That's what I said."

"OK, I think I have to go talk to the cops at some point soon."

"OK, just don't let them get to you, you've done nothing wrong and you're a good person. I love you."

Belle was escorted back to the holding cell she was being kept in. It was a small, bare room with the same painted brick as the rest of the police station. It had a bed that was six inches too narrow and a thin mattress with a rubbery coating. She lay back and let her hand rest on her bump. It was just reaching the threshold of being too big to hide, not that there was any point in hiding anymore. She felt a kick, like the beat of a bird's wing. The urge to cry rose again. She wanted to, it was like a weight sitting behind her eyes, a balloon that refused to burst. She squeezed her eyes tight but could only manage enough of a tear to blur her vision for a moment. She gave up and turned towards the wall, envisioning her back as a windbreaker protecting Yeshua from the world.

Closing her eyes for a moment, she heard bird song. She opened them again and her narrow bed was in a forest of a tall pine. The same place Gabe first took her to tell her about Yeshua. She sat up and swung her legs onto the moss-covered ground.

"Gabe?" She called out to the silent trees and her breath fogged in the air. She stood up and looked around. She found herself smiling as she took in the forest air. The air was far colder than she had experienced in years in Tennessee. She placed a hand on her stomach, a habit she was developing in times of fear and stress as well as contentment.

"Belle." A low voice came from between two trees around ten feet behind her. Even as she was turning round to see him she was in no doubt as to who was speaking to her.

"I don't want to speak to you. You've nothing to offer me."

A fire sparked in a pile of twigs between them, lighting Lucifer's face.

"Forgive the theatrics but I'm getting a little sick of total darkness."

"Just give it up, OK? I don't know what you expect to accomplish. I've said no enough, Gabe is nearby, you know you can't get through to me."

"This isn't about me anymore, Belle, It's about you." His face, now stubbled, seemed to morph into a hundred others in the jumping firelight. "I don't hate you, Belle, I feel sorry for you. All of these sacrifices you've made, your job, your home, your future, any semblance of a normal life, and now your freedom. You're a smart girl and you've thrown it all away."

"A lot of that is your fault" she snapped, the fire stinging her eyes. "You've been lashing out like a kid ever since I told you where to stick your offer."

He held out his hands as if to calm a growling dog.

"My point is, Belle, you deserve better. Do you think they'll thank you? They treat you like this, imagine how they'll treat Yeshua."

She bristled. Her baby's name coming out of his mouth stung like a curse word.

"He's not being sent here because people deserve it, he's being sent to help them get better."

He sighed.

"People will ruin it, Belle. Look at Brother Abel. He teaches from the same words as your good friend Adrian but you see how different they are. Humans take good things, pure messages, and corrupt them. In 100 years there will be men just like Brother Abel twisting the words of your son."

She wrapped her arm tighter around her stomach.

"Even if it's one person getting it right, it will be enough."

He rolled his eyes.

"You just won't listen, will you? I am trying to help you. I am the ONLY one trying to help you." His voice climbed in volume. "Gabe, your mom, your aunt, they all have their advice but have any of them tried to help you out of this? Has anyone shown you that you have the power to break free?"

His face was as twisted in anger as she had ever seen it. She felt strangely unafraid, seeing his own will weaken.

"They don't deserve any of this. They don't deserve a saviour. The few good people there are, like you, all they do is struggle to get by in a world made by people like Kitchering. You really think your son is going to magically change everything?"

She didn't say anything to him.

At that moment he stormed towards her, his face white with anger. He was far taller than her and within a few strides, he was able to reach out and pin her against a tree with his hand against her forehead.

The sensation was like being dropped in an icy sea as black as charcoal. The ill will of all of humanity, the callous and cruel actions people commit daily, murder and violence, abuse and rape, neglect and hatred. The malice and carelessness of each deed happening across the world shot through her and rattled her skeleton like the bass from a loudspeaker. She tried to scream but the sound was strangled. Her legs went weak but the force from his grip was strong enough to hold her upright all on its own. It choked every system in her body and her brain felt as though it was in a vice. Knowing that evil existed was one thing, feeling it rushing through your veins like an opiate was enough to stop your heart.

He finally released her and she fell to the floor. The autumn leaves felt disgusting, like flakes of skin. She choked on the cold air.

"And that's what I feel, every day, in my realm." He stepped back. "I'm sorry to do that, I truly am. You were strong to take it as well as you did, it's been known to kill."

Her whole body shook. She searched to find venomous words to spit at him but the energy to speak evaded her.

"I just want you to remember that feeling, what they're capable of, next time you throw your life away for them."

The fire shot up in the air and she heard him yell. She curled up and covered her head with her hands. When she peered through her fingers she saw Gabe standing between her and the devil, the fire surrounding them. For the first time, she saw a spark of fear in the fallen angel's eyes.

"Gabe," he said, "how long has it been?"

"You chose your path, leave the rest of us alone."

She heard him laugh.

"You're debasing yourself -"

Before he could continue a tongue of fire leapt up and knocked him to the ground with enough force to kill a person. Belle raised her head and saw something new, his eyes shining and red. He seemed to search his mind before the fire extinguished all at once, plunging the clearing into the pitch darkness of night, completely snatching away the daylight. When her eyes adjusted enough for her to see she was back in her holding cell, he was gone.

Gabe turned and knelt beside her. He opened his mouth as if expecting words to come out but nothing did for a moment.

"I know I said I wouldn't come unless you called me but..." his voice was weakening. "I felt this."

He reached out to touch her face and she jumped back. She lifted herself back up to being seated as her whole body shook.

"I can help, Belle. I can show you the good."

"No." She replied. "I need to remember this feeling."

His eyes widened.

"Belle?"

She stood up and banged on the door with both fists.

"Get my lawyer! Get Mr Gretszky! Tell him I plead not guilty!"

12
Untier of Knots

The next evening saw Belle's bail hearing. After talking to Mr Gretzsky, she refused to see or speak to anyone. She lay on her bed feeling as if her skin was on fire, shifting between tensing every muscle in rage and crying. They had given her a baggy orange shirt and pants, an outfit not made for women five months pregnant. Her belly strained at the synthetic fabric.

She knew what to expect as she was led into the room for the hearing. Sure enough, the spectator pews were packed. Gabe and her Mom sat in the front row behind her lawyer and they winced to see how she was dressed. One row behind them sat Abel and his wife. The other rows were a mass of faces and muttering. She picked out some she recognised from the day she confronted Abel. The rest were unknown to her. Word had gotten out.

The judge, Steven Krendle, was a man who looked to be in his late seventies. He had the greyest skin and the thinnest lips Belle had ever seen. She kept her eyes fixed on him as Mr Gretszky explained her lack of criminal convictions, her good character, and her fragile physical and mental state. She had read about Krendle before. He often appeared on local news bragging about how tough he was on drug addicts. She now knew the exact structure of the cruelty in his soul. It should have made her afraid, but she also knew of those who harboured worse things inside them.

When the state prosecutor got up to speak she could see the expression of the judge soften and his shoulders drop an inch or two. She kept her eyes fixed on the back of the prosecutor's head as he spoke, firing her rage out to him. Shortly after he started talking he scratched the nape of his neck, which she counted as a victory.

"Much has been said outside this courtroom of Miss Carter's apparent belief that she is pregnant with the son of God, that is not what we are here to discuss. Multiple witnesses have attested to her assault on an elderly man, who was hospitalised with his injuries. The attack was described by multiple witnesses as vicious and deliberate, in retaliation for an unknown comment made by the man during a moment of heightened emotion for all present. I believe Miss Carter presents a credible threat of further violence and, having previously gone into hiding with a friend, an obvious flight risk."

After he had finished speaking M. Gretszky stood up again.

"My client has asked to say something."

A murmur rippled through the crowd. As Belle stood she briefly turned and whispered 'don't worry' to her mother.

She faced the judge for a moment before speaking.

"Your honour, I did not attack Mr Tyson, and I don't expect you to believe me when I say that. Somewhere out there, as with everything Brother Abel does, there will be video footage that proves I was pushed into him by a member of his congregation. I was punched in the stomach by another. I'm sure Abel will be delighted to hear that both myself and my baby are perfectly fine."

She took a breath, there was silence.

"I don't expect to convince anyone that what I have claimed about myself is true, I know I would probably not believe it if I hadn't lived it. I only hope that people will believe I am innocent. Abel talks a lot about the devil, he believes I work for him. Or that I'm carrying him in my womb, I forget which one it is."

There were a few suppressed giggles in the room.

"But In recent days I have become far more familiar with evil than I ever hoped. It's not always deliberate, usually, it's just people not caring enough. What I ultimately want to say is that I'm done with looking away. I'm done with just trying to keep myself safe and running away from it all. So I am pleading not guilty. And I am promising that I am going to fight all of this. For my sake, my son's sake, all of us. I've seen the worst and I can't back away from it anymore. And a lot of people will laugh their heads off when I say this, but I do have God on my side."

She sat back down and there was an impenetrable silence for a moment. Then, a mixture of laughter and incredulity. She felt a hand squeeze her shoulder that she knew was Gabe's. The judge demanded silence.

"Miss Carter you are charged with aggravated assault against Mr Charles Tyson. Given the nature of the crime, the state will set the bond at $10,000.

Belle heard her mother begin to weep as Gabe reassured her they would pay for it. The chatter resumed as she was led away. She smiled at Cynthia and Gabe and fixed a look on Brother Abel. He and his wife were expressionless and unblinking.

In the studio.

Studio lights burned Brother Abel's skin as the make-up girl put the finishing touches on his face. He stretched his jaw and practised enunciating his vowels.

"You're on in thirty seconds."

"Thank you, Jennifer."

The crew finished their jobs and scurried into the background. He was left standing in the middle of a mock-living room set, an autumnal cornucopia on the repurposed driftwood coffee table and an abstract painting of Moses holding his staff aloft on the wall behind him. Lights behind the camera shut off and the crew remained as still as they could in darkness. A stage hand-counted down the last few seconds before the broadcast went live.

Abel's face broke into a warm smile.

"Good afternoon, my friends. Once again I welcome you to my home where you, and God, are always welcome." He took a seat on the large leather corner sofa that dominated the set. "Now, you've heard me say this many times, that our God is loving. This is true, our God's mercy is boundless, his love is boundless." The camera rolled closer to take in his face, tanned and powdered for the studio lights. "This does not mean that we do not fight when we see injustice. To fight the wrongs of this world as children of God isn't just permissible, it is our duty."

He crossed his legs and leaned forward at the waist like a father gently explaining to a child why what they had done was wrong.

"Yesterday Miss Maybelle Carter was sent to jail for assaulting one of our family here. Instead of showing remorse at her bail hearing, she continued to deny her guilt and repeat her blasphemous lies about carrying the Son of God. As I have explained before, nothing that she claims can be found in scripture and none of us is above the sacred word of God. While I do not agree that she should have been offered bail, I am reasonably pleased with the amount chosen by the state prosecutor. However, I fear that we are dealing with more than just a common criminal, her words in the courtroom yesterday have reinforced my fears that she is a representative of Lucifer himself."

"I fear that if more lost souls are taken in by her false message, God-fearing people could find themselves suffering similar violence and cruelty. I ask you all to make your voices heard and let your representatives know the importance of ensuring she stays behind bars. I am continuing to work with Governor Bob Kitchering to ensure his re-election and good work cracking down hard on violent crime. Now, I want to show you some of the missionary work our temple is doing in the deprived urban areas of Chicago."

"Cut to VT!"

The lights rebalanced in the studio and an assistant rushed onstage to hand Brother Abel a coffee.

"Thank you, Jennifer."

"There's someone on the phone for you in your dressing room, Brother Abel."

He swallowed his coffee and headed over to the small adapted bathroom grandly labeled a 'dressing room'. Picking up the phone he saw that the caller was Governor Kitchering.

"Hey, Bob."

"Just watching the broadcast Abel" Bob laughed, which crackled through the phone. "You really believe all of that spawn of Satan stuff?"

"I know you're not a man of faith, Bob, but it isn't just God who works in mysterious ways."

"Whatever. So, we tapped the Rabbi's phones as you asked."

"Hear anything we could use against her?"

"No. But he was asking questions about the footage."

"Footage?"

"From the day. He said to a friend of his that if they had footage it would show she's innocent."

"Hm."

"There isn't any footage is there?"

"No one has brought anything to me."

"Right, Right."

"What about the Aunt? The mother."

"The aunt is crazy. She believes this son of God crock 100%. The mother don't talk to nobody! All we got is two calls to the water company. I thought the MLK wiretaps were boring."

"So nothing?"

"We're looking into this guy Gabe she's been seen with. He worked with her at the gas station for a little while, he's the guy she's talking to in the diner video. We figure if she's running some kind of con he will know something about it."

"And?"

"Nothing. No birth certificate, medical records, previous jobs, or previous homes. There's no trace of the guy beyond a few months ago. He doesn't even have social media!"

"Creepy. He was there yesterday, he kept staring at me."

"But my guess is he's the key. If we can find something on him then we can discredit them both completely."

"He could be the devil" theorised Brother Abel, flatly.

Bob cackled.

"Are you serious? Be realistic for one second, will you? This religious crap wins votes but my son's reputation is at stake here. We must discredit her completely. Some people are actually starting to believe her."

Abel bristled at Governor Kitchering's casual blasphemy.

"Why the fuck didn't she just take a plea bargain? What pregnant woman would choose to be in jail?"

"It's like I said, she's evil."

"She's not evil, she's just an idiot. She could win this trial, you know, we got witnesses but no hard evidence. And people are rallying behind her. If she gets the right lawyer we're screwed."

"Well, you know I'm praying for your son."

"Yeah, yeah, we just need to find proof this is all a scam. Or she's nuts. Either way, I can't have her taken seriously ever again."

Lincoln County Women's Facility

Belle held back tears as she heard her mother's flow.

"I just wish you were home."

"I do too. More than anything. I just *couldn't* let them win that easily. If I wasn't in this situation I'm in maybe I would have taken it, but knowing what my son is going to be, I just couldn't."

"When he's here you might understand why a mother would have her child make these sacrifices."

She would have been angry at such a remark a few days

ago, but she couldn't muster it at that moment.

"I get it, mom. The awfulness of this place, of the thoughts and feelings that built it, I see it all so vividly that sometimes I get lightheaded. But that's why I can't turn away anymore."

Cynthia sighed.

"I guess I can't make you do anything. You are over eighteen."

"How is Vivienne?"

"Oh, she's like your damn campaign manager! She's got people to organise funds for you and everything."

"Funds?"

"Your bail money. She put together this thing online that people can donate to, Abel has been trying to get it taken down but it's starting to pick up some steam. People were really engaged by what you said, someone got a video of it, it's making a difference."

"Most people still just think I'm a nutjob though, right?"

"Oh, totally."

She giggled.

"I prefer that sometimes."

"Anyway I gotta go, I promised I'd help your aunt Vivienne with something. Call me whenever you can, OK?"

"Bye, mom."

Belle had thought it best to keep the details of the facility vague. She placed the phone back in its wall-mounted receiver and was ushered along to make way for the next woman. In the week she had been there she had asked herself constantly *why didn't I know about this?* She slept on a narrow bunk bed in a room with ten other women. Since she had been inside she had come across two other inmates who were also pregnant. She heard about another who had to wait six months before she could get out and see the baby she had given birth to on the inside.

Only a few of the women knew who she was, but all the staff knew. It hadn't taken long to find out who the county Sheriff had been before he had taken a more high-powered political position: Governor Bob Kitchering. He brought in the budget cuts, the two meals a day, the pink-striped uniforms designed to humiliate, the exercise time spent chained to one another, and the humiliating chants. He started off investing in private prisons with his father's money and used his political influence to make them cheaper to run. At night she built a timeline, with each blow to their conditions, he moved a step up the political ladder. She adopted an initial tactic of being on her best behaviour. After her bail hearing speech, she knew they would be waiting for her to step out of line so they could send her to solitary. Although, each day spent in a crowded cell made solitary seem more appealing.

"My two sisters and I have all been in here," explained Gia, her cellmate on an adjacent bunk, through whispers that night. "Mom took a lot of drugs, we took them too. My older sister got in for meth possession, my younger sister got done for prostitution, I got hooked on opioids and ended up on heroin."

"I'm sorry" Belle replied. Gia was thin in a way that immediately struck you as the result of something sniffed or injected. Her eyes always seemed half-closed, and they were the most hollow and sad eyes she had ever seen. During exercise time, Gia had to wear a shirt that read ADDICT so any passers-by would know why she was there.

"My grandma is looking after my son. She says she's gonna help me go to rehab when I get out."

"Did she help your sisters?"

"No. They stole money from her and stuff. She doesn't talk to them."

"What's he like? Scott?"

Gia's face illuminated for the first time since she arrived.

"He's real loud, he loves singing. He's kind of destructive, like he builds stuff out of lego and just breaks it, drives me nuts."

"How old is he?"

"Four. Had him when I was about a year younger than you."

She turned her head towards the bars to check for anyone listening in.

"How long have you got before your boy gets here?"

"Four months."

"Have you seen the OB/GYN in here yet? I hear he's real nice."

"Not yet. Everything has been so crazy I just can't wait to see him on the ultrasound again. He feels so far away right now."

"Who's the father?"

Belle stammered.

"Oh I'm sorry, it's none of my business."

"No, it's OK. It's pretty complicated is all."

"Isn't it always?"

A pillow hit Gia in the face from below.

"Shut the hell up!"

"You shut up, Dianne!"

A baton hit the bars with an echoing clang.

"Everyone better shut up!" Yelled a guard. They did so.

A week later Belle was given an appointment with the OB/GYN. She was cuffed and brought to a medical room that was the target of budget cuts. The same budget cuts Kitchering made before he won the most recent election. The window was covered in a metal screen thick with grime and the examination bed was protected with a trash bag. The doctor entered, a large-built south Asian man with greying temples. He smiled at her and introduced himself as Dr Ahmed.

"I'm afraid I only have a few minutes with you today, I have three other facilities to visit. We're just going to take some vitals, and check both you and the baby are healthy."

He took her temperature, heart rate, and blood pressure.

"You should be having an ultrasound at this point but budgets are..." He rolled his eyes. "But your vitals are good, so we can reasonably assume things are OK." He fetched a stethoscope from a repurposed filing cabinet. "At this point, the baby is about ten ounces, around six inches long. You should be feeling it kick a lot."

"Oh, I do."

"And not that you can in here, but you should try and take it easy where you can."

He took the stethoscope and placed it on her belly.

"Yeah, it has a good heartbeat. Here," he handed her the earpieces of the stethoscope and she shuffled up the bed to listen. The rapid heartbeat came through loud and clear, as well as the low-grade rumble of her cloying hunger. Her second meal of the day was three hours away.

Her strategic disassociation crumbled. Listening to his heartbeat and his movements broke through the protective barriers like a tank. She began to weep, and before Dr Ahmed noticed this she had dissolved into near-painful, full-body sobs.

"Oh, no, let me get you a tissue. Some water too." She thanked him. The crying was only providing partial relief. She felt a few tears on her face but it wasn't the cathartic wave she needed, it was muscular and skeletal, squeezing her whole body. As Dr Ahmed went into the next room to get her a styrofoam cup of water she lay on her side, wishing she could just cry like she used to. This was closer to wailing.

"I understand this can be emotional." He said, handing her the water. He took a seat next to her and spoke in hushed tones. "I know about...Brother Abel and all that stuff. I didn't wanna bring it up because I assumed you didn't want any differential treatment." She nodded.

"Look, I have to go, I'll see if I can get you to somewhere you can be alone for a little while, OK?"

She agreed and he stepped outside to talk to a guard. He shut down any suggestion of the sort, and she could hear in the Doctor's voice a frustration born from years of having his advice ignored. The guard entered.

"Get up."

She did so and he cuffed her. He led her back to the cell she shared with the other women and she tried to suppress the muscles in her face from twisting back into sobs. As she was ushered back into the cell Gia saw her red eyes.

"Are you alright?"

She crawled into bed and yanked the cover over her head, trying to drown out the voices of her fellow inmates and pretend she was alone.

That night she tried to sleep but her body was a steel knot. She didn't remove her hand from her bump for a moment.

A few days later she was woken up early by a baton at the bars of her cell.

"Time to go to work, ladies!"

Gia lifted her head and threw it back on the thin pillow with a sigh.

"What's happening?" Belle asked.

"It's our turn to go out and pick up trash."

"Pick up trash? Do we get paid?"

Gia scoffed.

"My sister did, 20 cents an hour. Since Kitchering became governor we don't get paid at all."

"Twenty cents an hour????"

"Yeah, she had to save it up to buy tampons. They give you like, ten free pads now."

They were loaded onto a bus and drove out to the middle of the highway, each with a shirt displaying their charge. As they exited they were given a trash bag and litter picker. The rain was pouring and the sky was as dark as dusk despite the early hour. As Belle was handed her trash bag she saw two guards erect a large pink sign reading PARTY TOO HARD AND END UP HERE. Cars beeped at them as they passed. One threw a coke can in their direction.

"I thought chain gangs weren't a thing anymore," Belle muttered to Gia as they swept through the long grasses to pick up torn-up magazines reduced to pulp in the autumn rain.

"I think it's not technically a chain gang since we're not chained."

"How have I never heard about this until now? I wouldn't treat my worst enemy like this."

Gia shrugged.

"No one gives a fuck about us. We're criminals."

"We're in jail, not prison, most of us haven't been proven guilty of anything."

"It could be worse, a cousin of mine was locked up in Arizona and they had to do this. She got heatstroke."

Belle squinted her eyes in the rain. She was beginning to shiver.

"Stop talking." Demanded a guard.

"We're still working, aren't we?" Belle snapped back. Gia's eyes widened as the guard came over.

"Do not get smart with me, miss Carter, I can throw you in solitary. In fact.-" He took her litter picker away "-pick it up by hand."

She exchanged a look with Gia. Struggling to bend down, she grabbed a handful of newspaper and shoved it into the trash bag. Her temples throbbed with anger.

After what felt like hours the hunger was agony. The guards initiated a call-and-response chant. The inmates would sing;

We don't run and we don't fight

To which the guards responded.

We got sticks and they got stripes.

Belle struggled to get the words out through her chattering teeth.

As the guards were loudly discussing how to incorporate clapping into the chant, a convertible Belle recognised pulled up behind the parked bus. Brother Abel stepped out, carrying a golf umbrella. He was followed by one of the cameramen she recognised from Adrian's house. Her anger began to tighten its fingers around her skull. She felt faint.

He shook hands with the guard nearest to her and they composed themselves for the camera.

"I'm here today with one of the law enforcement officers doing great work with the inmates at Lincoln County Women's facility. John here makes sure these ladies pay their debt to society by making our highways cleaner. And if I'm not mistaken there is a familiar face amongst these ladies today."

"Yes, Abel, today is the first day Miss Maybelle Carter has been out here putting work in."

From the corner of her eye, she saw them part so the camera could get a shot of her, stooping with her pregnant belly, picking up dirt with her hands.

"Is she a good worker?"

"All these ladies know better than to give us trouble."

A rush of blood went to her head.

"Who said I know better?"

She stood up and faced the camera, her hands and forearms covered in grime. She addressed the cameraman directly.

"You want to show people what's really going on here? None of these women has eaten today, most of them have done nothing worse than getting caught with weed, none of us are being paid -"

Abel interrupted "Well maybe you should have thought of that before-"

"Before what? I testified against Bob Kitcherings' son? Before you told lies about me when your followers assaulted me? One of them punched me in the stomach, you know."

She saw his resolve momentarily falter.

"If you want something to shoot, shoot this." She sat down on a relatively clean slab of rock "I'm not working anymore today." She turned to the other women "and neither should any of you."

"Do you want to go to solitary?"

"I don't care at this point. Hey, cameraman you know there's an 'except' in the thirteenth amendment? Slavery is abolished except as a punishment for a crime. That's what you're looking at here, slavery. And if you wanna beat or shoot a pregnant woman who hasn't eaten in fourteen hours on camera, go ahead John."

There was quiet for a moment. Gia sat down. John marched over to her.

"Get up right now."

"But she's right, I -" he hit her across the face with a baton, bloodying her nose.

"You have been brought here to do a job."

Gia got up and punched him in the stomach. A few shouts of laughter rang out among the women. He raised his baton again.

Instinctively, Belle ran over to assist her. Gia was small and thin. He had already landed another blow when she got to her and other guards were approaching. Abel had nothing to say, but his camera was fixed firmly on the developing situation.

Belle inserted herself between Gia and the guard and raised her arms. He flinched. Another guard raised a baton to Gia and she reached out to get it off him. Her adrenaline ran high, and she was close to getting it free. Then, a sting in her side became a full shockwave running through her whole body. Her muscles froze and she dropped to the mud, landing on her back. Before she realised what was happening she was dragged to her feet and cuffed, and put in the back of a car. She heard Abel say

"You tased her? She's pregnant."

As soon as the door closed in solitary, Belle dropped onto the small bed and began laughing. She lay there for perhaps an hour, just enjoying the silence. Eventually, she got up to wash the caked-in mud on her hair and clothes at the small chrome sink with its hotel-sized bar of soap.

She sat back down and felt Yeshua kick. She lay back and stroked her bump.

"I'm sorry, mom is putting you through a lot, huh? I didn't mean to, I just really don't wanna be a disappointment to you. If this is how they treat me, how are they gonna treat you." Her tears welled again. "And I'm sorry I don't talk to you enough. The books I read said you need to hear my voice as much as possible. They said I should sing to you too. And it's good therapy for me." She smiled, "Gabe says that when we sing it's like we give our souls a cuddle."

She stared at the ceiling for inspiration on what to sing, then it came to her.
"Listen, baby
Ain't no mountain high,
Ain't no valley low,
Ain't no river wide enough baby."

For three days Belle was content to be alone in her bare cell, away from the voices and complications of other people. She filled her days talking to Yeshua, sleeping sporadically, and doing half-remembered prenatal yoga from the books Gabe had given her.

The nights were more difficult. She finally grew tired of solitude as she was trying to sleep. The forming images of dreams to come began appearing behind their eyes as they often did. Then, she was hit with a vivid memory. Running hand in hand with Reece, the bang of the bullet that killed him, holding his hand to his side to stop the blood as he cried out. The memory was one she had avoided visiting, now it hit her like a falling tree. It was entangled with fear, an emotion she was too shocked to experience at the time.

She jumped up, her breathing rapid. In that moment the darkness was smothering and the walls were creeping closer.

"Gabe?? Gabe, I need you."

She turned and he was there. He wrapped his arms around her and told her to breathe.

"What was that?" She asked after she had calmed down and he had turned on the lightbulb dangling from the ceiling. "Was it Lucifer?"

"No, just the human brain being a bastard. It sounds like a PTSD flashback. If you think about it, it's a miracle you've only just had one."

She lay down.

"There are therapists and staff who know how to help."

"Gabe, I'm sorry, I should have called on you before. I just needed to be alone."

He stared at the floor.

"Did you know I was in solitary?"

"We did. Your mom tried to call and they told us. It's um..." He struggled to find the words. "It's been pretty nuts outside. I think the camera guy who filmed you getting tased had a crisis of conscience. He leaked the video."

"What?"

"It's been everywhere, national news, not just in Tennessee. You're getting attention."

"I don't know how to feel about that."

"Well, you should feel good, a lot of people are on your side. Plus, people are donating money. Your bail fund is starting to pick up steam."

She smiled, feeling a new spark of optimism.

"How's mom?"

"She's OK, she just wants you home. Vivienne has been going on the news and stuff lobbying for your release."

"Ohh no."

"She's doing a good job! She's persuasive."

"That she is. And Becky?"

"She's been trying to find you a good lawyer. The state defender they gave you, he's a good man, he just has so many other cases. He represents like half the women in here, it seems."

She puffed out her cheeks.

"Could you bring food in here?"

"Not really. Angels aren't like people, we're vibrations and light, not solid matter. I can move wherever I want, I can't do the same with things, people, food, that kind of thing."

"Dogs?"

He chuckled.

"No, but Carl does miss you. He sleeps with the stuffed bear you got him."

She beamed. Then she sat and turned to him.

"We need video. I bet there's a video. There's no WAY someone didn't have a camera on that day. Abel is followed by a camera crew all the time, not to mention people with phones. We find a video, I'm vindicated and then we can make sure Kitchering's son is charged."

"Yeah..." He nodded "I'll get right on it."

Brother Abel's Home.

Abel sat at his long, polished dining table with his wife as he did most mornings. He scrolled through his emails and she checked the schedule for upcoming services. There was a pounding at the door.

"It's Bob, open up."
He glanced at his wife and she let him in. He stormed over to the table.

"Bob! I don't believe you've been in my home before."

"Shut up, Abel, why is there a video shot by your cameras showing one of my guards tasing that woman."
He threw his hands up.

"Our cameraman leaked it, we fired him..."

"How could you let this happen? I need to trust you, we're trying to keep my son out of jail, I can't have shit coming out that makes me look like the bad guy."
Abel shrugged.

"I mean... they tased a five months pregnant woman... based on your policy."
He scoffed.

"Since when do you feel sorry for her, I thought she was the devil."

"Maybe, but, we have to work on the assumption the baby is innocent."

"Abel I can't put up with this psycho shit, she's absolutely fine, she's in solitary. I need to know you are 100% on my side."

"I am Bob, but my God always comes first.
Kitchering groaned.

Abel's wife chimed in with a smile "Can I get you a coffee, Bob?"

"Thanks, black with two sugars please."

She headed to the vast kitchen, the click of her heels on the flagstone echoing around the cavernous hall.

"The guard acted legally, Abel, she was a physical threat to him."

"She's like 100 pounds and five months pregnant, Bob, what damage could she do?"

"So you're some kinda BLM guy now?"

"Of course not, but I was there, she wasn't a threat."

"Just get rid of the video, Abel, it's your copyrighted material, get it offline."

Abel's wife returned with a mug of coffee.

"How about you just fire the guard?"

"What?"

"Just fire the guard, Bob" she continued, "Public opinion is against what happened to her, fire the guard for excessive force, and release a statement about it, it will make you seem sympathetic. Right now, people think you're doing anything to keep her in jail, if you speak out against her treatment it will make you seem moral. Caring. We need *her* to look angry and unreasonable, *you* need to look like a man of order."

The two men exchanged a look.

"Damn, Abel, has she ever worked in politics?"

He squeezed his wife's hand.

"I wouldn't be where I am today if it wasn't for her."

Jail.

For the next two weeks, Gabe would visit each day. They would talk, play memory games, and strategise. He tried to contact whoever was in the crowd from the few photos of the day. No one would talk. Someone was carrying the black box containing the truth, Belle was sure of it.

Her frustration increased until one morning when she was woken up by the county Sherrif. He had a grey look on his face.

"You're free to go, Carter?"

"What?"

"You made bail. C'mon, let's get you out of here without any fuss."

The morning air was cold and still as she was escorted out. She squinted in the cool early winter light and smiled when she saw the bare limbs of leafless trees. The gates opened and her mom was there, standing with Gabe and a tall woman she did not recognise. She would have to wait. She ran up to her mom and they squeezed each other tight. She stretched an arm out for Gabe to join the embrace. Eventually, Cynthia released her.

"Oh, god, you feel skinny, we gotta get you home and feed you! I tell you what when this is over I'm suing that sheriff for endangering you and my grandson."

She laughed.

"I've been dreaming about meatball subs. Who is this?"

She got a better look at the unknown woman. She looked to be in her late 40s, with an absurdly long dirty blonde braid laced with grey hairs. She wore a black sweater and jeans.

"This is Marnie," said Gabe, "she and her gang helped raise your bail money."

"Her gang?"

"The Tennessee scumbags. We're a biker outfit."

She put out a hand for Belle to shake and got a hug instead.

"I'll take it!"

Marnie laughed.

"We do a lot of work with incarcerated people, we just wanted to help out."

"Well, I owe you big time."

"You mentioned meatball subs, I know a place."

The two women got into Gabe's car and followed Marnie to a local BBQ joint. It was a small outdoor kiosk with plastic picnic benches, but Marnie insisted it was the best. Belle ordered a footlong and chocolate milkshake, relishing the simple freedom to eat. She tore into the sub and realised immediately that Marnie was right about the place. She could have wept.

"I owe you double, Marnie. Getting me out of jail and buying me this sandwich are both equally good."

"I'm always right about these things."

She finished the rest of her food in silence, Marnie and her mom shared a bowl of fries.

After removing all traces of barbecue sauce from her face, she resolved to find out more about her new rescuer.

"Why did you get involved? Did my aunt convert you or something?"

She laughed.

"Your friend Adrian got in touch. I was incarcerated at Lincoln too, and he knows how we do a lot for convicts in the area so he thought I could help out. I saw that video of you getting tasered and it got me and a lot of other folks angry. People around here know me and the Scumbags well. They wanted to help out."

"That's wonderful."

"Once Marnie got involved we had the money in no time," Gabe added. "They do this a lot, raising bail, money for lawyers, most of the Scumbags have been to jail so it's close to home."

"It's nice to gain a little faith in humanity again."

As they spoke a large man emerged from behind the kiosk with a trash bag. He put it in a dumpster and then spotted her at the table. He rushed over.

"Oh my God, Belle Carter! You're free!"

"Uh, yeah, hi!"

"I prayed for you, I prayed for you every day! We'll beat them! We will!"

She saw the passion in his eyes and smiled back.

"We will."

"Miss Carter, I know you're here with people but... could I...touch your belly? My mom is sick, I need your blessing."

She felt her face flush. She looked over and saw Gabe smiling and her mom confused.

"Sure, what's your name?"

"Marcus."

"OK, if you put your hand on the side here you can usually feel him kicking."

He knelt and did so. His eyes were fixed on her bump. She felt the flutter of a kick under his hand. He gasped.

"I can't believe it!"

She found herself grinning. He grabbed her hand and kissed it.

"You are the mother of God." He looked directly into her eyes. "We will get justice for you. Beshaah Tovah, Beshaah Tovah."

As he walked back to the kiosk Marnie and

Cynthia couldn't find the words.

"Well done." offered Gabe. "You handled that very well."

13
Mother of Perpetual Help

The next day Belle and her mom met with Gabe, Becky, Vivienne, and Marnie at Adrian and Yelena's home. Vivienne flung her arms around her at first sight and Becky immediately handed her Carl, who wagged his stubby tail and licked her face. The feeling of his little furry body in her arms stopped her from shaking at the prospect of a room full of people.

Yelena spoke quietly to her in the kitchen.

"I get it if you're freaked out by all this, if you need a moment alone, just nod at me and I'll get you out."

"I'll be fine, I guess it's good to see everyone again."

Yelena went to hug her but Carl bared his teeth and produced a low growl.

"Carl! No! She's our friend!"

"Sometimes dogs can get protective of pregnant women. It's a thing."

They went back into the living room and found Adrian in a corner having his face talked off by Vivienne. She was explaining her new work evangelising for her niece. He flashed Belle an awkward smile.

"I've been working the video footage angle."

Began Gabe. "Naturally, no one who was there is willing to give up any cellphone footage."

"Was there CCTV?" Belle asked.

He shrugged.

"I guess, I don't know how we would access that."

Adrian sat forward "A subpoena? If we can prove there's footage that would exonerate Belle we can force them to give it to us."

"I would guess he's probably destroyed it by now," added Becky.

Belle put Carl on the seat next to her. "It's worth a try. I say we get a good lawyer who can get it out of him."

Becky scratched Carl's ears, eliciting another growl. "And if he has destroyed it?"

"Then that looks super suspicious." Said Yelena. "If he's got rid of it his case doesn't look great, all he has is his culty followers backing his story up."

"What about the man who got hurt?" Vivienne asked, "he might remember something, did he see what happened?"

"He had his back to me, but I did try and help him up right after, he might remember that."

"Well we'd have to go easy on him, it can't look like intimidation." Said Cynthia. "So, yeah, a lawyer. Anyone know any lawyers?"

There was a pause in the room.

"I know someone," Marnie announced "she helped out some of the scumbags in the past, she's real good. We still have stuff left in the fundraiser so we can pay her."

Belle and Gabe exchanged a nod.

She grinned "Sounds great!"

Two days later a meeting was set up with Beverly Shannon. Her office in the centre of Memphis was furnished with large house plants but otherwise understated. Gabe, Belle, and Cynthia waited on a small leather couch before she called them in.

She was a tall woman in her fifties, with bright brown eyes and wavy brown hair maintained through regular salon trips.

"So you are the mother and you are the friend from the video." She shook Belle's hand. "Congratulations on the baby, by the way. I can't have any. Endometriosis. But I don't care. Take a seat."

They did so and she pulled out her files.

"I agree with you that there has to be footage. I can't force people to hand over cellphone video, so the best route is CCTV."

"And if he's destroyed it?" Cynthia asked.

"Then, as your friend said, it looks very bad on him. However, he has connections with the governor, so don't be surprised if he tries to wriggle out of it. I need to apply through the courts to get a subpoena."

"My main concern here is that I can testify against the governor's son again. If the assault charges are dropped will I be able to do that?"

"You could, but it would be helpful to find some new evidence. Unsurprisingly, the police are a little anxious about pursuing the case. Which is total bull, one of the cops who brought him in got fired for some administration-related stuff. But hey, one injustice at a time."

Belle leaned in. "...And what about the whole... religious angle, will that go against me?"

She applied hand sanitiser from a desk drawer.

"The case isn't about whether or not you are the mother of God, so as long as we can prove you're psychologically competent it shouldn't be a problem." She turned to Gabe "You, however, may be a problem. There appears to be no record of your existence whatsoever, which makes things difficult, legally speaking. So you're best staying out of any spotlight."

"I can do that."

As they exited the office a camera was shoved in Belle's face like the barrel of a gun.

"Miss Carter, how did you afford bail?"

She blinked in the sunlight and saw a local news reporter she recognised holding his mic an inch from her face.

"Uh...I..."

"Stay away from my daughter please, she's been through enough, she needs to be resting, please get out of our way."

As Cynthia turned her daughter away from the camera a second one was pointed in Gabe's face. A second reporter approached him.

"Sir, are you the man from the video?"

"No comment."

"Will you please get out of our way? You're harassing my daughter."

Belle heard the door to the building open and Ms Shannon's voice cut through the chaos.

"If you insist on a soundbite you can speak to me, I am Miss Carter's attorney."

The two cameras faced her and Gabe and Cynthia hurried her to the car.

That night the three of them watched her statement on local news.

"We will be issuing a subpoena for CCTV footage of the alleged assault. If Brother Abel has nothing to hide I suggest he hand it over and avoid any further legal complications. If, as we suspect, the footage exonerates Miss Carter then she would have grounds to sue for her imprisonment and the negative impact it had on her health and the health of her unborn child. I will recommend a full evaluation of her health by a trusted doctor to ensure her pregnancy is progressing as it should despite her well-documented mistreatment at the hands of Lincoln County law enforcement.

"As for her testimony against Rob Kitchering Jr, we will also be pursuing a psychological evaluation to prove her competency to testify in court. My client has made it very clear that her priority is getting justice for Reece Letsky. I say to Governor Kitchering that it will be far easier for him in the long run if he ceases using his power to keep his son from facing justice."

The footage cut back to the studio.

"Oh my God, she's amazing!" Gushed Cynthia.

"Wait, mom, they said there's a statement from Kitchering."

The anchor cut to footage of Kitchering outside Lincoln County women's facility.

"I was disappointed to learn that excessive force was used against a pregnant woman in one of the jail facilities in my jurisdiction and the staff member responsible has been fired."

Cynthia stood up and headed to the kitchen "Oh, he doesn't give a shit, it's all optics! He's been bragging about how tough he is on criminals for years."

"He's a real piece of work." Agreed Gabe.

Kitchering continued, "My son is innocent of the allegations against him and should the case go to trial again we are confident his name will be cleared. Thank you for your time, my family and I would ask for privacy during this period of our lives."

Cynthia re-entered with a pot of tea as the news anchor moved on to the weather report.

"As if! He's a bigger attention seeker than Abel! And what about *our* privacy! I had a reporter outside my work for a week! Is privacy just something rich people can afford?"

She poured out mint tea for Gabe and Belle.

"My phone has been making some weird noises too, I would not be surprised if they bugged it."

"C'mon, mom, I'm sure they didn't do that."

"Well, how else did they know where we were yesterday?"

Gabe and Belle exchanged a look.

"She has a point, Belle."

"Let's just try and deal with one disgusting abuse of power at once, shall we?"

The next day Belle visited the doctor as promised by her lawyer. She was mostly in decent health, but underweight, which did not surprise her. Yeshua was healthy too, as confirmed by a new ultrasound scan. At home that night, Cynthia carried the scan around with her and barely took her eyes off it. It made it all seem worth it, she said.

After a discussion with Beverly, Belle was able to arrange a call with Gia in Jail. She had spent her own time in solitary after the incident on the highway. She sat in her room waiting for the phone to ring at 9 pm on the dot. It did so, and she answered.

"Gia?"

"Hey, Belle."

"How are you?"

"I'm OK. I'm almost missing solitary at times, the privacy was nice."

She laughed.

"It is a relief at first."

"Oh yeah, you could not pay me to go back in there. Not that they do pay us in this place."

"Heh. How is everyone else? I heard they fired the guard who tased me."

"Yeah, I heard a bunch of the other staff bitching about it. I'm sure they'll rehire him when it blows over."

"Probably."

There was a pause.

"I didn't get a chance to thank you, by the way."

"Don't mention it."

"No, really, you could have gotten badly hurt. No one ever really stood up for me like that. So thank you."

"Sometimes you just can't look away anymore."

"I wish more people felt like that."

She shrugged.

"Everyone has their own stuff to deal with."

"Hey...Belle, could you do me a favour?"

She hesitated for a moment hearing Gia's shaky tone.

"Sure, what's up?"

"It's Scott's birthday next week, my grandma is having a little party for him. I've told her about you, do you think you could go along to it?"

"Sure! I'd love to! Could I bring my friend Becky? She has a little boy of her own."

Her voice brightened.

"That would be great! He doesn't have siblings so I'm always trying to find playdates for him!"

"Is it sad that I'm genuinely looking forward to it now? I haven't even had Yeshua yet and I already have no social life?"

Gia gasped.

"Yeshua? Is that the name you picked out?"

She smiled to herself.

"Yeah."

"It's gorgeous!"

The Temple of the Staff

The week that followed was the quietest Brother Abel had ever known. There had been no TV appearances, no new uploads to his channel and his wife had taken over preaching duties for half of his services, something she had never done before. She proved popular, a far less 'fire and brimstone' presenter who was closer to a motivational speaker.

Beverly had filed for a subpoena and his team of lawyers was searching for ways out of it. One morning he gave in and answered the third call that day from Governor Kitchering. He painted the perfect smile on his face before he answered, large enough for the stretching of his mouth to be apparent in his voice.

"Bob! How are you!"

"Abel, do not give me that good ol' boy shit, I practically invented it."

"You know, Bob, I don't approve of that kind of language."

"Just tell me, is there a video and if it gets out

will that be a problem."

He paused.

"Abel?"

"Well, it would depend on the angle of the tape?"

"Oh, God."

"Look -"

"You lied to me."

"I didn't lie"

"You told me there was no footage, no CCTV, do you have any idea how bad this will look?"

"I -"

"You know what, it isn't my problem. If this comes out I will drop you like a bag of rocks. You need my influence, Abel, I don't need yours."

"Look, my lawyers are going over all of this with a fine-toothed comb, this doesn't have to be the nail in the coffin."

"For your sake, I hope it isn't. How embarrassing will it be for you to have your sleazy Moses Mall taken down by some uppity teenager who couldn't keep it in her pants?"

"Don't get personal, Bob, I'm not the one caught up in a damn murder case."

"You wanna get personal? You fuck this up and you can say goodbye to your tax exemption. Goodbye, Abel."

The line went dead.

He paced his office overlooking the vast parking lot of the temple. His eyes fixed on the spot the CCTV camera had been filming. He reached into a drawer on his vast white desk and pulled out an address book. He tore a page out and headed downstairs to the Cadillac parked behind the building.

Twenty minutes later he showed up at an apartment building on a side of town he didn't frequent. His hands shook as he parked his car outside. The address matched. At the door of the building, he saw a buzzer marked 'G. Smith.' He pushed it.

"Belle?"

"I have a delivery for a Gabe Smith? I need your signature."

"Oh sure, come on up."

His loafers dragged on the stone stairs on the way up. The door to the apartment was down a green-carpeted hallway that felt stuck in the seventies. He knocked on the door.

Gabe opened it with a smile that quickly dropped. Abel was struck by the blue of his eyes. The will to call him the devil himself weakened.

"What are you doing here, Abel?"

He swallowed.

"I just...wanted to talk."

"I have nothing to say to you."

He tried to shut the door but Abel put his arm in the way.

"Look, we don't have to be blinded with rage here, we're both men, let's talk this out like men."

Gabe considered for a moment and fully opened the door. Abel looked around with visible confusion. Carl, sat on the old sofa, and lifted his head but did not rush to greet this stranger.

"Hell of a place you got."

"I know how much you love to poke fun at people with smaller homes than you."

Abel strolled over to the fridge and opened it. There was no food, no drink, just a stack of books on the top shelf.

He shot Gabe a look somewhere between confusion and disgust.

"I ran out of space for them."

"OK just...just... tell me who or what you are."

"*What* I am?"

"You got no food in your refrigerator, we can't find any record of you anywhere, and there seems to be no sign of your existence whatsoever beyond six months ago, you make no sense buddy."

"So you've been spying on me? You and Kitchering?"

"I haven't done anything illegal, buddy. You, I can't be so sure of."

Gabe said nothing.

"So what are you, some kind of conman? Worse?"

"I'm not a conman."

"And what is she? Your girlfriend? Your patsy?"

"She's what she says she is."

He laughed.

"Yeah, the Mother of God. It's a bunch of bull."

"I don't understand why you don't just leave us alone?" He took the trouble not to raise his voice. "We're not trying to steal your congregation, we're not trying to hurt anyone, if you think she's nuts then why can't you just let it go and move on?"

"I am a man of GOD." The full volume of his preaching voice would have made another person jump in such a small space. Gabe stood firm. Carl jumped off the sofa and ran to his master's side.

"I was placed on earth to protect people from the evils around us. She is *lying*. There is no scripture on this. God would never choose an unwed mother. She is corrupting people! The more I learn about you the more

I think you are the devil."

Gabe scoffed.

"You really believe it don't you? Sometimes I think it's just a big money-making scheme but you truly believe every word you say."

Abel picked up a kitchen knife. Gabe laughed.

"Abel, if I was the devil, what on earth do you think a crappy kitchen knife would do." He looked down at Carl. "Hey, buddy, am I the devil?" Carl kept his eyes fixed on the intruder. "Abel, I suggest you put the knife down and leave before I call the cops. Can you really afford an assault case right now?"

As he lead a sheepish Abel out the door he asked him:

"Hey, what is Gabe short for?"

He stared at him with a furrowed brow.

"Gabriel?"

"Right."

He closed the door.

Scott D'Acampo's Birthday party

Becky and Belle pulled up outside the small suburban home in Becky's car. The house in question had a small bunch of balloons tied to the front gate. Belle got Joey out of his car seat and Becky carried him across the street.

"Did you get him a present?"

"Legos. Gia said he likes them."

"Thanks for inviting me and Joey, by the way, it's hard to get out sometimes."

"Honestly, I've been looking forward to this wayy too much."

"Who doesn't like kid's party food? Besides, you have literally been in jail. If I were you this would feel like a trip to Vegas."

Belle rang the doorbell and a stout woman in her late 60's answered. She had Gia's eyes, only brighter. She smiled.

"You must be Belle and Becky, I'm Sharon, come on in."

"This is Joey by the way."

"Hi, Joey! I hope you like birthday cake!"

There were four other kids there around Scott's age but no parents. They sat happily in front of the small flatscreen TV watching cartoons.

"This is Scott," said Sharon, pointing to an olive-skinned curly-haired boy with cake frosting around his mouth. Belle knelt in front of him.

"Hey, Scott, I'm a friend of your mom's."

"Were you in jail too?" He asked.

Belle stammered.

"I uh... I was. Your mom was super nice to me."

He poked her belly.

"Are you having a baby?"

"I am."

"What's its name?"

"I am going to call him Yeshua. When he's born and I have birthday parties for him you and your mom can come."

He smiled. Belle reached into her bag.

"I got you a present. Your mom told me you like these."

He lit up and tore off the paper. He smiled and opened the box immediately, spilling coloured bricks on the floor.

"What do we say to Belle?" Interrupted Sharon.
He stood up and hugged her.

"Thank you, Belle."
She squeezed him back.

"No problem, buddy. Hey, I want you to meet my friends."
She gestured for Becky to come over.

"This is Becky and this is her little boy Joey. He's a little younger than you so play nice."

"He likes cake," explained Becky.

"I can get him a slice."

"Do you need a knife for that?" Asked Belle.
He nodded.

"OK, I can get that for you. We don't want you to hurt yourself, just watch your show."

After cutting slices of cake for the kids she retired to the kitchen with Becky.

"You are such a mom already, it's hilarious." Laughed Becky, making up a pot of tea. "Out here protecting babies from scary butter knives."

"Mom was always like that with me. I couldn't even eat grapes whole in case I choked."
She laughed.

"What about your dad?"

"He was kind of protective, but not as much. He used to rip my mom a lot for it. She used to make me wear SPF 50 sunscreen and not go out during the height of the day in summer."

"She's aware you're black, right?"
Belle laughed.

"We can still burn you know!"

"Whatever."

"I'm serious, you have to be careful."

"Are you gonna make Yeshua wear those weird sunhats?"

"Oh yeah, with the neck flap at the back and the visor? Why should he not suffer the same way I did."
Becky giggled.

Looking out of the window, Belle saw Sharon with a phone to her ear and a cigarette in her hand.

"This is nice, isn't it? Just being a normal mom."

"It is." Agreed Becky. "However they get here they all need the same stuff."

"What do you think Joey will be like when he grows up?"
She leaned back in her chair.

"He's kinda quiet, you know? Not like his mom." She smiled. "He's very gentle. He doesn't break stuff or kill bugs or anything. We were out in the park once and there was this dead bird on the ground. He just burst into tears." She was speaking more to the space in the room than Belle. "He was inconsolable. I had to bury it with some flowers to calm him down."
Belle relished the look of hope on her friend's face.

"I hope he keeps growing like that."

"Me too."

Becky craned her head towards the living room as if expecting spies.

"What's happening with Abel? Is he gonna have to give you the video?"
She shrugged.

"He's pretty much ghosted us. I think that's a good thing. It means he's scared."
Becky nodded.

"Let's hope."

"My lawyer is getting me a psychological evaluation. Prove I'm a reliable witness."

"How about a polygraph?"

She sucked in air.

"I don't know, seems kind of stunt-y to me."

"Abel does stuff like that all the time."

"That's why I don't wanna do it."

"He's a total stunt."

"Becky!"

"What! I didn't say it!"

Once their tea was finished Belle stepped outside where Sharon was pacing and glancing at the phone at regular intervals.

"Hey, Sharon."

Her face switched to a smile.

"Hey, sweetie! How is it in there."

"Good, peaceful."

"We like peaceful."

She looked at the phone again.

"Are you alright?"

She sighed.

"Trying to arrange a call with Gia. They're being a little awkward."

Belle stepped closer to her.

"I'm sorry."

Sharon scratched the back of her head as if it was burning.

"It's never enough for them in it? She already got a year in jail, they treat her like a dog. She made mistakes, but it's never enough." She didn't cry but her face grew red. "You fuck up and getting a punishment isn't enough. People won't rest until they make it hell on earth for you."

Belle put an arm around her.

"I get it. I don't know her as well as you, but I know she's not a bad person."

"She's a good mom, too. Better than the mom she had." She returned the phone to her pocket. "I had a baby young, then my baby had babies young. The opioids, they just burned through this family."

Belle hugged her properly. As she took her arms from around her she saw a single tear fall from her eye. She squinted as if trying to force out more, a compulsion Belle knew too well.

"Just feels like no one gives a crap about us. You can't change it."

"We can try."

She laughed.

"There's just so much. So much stuff in the way. It feels like if one thing gets better another thing comes along."

"I know how you feel." Belle stared at her feet. "Do think we need to fight everything at once? Just build a whole new world? Or take it one by one."

Sharon puffed out her cheeks.

"Hell if I know. But if it were easy to just make a new world it would happen ten times a year."

That night Belle got a call from Gabe.

"So, Abel showed up at my apartment today."

She closed the kitchen door.

"What? Did he want something?"

"He asked me who I was, if you're for real. He

says he can't find any proof I exist past six months ago."

"So he's spying on us?"

"He's been digging for dirt."

She kept her voice low.

"Did he threaten you or anything?"

"He picked up a knife, but he didn't do anything with it. I think he realised pretty quickly it was a bad idea."

"Did he seem...scared?"

"I would say panicked."

"Good. We're getting to him."

"He asked if I was the devil."

She laughed.

"What did you say?"

"I said if I was the devil what would a knife do?"

"You need to train Carl up as a guard dog."

"He doesn't have it in him."

Belle agreed.

After the conversation was over she texted Marnie.

Hey.

I wanna get involved in your work. Just let me know what I can do.

Belle.

The reply came through fast.

Sure, we're visiting a friend in rehab tomorrow and we try and say hi to other patients too. I can pick you up in the morning.

The next morning Belle found herself clutching Marnie's waist on the back of her motorcycle. The wind whipped and twisted the hair that hung below her helmet and the sun was low in the east. Belle's brow wrinkled as they pulled into a suburb ten miles west of Memphis. Marnie slowed down her bike as they approached a commotion surrounding a van outside a small home.

"What's happening?"

Marnie removed her helmet.

"I may have told a white lie, I thought you might chicken out."

"Chicken out of what?"

She stepped off the bike.

"They're trying to take this old woman into custody for missing rent, the group is here to protest it."

Belle's muscles tensed.

"How old is she?"

"82."

She swallowed.

"She's in the van?"

"Yeah, she's disabled so they had to get a special vehicle to... Belle?"

She was already walking towards the van, her mind was clear in a way that thrilled her. The voices of the crowd became distinct as she approached. There was a small gathering, she could just about make out the woman's frightened face through the tinted window at the back of the riot van. People shouted at the driver as neighbours looked on.

She paused at the window and locked eyes with the two men in the van. The man in the driver's seat was Officer Fleischer, the cop she liked when she was questioned about Reese's murder. She could tell he recognised her.

Without a word, she stepped in front of the

vehicle and looked both him and the other officer in the eye. Then, she lay down on the asphalt. The voices of the gathering were quiet for a moment, she heard the hum of the engine cease. The tread of the tyres was close enough to her face for her to smell the rubber.

Marnies' footsteps approached.

"Belle, you really don't have to do this. The plan was just to show our faces."

She didn't lift her head as she answered.

"I'm in a unique position, Marnie. I can draw attention to this."

"You know how badly Kitchering wants you back in jail?"

Her face didn't shift.

"And that would make him look terrible."

Marnie sighed.

"Your mom is gonna kill me for taking you here."

She stood up. "Anyone gonna join me at the back or what?"

The voices stirred again. Belle turned her head and saw Marnie's boots laid out at the other end of the van. She smiled.

"Get that girl a pillow and some water! She's fucking pregnant!"

An hour passed and three more of Marnies' biker friends joined, blocking the sides of the van. The crowd had increased and local news was arriving. Belle's view of the late autumn sky was briefly obstructed by a camera swooping into view. A redheaded reporter knelt beside her.

"Miss Carter, can you explain what you're doing here today for our viewers?"

"I think the situation pretty much speaks for

itself. You might wanna talk to officer Fleischer over there, I think he's about to call for backup."

The mic lingered for a moment until they realised she had nothing more to add.

"Brother Abel has called your treatment in jail an 'honest mistake', what do you have to say to that?"

"It's a mistake that served him and Kitchering pretty well. But I have bigger things to deal with now."

A slur rang out from someone trying to push through the crowd. Belle saw from the corner of her eye as two men pushed the man away. The news reporter scrambled to apologise to viewers watching live. Belle swallowed and rested two hands on her bump.

Her phone buzzed in her pocket. A text from Gabe.

I'm watching on TV. You need food?

She messaged back.

Probably best if you don't come Gabe, people talk about you enough.

The reply came fast.

Someone's coming, don't be mad.

Within ten minutes a familiar voice cut through the thickening crowd. Belle couldn't help but laugh as Aunt Vivienne's face broke through the sun shining directly in her eyes.

"Sweetie, I got you a sandwich from that deli near my house, it has grilled vegetables and nice lean chicken, it's very good for you."

She took a bite and thanked her.

"Does my mom know I'm here?"

"I don't think so, otherwise she'd have dragged you away by now. And don't tell her I came."

She smiled.

"I won't."

Two cops dragged away a man lying on the ground nearby. He kicked, then went limp as they carried him to a second riot van. Vivienne crouched lower over Belle. Before the crowd could fill the gap he left two more men lay down in his place.

"They're with me," Vivienne announced, proudly.

"With you?"

"People are listening to you Belle."

She sat up just enough to hug her.

"What about the lady in the Van?"

"They've been trying to get her food. The cops let someone pass through some water but that's it."

As the day carried on more were dragged away and replaced twice over. Some were pepper sprayed and then handed milk to pour into their eyes. Belle's heart stayed firmly in her throat. The sun had shifted to the other side of her eyeline. She heard a commotion at her feet and raised her head. Fleischer was threatening a man with arrest if he wouldn't let him through.

"Let him through," she announced, shielding her eyes from the sun. "I wanna talk to him."

The man sighed and stood to one side, not taking his eyes off Fleischer as he walked over to where Belle was lying. He squatted, blocking out the sun.

"You know why I haven't arrested you yet?" He muttered.

"Cameras, crowd, that little voice in your head telling you what you're doing is wrong?"

He exhaled. The crowd around grew quieter as muscles tensed, ready to defend the young pregnant woman.

"You're out on bail. This is enough to get you

sent back."

"So why haven't you arrested me? It would get your precinct a lot of new funding from the governor."

"Sounds like you want me to arrest you."

"I want you to do what you know is right."

She looked into his eyes until he snapped them away. She watched him as he stood up and speak quietly to another officer.

With little fanfare, he crossed to the back of the van. Belle turned her head and saw a pair of slippered feet join his behind the van.

A voice rang out "they let her go!"

A hand reached out to help her up as the jubilation began. It was Marnie's hand, and she placed an arm around her shoulder as the old woman was led back to her house.

Belle's back ached.

"What happens now?"

"Some friends of mine are trying to get her legal representation. It's not over but at least she can sleep in her own bed tonight.

Spots began to fizz in Belle's vision and her head went light.

"You OK?" Marnie asked.

"I think I may need to sit down."

Marnie helped her to a grassy verge by a neighbouring house.

"No no, don't lie back, put your head forward, let the circulation come back." She turned to the crowd. "Anyone have any water?" She rubbed her back as the blood returned to her face. "Are you in pain or anything?"

"No, I just overdid it I think."

"That was badass, I won't lie, but you don't have to be a hero all the time. I don't know about God or Angels but I remember what it's like to be pregnant." Belle chuckled.

"I think I need to go home."

As she approached her door and Marnie drove away she could sense all was not right. She rested a hand on her bump as she opened the door. Cynthia stood by the stairs, her eyes sore, phone in her hand. She waited until her daughter had locked the door before she spoke.

"Have you lost your mind??" Her voice was hoarse, and Belle's stomach dropped.

"Mom, I –"

"You are on bail. This could send you right back to jail."

"I had to."
She made a sound close to laughter.

"No, you didn't. You didn't have to do a thing. The only thing you have to do is rest, eat good food which *I* am providing for you, and grow a healthy baby. You can't change the world all by yourself, especially right now. And it kills me knowing you'll risk your well-being to try."

"I just –"

"Did you think about me? How I would feel seeing my daughter on the news like that when she's already been beaten, jailed, slandered? Everything you do, you do to me. I am your mother."
Belle turned her head away for a moment.

"It's because of all of that I had to. I laid low for so long, I'm sick of being weak."

"It isn't weak to be safe, Belle. I know what Gabe says, I know what God asked you to do but you're still a 119-year-oldgirl." She sighed. "Sometimes I hate that he picked you."

There was a moment of silence as they both digested what Cynthia said. Belle felt a spark of anger again.

"Well, I was picked. And I made the decision to start acting like it."

"I want you to act like my daughter."

"I am!"

Tears welled in her eyes again.

"Are you? Since you got out of jail something has felt different. What did they do to you, Belle?"

She sighed. The truth was owed.

"It's not what they did, it's what he did?"

"He who?"

She looked at her mother. She never looked older.

"The devil."

At first, she looked ready to laugh, but then the events of the last few months came flooding back.

"*The* Devil? As in Satan?"

Belle nodded.

"He came to me the night Reese died. He told me he made it so I'd be there when it happened. He said he thinks my son is a sacrifice and he wanted to offer me a way out in exchange for giving him information about my mission."

Cynthia sat on the stairs.

"And you said no."

"Of course." Cynthia exhaled. "But he didn't stop. He comes when I'm most vulnerable, that's what Gabe said. He came to me in jail."

"What did he say?"

"It's not what he said, it's what he showed me. All the evil in the world, all at once. It was like... falling forever. I can't –" she choked "I can't even put it into words. The ugliness. Gabe stopped him eventually."

"Why?"

"To show me the world didn't deserve me, or Yeshua. It backfired I guess, I just became stubborn. Make things better or die trying."

There was silence for a moment.

"Belle," Cynthia asked softly, "why didn't you tell me?"

"It's like you said, you're my mother. I didn't want to hurt you."

Cynthia began to weep. Belle joined her on the stairs and put an arm around her. She muttered 'it's ok, it's ok', as she cried into the crook of her neck.

Two weeks later. Vivienne's home.

Vivienne opened the door to find a slightly larger group than the previous week.

"Come in! Come in! It's chilly out!"

They shuffled in from the winter night and gave her their coats.

"I have some punch made up and some chips. There should be space for everyone to sit down but if not just let me know, I got some patio furniture out back I can bring in.

The group sat in the reddish glow of Vivienne's thrift store Tiffany lamps.

"Unfortunately my niece couldn't be with us tonight, she had some stuff to work through. But I'm seeing a couple of new people and I wanna get to know y'all." She turned to a man who sat next to her who looked to be in his mid-thirties. "Introduce yourself, we don't bite."

He smiled weekly, looking as though he wanted to disappear entirely into his large sweater.

"I'm Josh. I, actually don't know anyone here. I just wanted to find out more, I guess."

There was a pause while Vivienne waited to see if more information would spill out of him.

"Well, we are glad to have you!" She said at last.

After a few more introductions the discussion began. An older woman introduced as Manuela sat opposite Josh and spoke about her decision to come along.

"All my life I worked so hard and I had nothing to show for it, I never felt like God saw me. Then I see this young woman, she could be my daughter, and I see in her eyes that she is telling the truth. I can't explain it, I just knew. And the thought that God could come down and be with people like us, I just feel hope."

"That is what is so special about this," added Vivienne, "He's going to be one of us. Me and my family, none of us are millionaires, we're just working people. We struggle to pay our rent, we struggle to pay medical bills. My niece was working at a gas station with no hope of ever going to college when God came to her. And he is sending us his son because he truly loves us. Not just high and mighty men like Brother Abel. Servants like us. Because that's what we have to be. My niece is out being a servant right now, helping find representation for that poor boy's parents. And I don't mean a servant to a master, but a servant to one another. Until we go home to God all we have is one another. We are one another's duty."

As she spoke Josh kept his eyes fixed on the

floor. He didn't say a word until the meeting was over. As people were leaving he saw Vivienne collecting used glasses and plates.

"Can I help you wash up?"

She gave him a warm smile.

"Would you? Thank you, sweetie."

As he stood beside her at the kitchen sink passing her dishes to be dried, she talked continuously. He learned about Belle's first steps, her grades at school, and the framed scribbles she drew as a toddler. He didn't have to say a word until she took a breath to drink a glass of water.

"I wanted to... talk to you about something."

She swallowed her water.

"Sure, honey, anything."

He dried his hands on a dishtowel.

"I...used to work for Abel."

She turned to him.

"Well, sweetie, that's OK. I used to go to his services."

"I filmed stuff for him. He uh... he fired me."

"For what?"

"That video. The one where they tased her. I leaked it."

"Well, you did the right thing."

He wouldn't look her in the eye.

"He told me to leak it."

"Why?"

"He thought tasing a pregnant woman was wrong. He told Kitchering he fired me then when he found out Abel lied about that I got fired for real."

He folded his arms around himself.

"I really believed in him, you know? I was his biggest fan. Things would happen and I knew they weren't right, but I went along because..." He struggled for the words "because I believed in him. Even after he fired me I convinced myself that I was in the wrong."

Vivienne took his hand.

"What are you trying to say? I can help you."

He looked her in the eyes at last.

"I have a tape. It proves your niece is innocent. He threatened me, said I'd never work again... I'm not gonna lie for him anymore. I want to release it."

She threw his arms around him and squealed excitedly.

Belle woke up the next morning to a call from Beverly.

"What's up?"

"Your aunt came through for us! Turn on the TV!"

"What?"

"The news! Go watch!"

She hauled herself upright and pulled on a bathrobe. As she began her third trimester, mornings were becoming more difficult.

She kept the phone to her ear as she turned on the TV and switched over to the news.

CHARGES DROPPED AGAINST BELLE CARTER – ABEL CALLS IT AN 'HONEST MISTAKE'

She clasped her hand to her mouth and yelped with joy.

"A former employee showed up at one of your Aunt's meetings yesterday and said he had the footage. You're a free woman!"

"This is a miracle!"

"That would be your department, from a legal

perspective this is a big reduction in paperwork."

"And Abel? What's his take?"

"He said he never saw the footage, he encouraged your quote-unquote victim to come forward because he believed you truly had assaulted him, blah blah blah. Of course, now you have the opportunity to sue him for defamation and press charges against the woman shown pushing you in the video. And the guy who punched you in the stomach..."

"No."

There was a pause on the other end of the line.

"Are you sure? A settlement with him could set you and your baby up nicely."

"I appreciate it, Beverly, I really do. I just really want all of this to be over."

"I get it. Well, I will call you later and we can organise a psyche eval so you can testify against Kitchering Jr. I will speak to you then."

Belle ran into her mother's room like she was a kid on her birthday.

"Mom, come downstairs, I got a surprise."

Cynthia answered with a ragged, unused voice, "Can you bring me a coffee first?"

"I will make you a coffee downstairs, just get moving."

As soon as Cynthia saw the headline she squeezed her daughter tight. She ran to the kitchen and took the recent scan off the fridge and kissed it.

"You see that Yeshua! Mommy is staying right here!"

In place of champagne, they poured apple juice into wine glasses.

"So now you can just stay at home and get

yourself strong again, right?"

"No," Belle replied, "now the real work begins."
Her mom's face dropped.

"I was worried you'd say that."

The Temple of the Staff

Abel struggled to contain the hot feeling of rage searing the inside of his chest as he read the email from Governor Kitchering.

Consider this our last correspondence. It is truly staggering that a man of your means and influence got screwed by some welfare queen with a God complex. I will NOT be dragged down with you. I'm about to give a press conference denouncing you, consider yourself lucky I don't sue.

He slammed the laptop shut and began pacing around the room. He ran through options in his head for his next steps but the anger short-circuited each thought. He returned to his desk chair and prayed for guidance.

For perhaps the thousandth time that day his phone rang. The ringtone jolted him, and he could have sworn he left it on silent. The screen said the number wasn't known, but in his rage he answered, hoping for the opportunity to vent his feelings to an unsuspecting telemarketer.

"Whatever it is I'm not interested."

"Calm down, Abel, I'm on your side."
The low voice on the other side was one he did not recognise, but Belle would have. He scoffed.

"So you're trying to get money from me?"

"No, I'm offering you help. Guidance."

"Legal help."

"Divine help. You were praying just now weren't you?"

He sat upright.

"I'm a preacher. We pray a lot."

"For guidance, specifically."

"Are you watching me?"

"Of course, I'm your guardian."

An email notification pinged on his laptop. Opening it up again he saw a new message from 'The Man on the Phone.'

"Open the email, Abel."

Attached was a short, silent video. It showed Gabe knocking Lucifer down with a great tongue of fire in the forest. Abel felt a cold rush across his skin.

"What is this."

"Gabe. The man you tried to speak to."

In the video, the flames were reflected in Gabe's eyes.

"I knew it." His whole body shook. "A demon."

"I am your guardian, Abel. This is what you must fight."

He composed himself.

"I will, I swear."

Home

The next day Belle sat in Beverly's office as she poured Snapple into champagne glasses.

"Congratulations, you're competent to stand trial."

"Lachiam!" said Belle as they clinked glasses.

"Slainté" replied Beverly.

"Now how do we actually GET a new trial?"

Beverly finished her glass

"The best way is to secure new evidence. Or, get him to confess!" She laughed. "Rich kids aren't known for taking responsibility."

Belle thought for a moment.

"I guess." She drained her glass. "I may have an idea."

Later that day she arrived at the Letsky's household after calling ahead. Anette answered the door and hugged her.

Belle was led into a small house that had been lived in by the Letskys for decades. The walls were abundant with photos of Reece, him smiling in front of a pastel background at kindergarten, proudly wearing a suit at least a size too big at his Bar Mitzvah, as a newborn in Anette's arms. Belle swallowed her emotions.

Reece's dad, Andrew, got up from the sofa and shook her hand. He offered her a seat then went to make coffee. He returned with the drinks and sat next to his wife, holding her hand. Belle could see in his eyes that he had found it harder than her to maintain his composure.

Belle took a breath before she spoke.

"I know neither of you wants to go through a public trial again. It's messy. I feel terrible for running away after the last time."

Andrew looked at the floor.

"I wanted to suggest something to you, I hope you can help me with it. It's OK if you don't want to be involved, and It's OK if you don't want me to do it either."

She leaned forward.

"I want to us speak to Rob Kitchering in person. I know he's guilty. I want to get him to turn himself in."

Andrew let go of his wife's hand.

"Are you nuts?" He said at last "If he hasn't confessed already he never will."

"Andrew, I just think we can try."

"I don't want to see him, I don't want to talk to him." His voice began to crumble. "If I had my way he'd disappear off the face of the Earth."

Anette rubbed his back.

"I get it," Belle said. "I felt like that myself once."

"You don't get it. He wasn't your boy, you didn't see him grow up."

Belle felt a pang in her chest but said nothing.

"Honey, maybe we should consider."

Andrew turned to his wife with red eyes.

"No."

"I just want this to be over. He's got all those fancy lawyers, we'll be lucky if we even get a new trial. We need closure."

He said nothing.

"I just think if we can speak to him, face to face, he can see the human side of it. If you ask me, his Dad took over everything."

"So it's his Dad's fault?"

"No, Andrew, -"

"No one ever blames rich brats like him. It's always that he fell into a bad crowd, or some bullshit about 'mental health', or his mom didn't hug him enough, my son died and I had to watch shitty politicians talk about what a nice boy his killer was on TV. They put his graduation picture in the paper!" He half-laughed "My boy never made it to graduation."

Belle said nothing. Annette hugged him and took him to another room to talk. She was left alone for what felt like an hour. She didn't dare move, disturbing their home would feel like a violation. Her hand didn't come off her bump the entire time.

Anette returned to the living room alone and Belle stood to greet her.

"I wanna talk to him. I've been wanting to for a long time."

Her heart jumped.

"And Andrew."

She took a breath.

"He has...given his blessing."

Belle hugged her.

Gabe drove the two women to a block in the centre of Nashville the next day. It was a former factory building of red brick converted into apartments for Tennessee's wealthiest. Belle found it hard to comprehend the unkempt man she saw screeching away from the scene of Reece's murder living in the cultural centre of the state's capital. Her bones rattled at the thought of seeing him again.

She turned to Anette.

"You still want to do this?"

She nodded, keeping her eyes on the building.

The three of them ascended the black metal stairs to the third floor and an apartment at the back of the building, overlooking an office parking lot. Belle knocked on the door as she held Anette's hand. She stood tall, but Belle could feel her shaking.

There was a rustling and the sound of more than

one lock unfastening before he opened the door. Belle had never been this close to him before. His eyes were exactly like his father's. She expected him to slam the door shut but he stared at the three of them for what felt like an age.

Belle squeezed Anette's hand.

"Can we come in, Rob? We just want to talk to you."

He stammered for a moment.

"I...uh... I don't think that's a good idea."

"Please." Said Anette. "Hear me out. I think you owe me that much."

He ran a hand through his hair and stepped aside. He bristled as Gabe entered.

"Who is this guy?"

"He's a friend. He isn't gonna hurt you." Answered Anette with enough confidence to stop any further questions.

The apartment had minimal furniture but was still untidy. There was a white leather sofa with ornate arms, seemingly leftover from Governor Kitchering's last redecoration, facing a large TV. The coffee table in between was piled high with old letters and empty packets of chips. He hastily cleared similar junk off a heavy wooden dining table in front of a high window so they would have a place to talk.

"Is there a gun in here Rob?" Belle asked in the steadiest voice she could muster.

"No. My dad took em all after..." He didn't complete the thought "He has them."

Gabe stepped closer to him for a moment and stared into his eyes.

"He's telling the truth."

He pulled out four bar stools from under the dining

table.

"Are you going to be OK with this? You know, cos you're pregnant and everything?"

Belle was taken aback by his concern.

"No, I'll be fine."

Once they were sat around the table it seemed as though Rob would start speaking before he closed his mouth again more than once. His eyes were fixed on his hands. After a moment, Belle began.

"Rob, I brought Anette here today because she wanted to speak to you. You can imagine what she's been through these last few months."

"I didn't do it." He said, at last, making eye contact with Belle. "I'm not a murderer."

"I don't think you're a murderer," Anette said. He did not look at her. "I think you made a dumb mistake." She took his hands. "Look at me, boy." He slowly lifted his eyes to hers. "The problem is, your mistake, it took my boy away from me." Her voice faltered as she spoke but it didn't break.

She reached into her pocket and pulled out a stack of photos.

"Please, just look through these" Anette continued "I think it's the least you can do."

He didn't touch the photos. So, she reached over and pointed at the first.

"This is Reese with his grandma, that was his sixth birthday."

She flipped over to the next photo.

"This is him with the pet mouse he had as a kid. His name was Bruce. He kept that mouse alive for years. He was a caring boy."

She flipped to the next.

"This is him playing football at high school-"

"I didn't kill him."

Belle leaned forward.

"I was there, Rob. I called the ambulance. I saw you shooting, I heard your voice. I know it was you."

He said nothing.

"Rob, you're not like your dad. I can tell this has been weighing on you, it's so obvious. You can't even bear to look at these photos." Anette's voice sounded tenser.

"Because you're putting this on me!" His voice raised slightly and Gabe bristled. "Yeah, I've not been the best kid, but I'm not a killer! I'm not!"

"You know," interrupted Gabe "I could show you everything this woman has felt since you shot her son. I have that power, but I'm not going to do that. Because if you knew the pain you caused, it would drive you mad."

"What?" He laughed "What the hell are you talking about, dude,"

"Look at me."

He said it with such authority that Rob did so right away. Gabe's eyes, unblinking, fixed on his for a few heartbeats. His face twitched.

"What are you?"

"You can't bring him back, Rob, but you can do something to make amends." Promised Belle, snapping him out of the semi-trance he was under.

"What?"

"Hand yourself in. Give his family some closure."

He shook his head.

"No, no, no. I'm not going to jail. No."

"Your dad is the governor. You'd have a better time there than I did."

He laughed.

"My dad would never speak to me again, he already hates me."

"No father hates their son," Gabe said.

"Rob, please." Anette pleaded. "I know you're scared. I know why you want to run. I can't forget what you took from me. But if you admit it, if you do your penance, if you let me and my family put an end to this, I can forgive you."

He stared at her with wide, sleepless eyes.

"How?" He whispered.

"Forgiveness doesn't get rid of what happens, but it gives us peace."

She took his hands in hers.

"But I can never forgive you until you end this. Until you apologise."

His eyes squeezed shut and his face reddened. He dropped his head.

His voice came in a broken whimper. "I've barely slept. I can't stop thinking about it." His shoulders shook. "My dad has thrown money at it but he just wants to save his reputation. Well, you know what?" He lifted his head. "Fuck him. He dropped me like a rock when I was in rehab, he only cared when I was making him look good."

He swallowed.

"I'm sorry, Anette. I'll tell the cops it was me."

She broke out into a smile.

"Thank you, thank you, Rob." She stood up and took him in her arms, resting her chin on his head. "I forgive you."

14
Full of Grace

Belle held her mother's hand as they watched Rob Kitchering on the news. Smiling in handcuffs as he was escorted away by police under a strobing light of cameras flashing. Occasionally it cut to footage of Governor Kitchering marching to his office under similar flashing cameras, his red face pointing down.

"You know what the best thing is?" Belle said, "They haven't mentioned me at all."

Cynthia kissed her head.

"I don't know if I could do what Anette did, if someone took you from me I'd probably want them dead."

"His dad couldn't forgive him, who can blame him?"

Cynthia sighed.

"Thrown his life away. What a stupid boy."

"Better he makes up for it down here than up there."

"Please don't get theological with me, Belle, it's a Tuesday night." She sighed.

Belle giggled.

"Anyway, what we need to focus on is you and my grandson." She sat forward and opened up her bulky work laptop. "I was thinking we throw a baby shower. Just a small one, close friends."

"Sounds like fun."

"I was looking at these sheet cakes they do at Costco, you can get any picture you want on it. We could have one of your baby photos! That would be fun."

Belle smiled as her mother reeled off ideas for party favours, imagining her singing songs to Yeshua and playing board games with him as she did with her when she was small.

That night Belle, Cynthia, and Gabe were invited to Adrian and Yelena's home for the final night of Hannukah. After lighting the menorah and placing it in the window, they sat on the mismatched sofas to exchange small gifts.

"I hope everyone stuck to the ten-dollar limit," Yelena began, "I don't want anyone to look bad."

"Can I start?" Asked Gabe.

"I think you'll bite our hands off if we don't let you, Gabe," Adrian replied, "Go ahead."

He reached into the grocery bag he brought with him and handed each guest a gift. Before they began tearing the paper he halted them.

"Carl goes first."

Carl was handed a small but exquisitely wrapped package. He sniffed at it and started to paw at it before Gabe helped him. It was a little white collar, embroidered with his name in gold. He sniffed at it curiously, and Gabe put it on him. He transferred him to his lap.

"Ok, the rest of you can go now. Counter-clockwise order, please."

Cynthia was next. She did her best to open the cube-shaped package without tearing the blue and gold paper. It was a snow globe with a photo of her, Gabe, Belle and Carl in the backyard of her home. She beamed.

"You next, Belle." His excitement was palpable. Belle smirked, getting flashbacks to waking up her parents at 7 am to open her birthday presents. It was a small blue blanket.

"I knitted it." He said before she had a chance to react.

"Gabe, that's so nice!" She lay it across her bump "You did such a good job!"

For Yelena, there was a set of fountain pens with her initials. Adrian laughed as he opened his, a rare sound that made Belle jump. He revealed a small wooden dreidel. Yelena cheered sarcastically.

"I know you have hundreds, I made this one myself though."

"Are these teeth marks?"

"Carl tried to eat it."

He laughed again.

"Thank you, Gabe, it will have pride and place in the dreidel drawer."

"I'm honoured."

For Sarah, there was an old vinyl Dean Martin record. Her favourite singer. Adrian lowered the needle on the old record player and the song began. Everybody Loves Somebody. Sarah sat up in her wheelchair and beamed, and began singing each word.

As the song faded out they applauded

"You want to go, next Belle?" Yelena asked.

"Yes, I will start with Gabe because he's nearest and I don't wanna get up."

She reached into the tote bag but was interrupted by a knock at the door.

Adrian went to answer the door. There was a polite conversation with whoever was standing outside before he stuck his head back around the partition.

"There are some people here who want to see you, Belle."

She felt a flip in her stomach.

"See me?"

He reassured the people outside that he wouldn't be long and walked over to her.

"You don't have to go and talk to them if you don't want to, but for what it's worth, they seem harmless, and I think you should."

She turned to Gabe, who had the look of a parent watching their child take their first steps.

"Ok. Will you help me with this, Adrian?"

He gave a rare smile.

"Of course."

Outside a group of about five people stood under the glow of the porch light. Their faces lit up when they saw her.

"It's really you!" Proclaimed a woman in her 40s.

"You guys must be freezing, you should come in. Is that OK, Adrian?"

He nodded.

"Come upstairs, you can use my study."

As they passed the entrance to the living room Gabe and Belle smiled at one another. She caught her mother's eyes. She mouthed 'be careful'. Belle replied, 'I promise'.

Adrian's study was small but it had a reasonable-sized sofa and enough space to sit everyone. A woven rug almost completely covered the wooden floor. Ikea shelving units with bending shelves full of books lined the walls. Belle took the middle of the sofa and Adrian sat behind the desk.

"What did you guys want to talk to me about?"

A young man with red hair spoke first.

"First I want to apologise for dropping in on you like this, and thank you, Rabbi, for even letting us in."

He smiled.

"Well, Belle is my friend."

The young man continued.

"We know your aunt, she said you were coming here tonight for Hannukah."

"Did she suggest you come?"

"Yes," he giggled, "I said it might be presumptuous but, she said it would be good to ask you."

"Ask me what?"

"To pray for us."

She paused.

"Pray for you?"

An older man spoke.

"You are closer to God than anyone on Earth, we want you to take our prayers and give them to him."

She felt her face flush.

"I don't know if my prayers would come through any louder than yours." Instinctively, she looked to Adrian. He crossed his arms.

"I still don't fully understand what you are, Belle, but I do know there is always some value in bringing people comfort."

With that, she felt her nerves settle.

"OK, tell me your prayers."

The old man swallowed.

"My wife, she doesn't have long, I want you to ask God to give her peace, and to take her home."

When she had heard all their prayers they returned downstairs. Each person shook her hand as they left. As she reentered the living room Gabe threw his arms around her and squeezed.

"You did good, kid."

"Very well," agreed Adrian. "It's tough when people tell you things like that, you were great."

She sat back down between her mother and Gabe. Cynthia held her hand.

"You OK?"

She nodded.

"Yeah, it was kinda nice. They trusted me, it was nice to be trusted."

She gave her mother's hand a squeeze. She remembered what they had been doing before the interruption.

"Oh! Gabe, your gift."

She handed him a small box wrapped with gold paper. Inside was a velvet ring box, he opened it and saw the pewter ring, bearing the design of two hands holding a heart with a crown.

"A Claddagh ring!"

She was momentarily surprised that he knew what it was by sight, but what could surprise her about an angel?

"My lawyer has one and I asked her about it. It's supposed to represent loyalty and friendship."

He put it on his right index finger. She was relieved to

see it fit.

"I'll never take it off."

She knew he meant it.

That night as she was about to get into bed, Yeshua kicked as if to remind her. With some difficulty, she knelt by her window and took a moment to observe the full moon before closing her eyes.

"It's me." She whispered. "I have some things to ask you for, on behalf of some friends."

The next morning Belle woke up early. She lay in bed on her back for an hour, content to stare at the ceiling and feel Yeshua kicking. She thought about how she would be beginning maternity leave if she had a 9-5 job. Eventually, she made her way downstairs. She decided against turning on the TV or playing music and sat in the living room sipping tea with nothing but the sound of the clock ticking.

Then, the silence was broken. The living room window her back was facing shattered, showering her with glass. Instinctively she jumped away from the window and spotted the brick on the carpet. She saw a black-clad figure running away from the house, and ran to the front door to find the key.

Throwing it open and running out into the cold concrete driveway, she saw no sign of the assailant.

"Belle? What happened? Are you OK?"

Cynthia's voice rang out as she descended the stairs. Belle ran back inside and locked the door.

"What happened?"

"Someone threw a brick through the window, I didn't see them."

"Are you hurt? Did you step on any glass?"

She inspected Belle's hands for injury.

"No. I mean I don't think so."

They both turned and saw the brick. It was wrapped in a piece of paper and tied up with a rubber band. Belle stepped towards it.

"If it's an envelope don't touch it, you don't know what's in it."

She attempted to bend down and pick it up but when it was difficult Cynthia stepped in.

She unfurled the paper. In scrawled, large blue ink was written SATAN WHORE. They exchanged a look.

"Abel's done something." Assessed Belle. Cynthia agreed.

The video was not difficult to find. Shaky, front camera footage of Abel against a blank wall. Like a film from a bunker.

"My friends, this video is both a warning and a call to arms." He paused to swallow his emotion.

"This isn't good." Noted Cynthia.

He continued.

"I believe a messenger came to me, an angel if you will, and gave me the following footage as a means of showing me the truth."

A short but unmistakable video of Gabe throwing fire as Belle cowered behind him played. Belle's heart dropped to her stomach.

"I'm sure you recognise the woman as our friend Belle Carter. But many of you have not seen the face of her friend. He calls himself 'Gabe', but it's a lie. He is the devil himself."

"Oh no." Whispered Cynthia.

"This messenger, my guardian, gave this to me so that I could show you the truth. The devil is walking among us." His eyes were red and he began to well up. "We must protect ourselves. We must drive out this evil. I am calling on all of the faithful in this nation to join me and reject these liars, to push them away, to cast them out like snakes in the grass." He sighed and composed himself. "Please stay with me for any future updates. I will pass on whatever information I can." The screen returned to black.

Belle paced the room. Cynthia seemed to struggle to remember how to speak before she said anything.

"I just... I don't understand, Belle, what is he talking about? How did he get that video? None of this makes sense."

"I know what he's talking about."

Cynthia turned to her.

"What?"

"I told you the Devil came to me in jail? Well, the video is Gabe protecting me from him. I guess he's convinced Abel the opposite is true."

Cynthia continued to say nothing.

"He was-"

"I don't want to know." Her voice was quiet. She put her head in her hands. "All this stuff, Belle I..." Her lip quivered "How can I be a mom to you when this is what you're facing?"

"You're always gonna be my mom. Abel is never taking that from me." She felt a sting in her foot and looked down to see a small piece of glass sticking out of the side. "We're getting out of here." She said. "We're gonna go somewhere safe until we can come home and be a family again."

Gabe arrived at the house half an hour later and boarded up the smashed window. Once the glass was swept away he was able to look them in the eye.

"I'm so sorry. I failed you both."

"I won't have that kind of talk," reassured Cynthia. "We're all in the same boat here."

"It's my job to keep you all safe though." He sighed. "I've had 6,000 years of this crap and I still can't predict him. I still underestimate how low he'll sink." He looked into Cynthia's eyes. "I'm sorry it took so long to tell you."

She swallowed.

"Just don't leave me out of anything anymore."

"So where do we go from here?" Belle asked.

"I don't feel safe here. When they thought we were liars that was one thing, but Satanists?" Cynthia shuddered "they may want us dead."

"I spoke to Marnie, she knows of a safe house used by another gang that owes her a favour."

"Where is it?" Asked Cynthia.

"Detroit."

"Detroit??"

"It's far away. Abel is a big deal in Tennessee but the further out you go the the less people care. Plus, Kitchering has no authority in Michigan."

Belle sat on the steps to relieve her legs, which were becoming sore.

"I've not been further North than Virginia."

"It's snowy in Detroit, you like snow. Plus, the neighbourhood the safe house is in is almost abandoned."

"Well, that's just sad."

Gabe shrugged.

"The decline of the American working class works in our favour at this point."

"What about Viv? She could be a target?"

"We'll drop in on her. She'll probably be too stubborn to run, though," Cynthia said.

"I can call her."

"No, Gabe. I'm still not convinced they weren't bugging our phones."

Belle puffed out air.

"Well, I guess weirder things have happened."

"How far is it to Detroit?"

"11-hour trip. I'll drive, it's the least I can do," he shrugged "plus, Angels don't get tired."

"What about your job, mom?"

"I emailed my resignation before Gabe got here."

Belle stood up again.

"What?"

"I say resignation, they were making redundancies. I get a pretty good payout." She smiled. "Kitchering announced a lot of budget cuts in our department, which I'm sure is completely independent of anything he feels towards our family."

After half an hour of hasty packing, they loaded into Gabe's car. Carl was already sleeping in the passenger seat. They pulled away and Belle kept her eyes on the house until it disappeared completely.

Belle volunteered to knock on Vivienne's door. She greeted her with a hug.

"Sweetie! I saw what that awful man said but don't you worry, I'm going on TV in a week, I'm going to stand up for you."

She smiled.

"Actually, Aunty, me and mom are gonna go somewhere safe for a while. Marnie knows a place in Detroit."

"Oh, honey, but you have God on your side."

"They put a brick through our window this morning. Mom doesn't feel safe." She sighed. "Come with us, Viv, I'd never forgive myself if they hurt you." She pinched her cheeks.

"Everything I got into, I did on my own. I appreciate the care, but I'm staying right here and standing up for you."

Belle grinned.

"Mom said you'd say that."

They left ten minutes later with a stack of hastily made sandwiches in Tupperware and a plate of deviled eggs covered in saran wrap. Belle fed a piece of her chicken sandwich to Carl as they pulled away.

The sky was blushing pink at the horizon as they arrived in Springfield Illinois. By this time Cynthia was travelling in the passenger seat so Belle could stretch her legs across the back seats. Gabe found a nondescript motel and pulled up.

"Remember when we met and you told me you were from Illinois?"

Gabe smirked.

"Oh yeah! I guess it sounded good."

The room was clean and comfortable enough. There was an armchair for Carl to sleep on, two double beds and a TV. Belle lay on her side and Cynthia rubbed her back as Gabe got the bags from the car. Belle pulled out her phone to update Becky on the situation.

Gabe arrived with sandwiches and snacks from a gas station across the road.

"It's a sandwich day, ladies. Life on the road."

"We used to do this with your father when you were little, Belle."

"Oh yeah. In the hotel rooms."

Cynthia explained to Gabe, "Abe would work away and sometimes we would go with him when Belle was small. We'd get snacks and have little hotel picnics, maybe watch a movie." She smiled at the memory.

"Well, I know for a fact they meant a lot to Abe too," Gabe replied.

Cynthia swallowed.

"Thank you, Gabe."

He grinned.

"You're welcome."

They set off early the next day and drove solidly to Detroit. The closer they got, the colder it became, and once they were in Michigan there was thick snow everywhere under a crisp blue sky. Cynthia shook Belle awake from her backseat nap. She had always been in love with snow. Carl had never seen it before, and stared out the window for the remainder of the journey, barking whenever he saw another dog playing in it.

Detroit sprouted out of the ground as they approached their destination. It was busier than Belle expected, plenty of neighbourhoods looked like any other. Occasionally, abandoned industrial buildings made into explosions of colour with street art revealed a dying manufacturing history. The skyscrapers in the centre of the city loomed like huge gravestones.

The neighbourhood they were staying in had been forgotten. It was a working-class suburb not unlike the one Belle had grown up in, but only a few houses were occupied. Those were brightly painted and well cared for. The safe house was a former general store near where the suburb met a road going straight across the Canadian border. Gabe parked up and Carl ran out to dive into the snow. Belle was blindsided by the biting cold. The icy wind thrashed her face.

"It has heating, I checked," reassured Gabe. "Marnie gave me the number of the lady who owns it. She lets bikers use it, they pay her I think."

"Do we have to pay her?" Cynthia asked.

"No, the gang owes Marnie a big favour. She wouldn't say what it is but I think ignorance is bliss in this case."

Gabe unlocked the door with a key under a flowerpot. The outside of the building wasn't derelict, but most of the windows were boarded up. The inside was a pleasant surprise. It was clean, there was a TV, a kitchenette, a large corner sofa, and a pool table. The carpet was a little worn and there were faded lines on the wall from where shelves of produce had once been.

"There's a bathroom with a shower and a couple of camp beds. A little store nearby we can buy food from, we're all set," announced Gabe.
Cynthia inspected a small bookshelf of paperbacks and DVDs.

"Who knew biker gangs lived so well."

"It could be fun, hotel picnics right?"
Cynthia smiled at her.

"Our priority is medical care. Figure out how Yeshua is going to get here."

One week later

Studio lights buzzed on and Adrian and Vivienne squinted. Their debate partner, Angela, was used to the spotlight and unphased by it. She already had her camera-ready smile ready to go. Adrian turned to Vivienne.

"Are you nervous?"

"No, honey, I can talk the hind leg off a donkey. You?"

He waved his hand from side to side.

"I've done this kind of thing a thousand times, but TV is different. I'm not a performer."

"Well, I got you, sweetie."

He found himself reassured.

"Welcome back to Talking Tennessee, I am here with a panel to discuss the great theological debate sparking up in our state concerning, of all things, a pregnant nineteen-year-old girl. Normally, the pregnancy of a gas station worker wouldn't be of such concern but earlier this year she was seen in a video claiming she was pregnant with the Son of God.

"While most of us wondered just what the heck that meant, preacher Brother Abel has gone as far as claiming she is working with Satan himself! This story has everything, folks, murder, prison, local government, and God.

"To discuss the latest developments in this story I am sitting with Vivienne Carmicheal, Belle Carter's aunt, Rabbi Adrian Sanders, Author of *Olam Ba Ha: The World to Come and the Messiach,* and Angela Slater, speaker at The Temple of the Staff and wife of Brother Abel."

The three of them smiled with varying levels of confidence. The host turned to Adrian first.

"Rabbi Sanders, what exactly does 'Son of God' mean?"

He took a breath.

"Well, Jonathan, I can't say I know the answer. The idea of the Messiach is pretty prominent in Judaism and throughout history, several people have claimed to be the Messiah. None of them has ever claimed to be the Son of God, however."

The host raised an eyebrow.

"So you're undecided on the subject? Do you think she's lying? She worked for you, didn't she?"

"She did, and no, I don't think she's lying, or insane, or in league with the devil. The idea of the devil is more folklore than theology, but that's a different discussion for a different time. The exact details of her mission I don't know, but she seems self-assured and smart." He leaned forward, beginning to find his flow. "The Messiach as described in the Torah fulfils a very specific purpose, he's a king and a ruler of David's line, leading us into a new age."

"So you really don't know?"

"I think the word of God is there for us to interpret and try to understand, not necessarily treat as black and white. I don't want to cast any great titles onto a fetus."

There was a small giggle from the camera crew.

"I will say that I met with Gabe and I don't think he's the devil."

"He isn't!" Vivienne near-shouted, "he's been nothing but a friend to our family, demons don't care for people like he does!"

"The greatest trick the devil pulled is convincing mankind he doesn't exist," insisted Angela. Adrian scoffed.

"I would say the greatest lie mankind told itself is that a supernatural entity is responsible for all of its evil. What we should really focus on here is an abuse of state power and what happens when it mixes with religion."

Angela let out a patronising laugh.

"You sound less like a Rabbi, more like a leftist college professor."

"I'm both, Angela."

"I've been a woman of faith my whole life, and I know my niece. I know she's telling the truth and I'm not alone. And I'm not the only person who has turned away from the Temple of the Staff." Vivienne turned to Angela. "I followed you and your husband once, but good men don't drive innocent people out of their homes. They don't lie and get people sent to jail. They don't whip up angry mobs."

Angela smiled again.

"My husband and I have been blessed by God too often to doubt his love for us. Abel has always been a passionate defender of God's children. He condemns acts of violence towards anyone, but he knows he has to do what he can to protect America."

"Against a baby?" Adrian retorted.

"What about when one of your followers punched my niece in the stomach? Who does that protect?"

"The Temple of the Staff believes in the rule of law, we condemn all violence."

"You can't play dumb, Angela. He knows the influence he has, he knows how people will react. It's irresponsible to incite people like this. I saw cops digging their knee into her back and you were stood in my front yard calling it a victory." He looked directly at her, she seemed to waver for a moment. "And you knew she was innocent."

"I didn't know. We did what we thought was a proportionate response to one of our congregation being assaulted."

"We all saw the video, it was obvious she was innocent. And you were THERE." Added Vivienne.

"You can't blame us for the justice system taking the action they felt was appropriate."

"Not a good idea to throw cops under the bus Angela," Adrian pointed out, "that's a big portion of your congregation."

She opened her mouth to retort but the host interrupted.

"I'm afraid that's all we have time for today, we have to go back now to Tom for the weather."

That night the Temple of the Staff uploaded a version of the debate with the title 'Angela SCHOOLS leftist Rabbi on Scripture and the rule of law.'

Detroit

"Is it not super boring being shut up inside all day?" Asked Becky.

"Eh, once you've been in solitary this feels like a stay in a resort."

"True, and you have Gabe. Lovely Gabe."

"What has Abel been saying?" Asked Belle.

On the other end of the phone, Becky sucked in the air.

"I know, I know, I should ignore him, I just want to know how crazy things are."

"Well, pretty crazy. He veers from you being controlled by the devil to insisting Yeshua is the devil

and he's going to destroy us all."
She adjusted the sofa cushion behind her back.

"Oh, man."

"And he keeps asking where you are, but I don't know what exactly he wants with you? He always says he doesn't condone violence against you blah blah blah, but then he keeps saying 'we need to fight' and acting like this is the death of all God-fearing people. How does he think people will react?"

"Oh, he knows exactly what he's doing, getting them to do his dirty work and claiming plausible deniability."

"What blows my mind is he genuinely seems to believe it. I used to think he was just in it for the money, but now, who knows." Joey babbled in the background. "I gotta say, there's a lot of support for you, more and more people believe you."
Belle smiled.

"It's kinda nice, you know? I just wanted to be left alone before but it feels good to have people on board with this."

"Well, thank your Aunty Viv. She's kicking ass."
She giggled.

"I did see that TV debate. She and Adrian did so well."

"That woman creeps me out."

"Me too."
Joey began to fuss.

"I better go, he needs his dinner. I wanna be there for the birth."

"We'll arrange something."

Cynthia arrived a little later with groceries. She

rushed about, rustling packets and cursing as she nearly dropped things.

"Are you OK, mom?"

She looked off into the distance while considering her answer.

"I got recognised at the grocery store."

Belle sat up.

"What did they say??"

"She was a believer. She asked if she could meet you."

"Well, that's not too bad."

"But she could tell someone, Belle, and it could get back to Abel."

"Not necessarily, she would know not to tell anyone."

Cynthia sighed.

"Where's Gabe?"

"He took Carl for a walk."

Gabe entered the room at that moment. Carl shook the snow off his coat and trotted in to curl up in front of the space heater.

"What's up, gang?" He trilled.

"Mom got recognised by a believer at the grocery store, she's freaking out."

He blew out air.

"Well, if they're a believer, that's not too bad."

"All we need is for her to tell the wrong person."

Gabe ran a hand through his hair.

"We just have to accept some risk, I guess."

Cynthia sighed.

"We're just so close, I can't face someone..." She waved her hands around to find the words, "...attacking us right now."

She sat down.

"What about when he's here? Are we just going to have to keep hiding?"

Gabe hung his head.

"He's my grandson. If I can't protect Belle how can I protect him?"

Gabe sat down on the edge of the sofa by her.

"I wish I had easy answers. A lot of this is new to me, too."

Belle considered.

"I think all we can do is show the world we're bigger than Abel."

"How?" Cynthia asked.

She shrugged.

"I don't know yet."

That night, Belle struggled to sleep. Yeshua was awake and wriggling. The position of his kicks had changed, he was getting in place to make his entrance. She knew Gabe would be awake. Leaving the small room she slept on a camp bed alongside her mom, she found him sitting in the dark staring at a laptop screen, Carl curled up beside him.

His expression of concern melted into a smile when he saw her.

"Hey! Trouble sleeping?"

She nodded.

"What are you looking at?

He sighed.

"The Temple of the Staff Website. I know, I know..." he lifted his hands, pre-emptively responding to her criticism, "it's not good to pay him attention."

"I get it. I guess you have to know your enemy."
He closed the laptop and switched on a lamp next to him.

"At least *I'm* the enemy now. Once I'm gone, he might leave you alone.

"Once you're gone?"
He nodded.

"Once I'm gone."
The expression on her face must have inspired him to change the subject.

"You know, it's a really clear night, why don't we go for a little walk."

"It's one o'clock in the morning."
He grinned.

"Exactly! No one else around. Carl needs it, too, he had a nap earlier."
As soon as he stood Carl leapt to the floor, ready to get going.

Outside was icy but pleasantly still. There was a new dusting of snow on top of spots where patches of the previous layer had worn away. The sidewalk had been cleared.

Gabe kept his eyes on the stars as they walked. There was a glow obscuring some of the night's sky by the city centre, but out in their suburb enough of the houses were empty to keep them shining as clear as they would out in the fields around Memphis. They walked around the dying neighbourhood, some parts better lit than others.

They came to a hill, with steps leading up to a lookout point over the city. At the top, they could see where the city stopped and lake Michigan began. The space in between was a sea of tiny yellow and white lights like any other metropolis, made far brighter by the snow. Again, Gabe looked up at the sky.

"It is just astonishing. Billions and billions of them." He turned to her. "It amazes me too, all that he made."

Belle allowed herself a moment to appreciate the night sky. She only knew a few constellations, Cassiopeia, the Big Dipper, and Orion's Belt. The tiny pinpricks of light in between these bodies interested her, how distant they were.

"I was thinking about what happened with mom, getting recognised and all."

"Uh-huh."

"I wish I could have met that lady."

He turned away from the sky.

"You do?"

She nodded.

"It feels a little weird when people act like I'm some kind of celebrity, but it also feels good." She struggled to find the right words. "It feels like I'm giving them some kind of comfort."

He smiled.

"You were right about how scary it can be, existing without knowing why, or if there's anything that comes after. When I got to talk to my Dad it was like I finally got some relief from that. It feels good that me and Yeshua can offer that to other people."

He picked up Carl, who was beginning to shake in the snow.

"You are gonna do just fine."

She exhaled, her breath visible and twisting its way towards the city.

Tennessee

As Governor Kitchering pulled up in front of his grand Nashville McMansion he spotted a man waiting at the door for him and rolled his eyes.

"What do you want, Abel?" He asked with a flat voice as he exited the car.

"I need a favour, Bob."

He chuckled.

"A favour? You're poison, Abel, half the media has written you off as an amusing nutcase. Just hand the temple over to your wife already."

"I don't care about that anymore, I have a mission."

As he walked closer to him, Kitchering was taken aback by his red, wild eyes.

"And I have an election coming up. Just being mentioned in the same sentence as you is dangerous. My campaign team is having enough trouble with the shit my son is in –"

As he went to unlock the double door Abel stood in his way.

"I can help you with the election. I still have a big congregation, I can still endorse you."

He laughed.

"I'm not worried about the paranoid freaks who go to your church voting democrat any time soon."

He pushed him aside and entered the house, only for Abel to follow him. Even with their hushed voices, their conversation echoed around the cavernous hall.

"I want to know where she is."

He turned, considering calling the cops.

"What makes you think I know?"

"You can tap phones, I know you can find her."

Kitchering groaned.

"For God's sake, Abel, give it up. What are you gonna do when you find her, kill her? Perform an exorcism?"

"I find her, I find that man she's always with. I can drive out satan himself, Bob."

He laughed.

"You're insane."

"I've exhausted every lead. I've had people attend her aunt's meetings, I've been interrogating her followers, I even paid private investigators, it's like she's vanished."

"You want my advice, Abel? Just let it go. And get out of my house before I call the cops."

"I can't let it go!" His raised voice temporarily silenced Kitchering and filled the huge entrance hall. "This is about humanity's future!"

Kitchering sighed.

"Look, I don't know where she is. Go waste someone else's time."

He stormed into his living room, a faux-hunting lodge space with canvas prints of family photos on the walls. Of course, Abel followed him.

"Don't you want revenge? She sent your son to prison, she may have cost you your career."

He paused before turning to him again.

"That boy did it to himself. We are currently setting up a scholarship in Reece Letsky's name. All I gotta do is cry on TV about how bad I feel for what my son did and all is forgiven."

He sat down on the cream leather corner suite, artfully draped with fur throws.

Abel sighed.

"I don't want to have to take this route, Bob."

"What route?"

He pulled out his phone and began scrolling through screenshots. He held it up to Kitchering's face so he could see. Emails between the two discussing the wiretaps on phones. Kitchering's face hardened, blushing to a purplish shade.

"It'd ruin you too, Abel."

He shrugged.

"You're not the only one who can cry on TV and ask for forgiveness. It worked for Jimmy Swaggart." He put the phone back in his pocket. "As I said, my mission is bigger. If I martyr myself, so be it."

He continued to glare, his jaw muscles tight as bowstrings.

"Preachers and politicians are not the same breed, Bob. You're incapable of sacrifice."

Kitchering stood up and smoothed his grey hair.

"I find out where she is and tell you, you stay away from me."

"Consider it done." He turned to walk out. "She's due pretty soon, so get to it."

Detroit

As her due date approached, arrangements were made for Vivienne and Becky to arrive in time for the birth. One day, Gabe agreed to scout the local hospitals to see which would be the most suitable. After an hour he returned with a drained expression.

"What is it?"

"They found us, Belle, those bastards found us."

"Who?" She asked, although she already knew the answer.

"I went to the hospital and there's a bunch of people outside with signs and one of them has a megaphone screaming about Satan coming."

"Shit..."

"So I went to some other hospitals and it's the same story."

"Did you see Abel?"

"No, but I know he's involved."

"Check his website, see what he has planned."

The latest entry was an untitled video. It was shaky, filmed on a phone against a plain background. It was titled 'the fight against darkness'.

It began with a moment of silence while he set up the camera and took a seat.

"He's completely lost it." Gabe murmured.

"My friends." He began, "I have discovered the whereabouts of Belle Carter and the demon protecting her. They are in Detroit, hiding like cowards. I need all believers to come with me and drive out this evil, only our strongest fight will be good enough."

His voice broke with emotion before he continued to speak. Belle felt her blood run cold.

"People may call me crazy, call me all kinds of names but when the doubters and the blasphemers come to your door and try and block your path to righteousness, you push them down. I am coming for you, Maybelle Carter, and I will stop you and the demon you call a friend. Those of you who signed up to my mailing list will receive instruction, I urge you to help me. God be with you."

They were both silent for a moment, which she eventually broke.

"What do we do?"

The door opened and Cynthia came through and slammed it behind her. Her eyes were wild.

"He's outside, he found us."

Belle and Gabe peered through the window. Abel was standing in the snow, ranting into his phone camera.

"Myself and my people are going to keep watch outside this den of outlaws and demons until they stop being cowards and face us."

Over the space of a few hours, members of Abel's congregation who had been guarding the hospitals arrived outside the safe house. A few of them threw stones at the door and shouted threats until the press arrived. As soon as local news cameras showed up Abel straightened himself out, reduced his volume, and gave interviews to the camera. The three occupants of the house watched one on a local Detroit news bulletin.

"We are people of faith. We know some folks might think we're crazy, but we are here to protect them from what we believe is a great evil."

"A baby?" asked an incredulous reporter.

"God works in mysterious ways but so does the Devil. He appears to us in the most innocuous places."

As he continued to speak, Belle recognised a man standing in the crowd behind him. He seemed to lock eyes with her through the screen.

"It's him."

"Who?" asked Cynthia.

She pointed to his face on the screen and he smiled at her.

"That's the Devil."

She rushed to the window but could not see him in the crowd.

"Oh my God" muttered Cynthia, leaning in close. Gabe didn't move. Belle rushed back and saw his face still locking eyes with her through the old screen, slightly blurred by the grainy low-pixel display. An electric shot of static lit up the screen as his face disappeared, making the three of them jump. Then, an image of a man being gunned down by police, the camera lingering on his open, dead eyes. Static again, Then the face of Hannibal Lecter.

"Amputate a man's leg and he can still feel it tickling. Tell me, ma'am, when your little girl is on the slab, where will it tickle you?"

More static. Then, Billie Holiday's pained face, her mouth somewhere between a roar and a cry, as she sang Strange Fruit.

Belle felt a squeezing pain inside her. She tried to suppress it, but Gabe saw her hand clutch her stomach. Cynthia yanked the TV plug out of the wall.

"Belle?" Gabe asked. Carl leapt from the dog bed he had been sleeping in and began to bark.

"It's probably nothing, I have a little while to go."

"OK, just lie down."

She did as she was told.

The pain rolled like thunder and died away, but it wasn't severe yet. She repeated to herself that it could be nothing and that even if it was labour it could take a long time. Cynthia got her a glass of water and Gabe took stock of who was outside.

"What's it like, mom? Giving birth?"

"Well, mine was long and painful, and gross. But you have an in with God himself, so yours should be easier."

She chuckled.

"Did you have an angry mob outside?"

"I had my family, so yeah, kinda."

Gabe's phone beeped.

"It's your Aunt. She says she's on her way with Becky."

Belle felt a jolt of excitement. It felt as if she hadn't seen them in years.

"We need a doctor." Cynthia insisted.

"We could have hours, yet."

"I don't want to risk her leaving." Gabe said.

An hour passed where the three of them hardly spoke. They could hear Abel preaching outside, interspersed with a cheering crowd. Belle hadn't experienced any more pain, but her body was tense in anticipation. As she reassured herself that it was probably a false alarm, a pain not dissimilar to a cramp started building. It came like a rolling wave, rising to a point where she felt like a balloon about to burst before crashing and subsiding. She leaned forward and grimaced, as Cynthia rubbed her back.

"Oh man that sucked," she said as the pain melted away again.

"I hate to tell you sweetheart but that is just the beginning. Look, I found a number for a midwife, she might be able to help us.."

Belle nodded and Gabe sat beside her.

"Hey, you remember when I saw you throw up when you had morning sickness?"

She nodded.

"Well if I see you crowning or whatever I will immediately leave the planet."

Belle giggled.

"I wouldn't blame you. We watched a videotape of it in sex ed, I couldn't look at my mom the same way after. Me and my friends all swore we'd never let a boy near us."

"Speaking of, I'll call Becky. They should be here in a couple of hours."

"Wait, stay here for a little bit, I want to ask you something."

Gabe peered around the corner to see if Cynthia was in earshot.

"What is it?"

"Are you really going to leave when the baby is here?"

Gabe ran a hand through his hair.

"Not immediately, but yeah. I should never have stayed this long anyway, the plan was to tell you and then leave. I managed to squeeze a little vacation out of it."

Belle's heart sank.

"Well, I don't need to tell you that I'm grateful for the help you've given me."

He smiled at her.

"I'm gonna miss you too. But, it's not las if you'll never see me again. And if you feel stressed or unsure when you're raising your boy, just know me and your dad will be watching and we'll be talking about you."

She smiled at the ceiling.

"And hey, I can actually confirm that your father is watching you from above, it's not just a platitude."

She adjusted the pillow propping up her back.

"Sometimes I forget that in a way I'm still the luckiest person on the planet."

Her mom re-entered the room.

"I can get a midwife here in two hours."

Time passed and the crowd outside increased with onlookers and reporters. Curious neighbours craned their necks to see what the fuss was about but took a step back when they heard Abel talking about God and Satan. There was perhaps nothing more off-putting than making eye contact with a street preacher. Members of the press shoved notes under the door, demanding an interview. Cynthia shoved them back out.

They were around half an hour apart, and not as painful as she had expected. She gave up any hope of being able to get to a hospital and instead began praying inside her head that the midwife would make it through the crowd. Cynthia had warned her not to make herself conspicuous. Gabe refused to leave Belle's side and Carl refused to leave his. After some time his phone rang. Gabe answered.

"Becky, thank God."

Belle sat up.

"OK, just park down the street and go round the back of the building. Do not talk to anyone. I know you won't, it's Viv I worry about."

Belle laughed. There was a soft knock at the back door a few minutes later and the three women entered silently and saw Belle grinning on the sofa. Vivienne hugged her as Gabe locked the door. She pulled back to get a better look at her.

"You're so much bigger now!"

"Well, the finish line is very much in view. A midwife is on her way."

Vivienne stood up and threw her arms around Gabe, thanking him for keeping her niece safe. Becky giggled and took a seat by Belle's feet.

"Where's Joey?"

"He's with his dad."

"Wow, he's finally stepping up?"

Becky smiled.

"He said he saw me helping you out on the news and he thought that if you're telling the truth he should probably get in your good books."

She shrugged.

"Whatever works I guess. I'm just happy for Joey."

"How far apart are the contractions?" Vivienne asked, stroking Belle's hair.

"Pretty far, I think we could be here a while."

She kissed her forehead.

"I'm just happy you've found people who are gonna keep you safe." Becky added.

Vivienne squeezed her hand.

"Look at you! You are glowing!"

"Well, I just wish I was in a hospital."

"Child, you have God on your side, you are gonna be just fine."

She smiled at her aunt.

The sound of crunching snow spread from the front of the building to the sides.

"I just saw someone go through the back! There's a door here!"

More voices could be heard through the door the three women had just entered through. Belle groaned and lay back.

"Don't worry, we will not let anyone get to you," Cynthia reassured her.

"I'm just worried about the midwife. Plus, when they realise I'm in labour I feel like all hell is gonna break loose."

"It already has by the looks of things." Added Becky. "You know I think that guy Brother Abel tapped my phone? I'm suing him when this is over, I swear."

By the time the midwife arrived the building was fully surrounded. Abel had managed to obtain a microphone and was relishing the publicity.

"She's here," Cynthia announced, peering through a gap in the curtains by the front of the building. With Gabe's help, Belle stood up and walked to the window. A middle-aged woman carrying a large bag made her way around the outside of the crowd. She assessed the building.

"Call her." Belle said, "It's probably best if she goes through the back."

"She'll be noticed," Cynthia replied with a tremulous voice.

"As long as we get her inside."

"I think it's best you lie back, Belle," Gabe advised softly. She made the arduous journey back to the sofa and took up her position again.

"Yeah, through the back. As long as we can keep everyone else out, we should be OK. Knock four times so I know it's you."

Cynthia hung up the phone and she and the rest of the group made their way to the back door. Belle felt her heart dancing in her mouth. Voices at the back increased as the midwife came closer. Becky kept her hand on the handle and the key poised at the lock waiting for the signal.

"Someone's trying to get in!" A muffled voice from the front halted the flow of Abel's preaching.

"Everyone, to the back!" He said through the microphone.

The midwife knocked four times. Becky scrambled with the key and opened the door by a few inches. Grabbing hands reached in and the others pushed them back out as Becky took hold of the midwife's arm and tried to help her through. She threw the bag through the door and squeezed inside. The others pushed on the door but the tide of bodies was too much. It swung open halfway and Belle cried out. One man, a barrel-bellied trucker type wearing a camo coat too thin for the weather made it through and pushed Gabe to the floor. Cynthia turned to help him.

"Just keep them out, Cynthia, I can deal with him!"

She resumed her position, retaining the flow of people by pushing against the door. The man in camo faced Gabe with burning eyes as he got back up on his feet.

A new contraction started as he pulled out a knife. Belle did her best to hide it.

"Demon!"

"I don't want to hurt you," said Gabe, his hands outstretched.

"You will not take these people! We are God's children!"

He swung at Gabe, who stepped back. He swung again and caught Gabe's arm. Carl barked furiously at him as Gabe stared wide-eyed at the blood.

"It's good to know you do bleed."

"It's news to me too, man," Gabe replied.

The man swung again and Gabe halted his hand mid-air with an unseen force. The knife became water and splashed on the ground. The man stared at his empty hand.

"You unholy demon!"

Belle cried out as the wave of her contraction crashed.

"She's in labour?"

Gabe took advantage of his momentary distraction to try and grab the man. He fought back well, raining punches down on Gabe's face until his nose and lips were bleeding. Carl pulled at the hem of his pants with little effect, growling as best he could.

The man pushed Gabe to the ground again and pulled his arm back to land another punch. Gabe reached his hand out again and halted it. The man growled in frustration.

"Fight back properly you fucking coward!"

At that point, the four women managed to shut the door and Cynthia locked it. Without hesitating, Becky grabbed a heavy saucepan from the top of the stove. She ran over and smacked the man over the head with it before Belle could yell at her to stop. The man flopped forward onto Gabe.

"Is he dead?" Becky asked.

"No, he's drooling on me," Gabe answered, rolling him off.

Cynthia rushed to Belle's side, followed by the midwife, as the other three women helped Gabe up.

"What are we going to do with him?" Becky asked.

"Tie him up," Gabe suggested. "I'm forbidden from hurting humans but restraining them is a grey area."

He walked towards the mirror, inspecting his bloody face with curiosity.

"Belle, my name is Angie. I'm retired but I worked at the Henry Ford Hospital for fifteen years so you're in good hands. How far apart are your contractions?"

"About half an hour." Belle was reassured by her matter-of-fact tone. She stared at her face. "This is gonna sound odd but I feel like I weirdly recognise you, like you were in a dream I had once."

Angie chuckled.

"Well, that is certainly a new one." She leaned in and whispered, "help is on the way."

She opened her bag and pulled out a blood pressure monitor. Gabe took a seat next to Belle and rolled up his sleeve, poking at his wound and sucking air in his teeth when he realised how much it hurt.

"Is this what you had in mind when you took a vacation on Earth?" Belle asked as the blood pressure cuff was placed on her arm.

"I assume it will heal up pretty quick. I suppose it's a way of making me seem more human, huh?"

Angie took Belle's vitals and listened to the baby's heartbeat, announcing everything was on track. Outside, the crowd continued to roar and stones pinged off the doors and windows.

"Oh my God, look!" Becky cried. Belle craned her neck to look out of the one unboarded window as Becky drew back the blackout drapes. The people closest to the building pressed their bodies against it and linked arms. They kept their eyes shut and were silent as the missiles from the crowd and poisoned words began raining down on them.

"They're all around the house!" Announced Cynthia, peering out through a crack in the plywood covering another window. "They're protecting us!"

Belle felt a cool sensation rush over her as the pressure inside her eased.

15
Queen of Heaven

Brother Abel's voice outside was louder and more passionate than ever.

"These people have been deceived by Satan! They are protecting him from God's justice!"

The people surrounding the house didn't flinch. Belle would hardly have noticed if they had.

The midwife instructed her when to push. She felt as if her pelvis was on fire. Gabe paced the floor behind her, Carl under his arm and Becky encouraged her to curse out loud if it helped.

"You're doing very well," encouraged Angie, "just keep taking deep breaths. You can do this."

Her brain was a fog. She tried to keep her eyes on some old license plates nailed to the wall opposite but they blurred in and out of focus. The voices around her felt like they were coming through ten feet of water. She preferred this, all that she wanted to think about was hearing Yeshua's first cries. The license plates continued to blur as the pain increased, like a clawed hand reaching inside her and tugging furiously at her insides. Then, the room went black.

All other voices were silent except for Abel's, she could hear his lips smacking against the microphone as he denounced her. She felt a close, muggy heat, like the humid summer days back in Tennessee. As Abel's voice died away she could hear distant screams, people begging for mercy. She was floating in a void, hearing them in all directions. She remembered how Satan had described his kingdom to her. Then, a golden light like the spring days when she was a child, her feet stood on the cool grass and a breeze lifted her hair. Her pain was gone, and looking ahead she saw her father. He smiled at her but said nothing. As she tried to walk towards him she fell through the ground, as she had often fallen in dreams. She was in a cool forest like the one Gabe had taken her to. Turning to her left she saw a man. He was in his thirties, with skin as dark as hers and her father's eyes.

He wore a white robe that seemed to glow, and plants leaned into him as though he were the sun. He held out his hand and she took it.

"Pray." He instructed.

She took his hand and kissed it, and closed her eyes. She prayed into his hands, begging God to keep him safe. The pain began to creep back into her reality, and he loosened his grip and let go of her.

The cold returned and she could hear nothing but the sound of her breath. She dared not open her eyes as she knew she would see nothing.

"It's nice to have some alone time."

His voice sounded as though it was coming in all directions, as if she had been swallowed. She felt a rush of energy to her stomach, and clutching her hands to it she found it was flat. Opening her eyes, she saw nothing but her own body, her feet dangling. Where black is the colour and none is the number.

"Here's a lesson about those of us who find ourselves involved in God's business. We're different things to different people."

She shut her eyes and clapped her hands to her ears, but his voice was as loud as ever.

"Take me for example. Before Dante mapped out his inferno, people talked about the mouth of hell. Not the gate. Hell was the belly of the beast, and I was the beast."

There was a sound like blood rushing and she sensed him in front of her. She opened her eyes and the devil was there in the shape she knew him as.

"Sometimes I'm a man, dangerous because I am inconspicuous." He shifted his form again, growing to a towering height and sprouting a crown of twisted horns. His skin turned blood red and his body was ridged with hard sinew. Belle stepped back, determined not to break eye contact.

"I think this form actually comforts people. They think I'll be easier to spot." He laughed, flames spitting out of his mouth. "You and I know it's never that easy."

A sharp pain clawed at Belle's stomach. She doubled over, feeling the ghostly sensation of her mother's hand squeezing hers.

"That's supposed to be your punishment, isn't it? Women caused mankind to fall, the agony of childbirth is her punishment. I thought you were here to fix that?"

"Shut up!" She cried. She hoped she hadn't said it out loud to her family.

He was silent for a moment, then shrank back into his human form.

"You know my truth and I know yours." He stood beside her as she struggled to regain her upright position, breathing through her contraction. "But what people believe changes. What will people believe about you in one hundred years? One thousand years? Will you be a God? Or just a fallen woman?"

"I don't care" she choked. "I care what the world will be like."

He rolled his eyes.

"You think that matters to the big man?" His eye twitched. "In fact, forget about him for a second, what about all the little people?" He scoffed. "All this time you've been worried about them hating you. What about when they love you? What then?"

She strained to focus entirely on breathing and not on what he was saying.

"How many non-believers have been hung, burned, genocided, and had their homes stolen? Why would YOUR believers act any different?"

"What are you talking about?"

A ball of light began swirling between them. It lit up his face from beneath, making him appear little more than a smirking skull. It throbbed and warped until it formed a frozen vision of the scene outside the safehouse, a holographic miniature of Abel and his followers. The devil reached in and began lifting and reshaping the images, like a chessboard.

"Take Abel here. One time he was a good kid who wanted to make the world a better place through God, through his ministry. Let's say YOU were born 500 years ago. Let's say he tried to do it through Yeshua."

He blew on the back of Abel's head like he was a dusty action figure. He placed him in the scene and he animated and began to speak.

"Our great mother Maybelle brought the Son of God to us as a sacrifice! Our redemption is through him! Those who tarnish his good news should be cast out!"

Her heart froze.

"But" She stammered "Who would he be trying to drive out?"

He shrugged.

"Maybe someone like you, some poor kid, given my experience of human history it's usually someone like your friend Adrian." He cocked his head. "He still doesn't believe you fully, does he?"

She shook her head.

"Adrian helped me. He's my friend."

"That won't matter. When you and your son end up with your own followers like Abel he'll just be a heathen."

A feeling of lightheadedness crept in and she sank to the floor.

"Especially if they're poor, or foreign, or the wrong colour, or gay, or mad, or disabled, or on the wrong side of a war, or the wrong side of politics, it will all just be another excuse to destroy the nonbelievers."

"What is your point here?" She snapped. "You know as well as I do free will can be a real bitch sometimes but isn't that the point? The message is there, they can choose to follow it."

He rolled his eyes.

"Will that comfort you? When he's a sacrifice? I'm trying to stop that, Belle, I'm trying to help you."

She stood up, her strength returning.

"What do you care? You're the *devil*. The human race is an undeserving plague to you, ignorant creatures basking in God's light who don't understand it, let alone deserve it, what does it matter to you if you help me?"

A thought struck her.

"Sacrifice..."

"What?"

"You keep using that word... the whole point of sacrifice is you give something up and you get something in return, so what does the universe get out of my son sacrificing himself?"

"Nothing." He interrupted.

She shook her head.

"Not nothing. You wouldn't go to all this effort for just nothing. The gain of the universe has to be your loss." He said nothing. "What are you afraid of?"

"I'm not afraid of anything."

"Gabe told me you're the most pitiful creature in existence, the furthest thing from God's warmth. The souls in hell, keeping them in the darkness with you, torturing them, makes you feel powerful. It's the closest thing you have to what you gave away."

There was silence, save for the humming of the light.

"Yeshua, he's being sacrificed for them, that's what it means, taking on our sin. I never understood it til now. God reaches out to us so we can be closer to him, so we can spend eternity with him – something you can't ever have." She laughed. "He suffers their damnation for them." She faced him. "And if souls aren't being damned as they used to, where does that leave you? Alone in the dark."

The scene of Abel's protest disappeared. His face bore such an acidic glare that her confidence briefly shook. He lurched forward and grabbed her jaw in a vice-like grip, nearly lifting her off the ground.

"He'll have to come to my realm for that, and when he does, he will get all my attention." He laughed. "You think I made it hard for you? I will break him in a thousand ways."

She looked him square in the eye.

"It will be nothing compared to what you've done to yourself."

A contraction rolled upon her again. She cried out. A white light grew around them.

"Gabe? Are you doing this? Stay out of it!"

A force pulled her back painlessly, through a blinding white tunnel. The voices of her family grew louder as the face of the devil disappeared into the distance.

Again she fell, back into her body laid out on the sofa, her hands squeezing her mother's and aunt's and a cacophony of angry voices outside. She cried out in pain. Then, there was another cry, piercing and high.

"You did it," Angie said.

Cynthia leaned over and kissed her forehead. Her eyes were still blurry as the squirming bundle Angie was dabbing with a towel and draping a cotton cloth around came into view. He had wisps of black hair and his hands reached out as if to grab onto something stable. His mouth was wide and he cried out as the cold air hit his skin.

Belle sat up. Her entire body ached.

"Sweetie look!" Cynthia cried, her voice beginning to falter, "he's finally here!"

Angie passed him to her as his cries began to die down. They would have heard him outside had there not been so much shouting. Yeshua looked up at his mother with his inky-black newborn eyes. His arms still flailed around, making sense of this gaping, open world.

Belle crumbled and began to sob as she held him close. Cynthia stroked her forehead and Vivienne began to whisper a prayer.

"Oh my God," Becky said. "You did it."

"You poor thing," Belle said between bouts of sobbing, "You poor, poor thing."

Gabe was silent. Vivienne got out of his way as walked over. He knelt down and placed a hand on her shoulder. "It's done," Belle said.

"Now the work begins." He answered. He looked at Yeshuas' face, his big eyes wide with confusion. "He already looks like you."

"Belle, would you like to cut the cord?" Angie asked.

"Let my mom do it."

Angie handed her the long-handled scissors. Cynthia cut through the chord and placed a towel over Belle's legs.

"There you go, honey. He's all yours." Angie announced, bundling up some of her things.

As Yeshua's lungs fell silent, the noises outside seemed louder. Belle took deep breaths as her own crying began to subside.

"Congratulations," Becky said, "and welcome to hell."

Belle felt as though her heart was about to crack through her ribs like a flower in concrete. Yeshua's eyes opened and shut, staring up at her as if trying to place where he may have seen her before. Vivienne took her hand and kissed it.

"Sweetheart he is perfect! Let his grandma hold him."

She supported his head as she transferred him to Cynthia, who sat on a wooden chair pulled up next to her. She put her finger out to him and his tiny hand closed around it.

"Hey sweetie, it's nanna!"

Belle had never seen her smile so wide. Becky fetched her a glass of water. Gabe was silent, switching his gaze between Belle and her newborn son.

"His fingers and toes are so tiny."

"Don't let that fool you," Cynthia said, "their nails get super sharp, and their grip is stronger than you think."

Belle let him hold her finger. She turned to Gabe, his eyes shining through the bruises blooming on his face.

"Do you want to hold him?"

He half-laughed.

"You would really let me do that?"

"Of course, mom, give Yeshua to Gabe."

Cynthia stood up and crossed the room to him.

"Just support his little head in the crook of your elbow like that, and hold him steady with your other arm.

Gabe stared at the baby in his arms, now sleeping with his fingers stretching around his tiny face. He yawned, revealing his bright red gums.

"I can't believe I'm holding him."

"Well, why wouldn't you be?" Becky asked, "You've done more than most fathers' have."

"It's just, he's so much bigger than me, you know? I'm just a messenger and he's... he's like a king. More than a King." He laughed out loud. "I'm not worthy, and here he is in my arms. I should be bowing to him. And he's just so beautiful."

"He's super cute." Agreed Becky. "He's gonna look just like his mama."

"I think he'll look like his Grandad." Answered Belle.

Angie checked Belle's vitals and advised her to rest. Outside, the crowd had quietened down a little but the chorus of voices was still strong and stones still bounced off the door. The believers surrounding the house stood strong. Some of the theme were praying, and some were singing. The sun was setting, but it didn't seem to make any difference to the numbers. Belle was shown different ways of soothing her baby by Angie and her mother. She found it impossible to take her eyes off him, as did Gabe.

There was a groan from the room where the attacker was being kept. Belle and Becky went to investigate. The man was tied by his ankles and arms to the camp bed she had slept on, in something similar to the recovery position. He saw the two women at the door and thrashed for a moment like a fish in a net. The two of them jumped, but the man realised he was tied fast.

"What's your name?" Belle asked.

He didn't answer.

"She asked you a question." Becky snapped.

"Fuck you."

She lurched at him but was held back by Belle.

"Why did you attack us?"

"Because you're Satanists."

Belle stepped closer to him.

"I had my baby. His name is Yeshua."

The man said nothing.

"How about you take a look at him, see if he looks like a demon to you."

Again he said nothing. Belle went back into the main area of the safehouse where Cynthia was holding Yeshua. She took him in her arms and returned to the room.

The man averted his eyes as she approached him. She knelt beside the bed and moved the swaddling fabric away from his sleeping face.

"Please just look at him."

He continued to look away. Belle placed a pillow next to his head and lay Yeshua on it. Becky frowned.

"Belle, I don't think that's a good idea."

"Let's just see."

Yeshua's face was inches away from his, squirming a little as he opened his eyes. The man opened his too and looked into the baby's face. His face crumpled, and he began to weep.

"Forgive me, please" he begged, "please forgive me."

Belle placed a hand on his head.

"We forgive you."

An idea came to her. She picked up her son again. "Becky, could you untie him?"

The three of them re-entered the room. Gabe stood straight when he saw the man. The stranger looked at the ground and mumbled an apology. Belle pointed out the key to the front door to the man. When the rest of the room realised what she was planning they ran forward to stop her. Gabe stood in their way.

"I think she knows what she's doing."

The man unlocked the door. Outside it was dark and the air was cold. The people linking arms in front of the door stared wide-eyed as they saw her. Abel's followers faced the other way, engrossed in his speech. He was standing on a hastily constructed platform now, his wife at his side looking more than a little cold and fed up. Belle wrapped her arms tightly around Yeshua, against the cold air. Wordlessly, those protecting the door broke off and formed a circle around her.

"Thank you." She said.

One by one heads turned as they exited the safe house. No one attacked them, perhaps out of confusion when they saw one of their own leading her. Her protectors held one another's hands as they moved towards Abel. The others inside the house stood at the door and did not exhale. Belle approached the platform.

Abel fell silent as he saw heads turning and the young woman with a newborn heading his way. As she approached she could see the expression in his eyes shifting, from horror to bemusement, to something else she couldn't define but hoped to. She felt still as she ascended the steps to the platform. The human chain around her broke to let her walk up, then she stood facing the crowd. The press, thankfully, had gone.

She did not use the microphone as she stood in front of the crowd.

"His name is Yeshua." She announced. She did not go unheard by anyone. She turned to Abel. His brow was knotted and for once he seemed to struggle to find words.

"Put your arm like this, you need to support his head in the crook of your elbow."

Yeshua's tiny body was at no point unsupported as he left his mothers' arms and entered Abel's. His wife bristled as the transfer was made, reaching a protective hand forward. Belle took a step back, leaving her son with Abel.

The preacher stared at her for a moment, then turned his eyes to the baby in his arms. It was sleeping again, making snuffling sounds and twisting its hands. The baby's eyes opened for a moment, taking in the strange new face, then closed again, content with the new world. Abel lifted a finger to Yeshuas's hand, allowing him to grip it. He swallowed, stifling some involuntary gasp or sob or choke as it rose in his throat.

"Is he a demon?"

His head began shaking as if against his will, stiff at first then loosely.

"No."

"Is he Satan?"

"No."

"What is he?"

He did not remove his eyes from Yeshua.

"He's a baby."

Belle allowed herself to smile.

The preacher adjusted his arms slightly to better support the child. He lifted his gaze to meet Belle's eyes.

"Who are you, Belle?"

She kept her back turned to the crowd as she spoke.

"I am his mother."

Abel stepped towards his wife and transferred the baby to her. As he opened his eyes she lifted the tips of her fingers to wave at him, welcoming him.

Gabe turned to the women in the safehouse as they watched through the cracked open door.

"This is it." He said. "This is why she was chosen."

Belle gestured for him to come over. He walked slowly, some members of the crowd jumped back from him as he approached. He rose the steps to the platform and approached Belle and Brother Abel.

Abel stared at him with an incredulous look as he stepped on the platform. His wife was similarly dumbstruck as he took the baby from her arms with gentleness no demon would surely be capable of. Belle whispered instructions to him and they stepped into the crowd together.

One woman stepped forward hesitantly.

"Come say hi, it's OK," Belle reassured her.

The woman came closer and peered into the bundle Gabe was holding, Her eyes widened when she saw a very human baby and not a hellish abomination.

"He's a cutie." She said at last. "What's his name again?"

"Yeshua" answered Gabe.

One angry voice rang out "Are you all insane?" A man with a buzz cut fought his way through and pulled out a handgun. Belle jumped in front of her baby. She squeezed her eyes shut. If this is how it ends, Yeshua will be safe. The gun went off as if it was next to her ear, when the shot finished ringing out there was a deafening silence.

She stopped holding her breath and opened her eyes. The face of the man who shot was white as a sheet. Yeshua let out a piercing cry. She looked down expecting to see gouts of blood. Instead, she saw the bullet suspended, stopped in its trajectory mere inches from her chest. It vibrated as it lingered, eventually dying down into complete stillness and falling to the asphalt with a sound no more remarkable than a spoon being dropped.

"Oh my God." A woman to her right muttered. "Oh my God, you were telling the truth."

Belle had no words. The woman then dropped to her knees, almost dragging her down as she clutched at her coat.

"Oh God, mother of God, please forgive me." She began to weep.

Her face became unbearably hot.

"What? No, please, just get up."

Two more to her left did the same.

"Please, forgive us."

Arms in the crowd reached out to touch her. She turned and saw Brother Abel and his wife, dumbstruck.

"I have him!" The woman holding Yeshua cried, "I have the messiah in my arms!"

Those who stood near her rushed forward to get close to her son as he continued to cry.

"No, get away! He's too small!"

Her voice was drowned out by frantic prayers and adoration.

"You!" The woman kneeling at her coat cried "You tried to kill the mother of us all!"

She turned and saw the woman and others descend on the man who fired the gun. They kicked at him, clawed and tore at his clothes. Gabe, Becky, Vivienne and Cynthia rushed forward, trying to penetrate the dense ring of people reaching towards Yeshua.

"Please, stop!"

Again her voice was drowned out. She remembered what the devil had shown her. She ran to the stage and tore the microphone from Abels' hand. He was still frozen to the spot.

"Stop, all of you stop, right now!" Her anger surprised her, it was the same she had felt confronting Abel outside the Temple of the Staff.

To her relief, the commotion stopped. The people surrounding Yeshua dispersed enough for her to see that he was unharmed. The man who fired the gun was left on his knees, blood streaming from his nose and dirtying the snow.

Cynthia stepped through the crowd and took Yeshua. The look she gave the woman holding him could have melted her. His crying eased a little in his grandmother's arms.

She ascended the stairs and stood by her daughter. Belle rushed forward to hold her son. She rocked him for a moment and his crying ceased. Then, without a microphone, she spoke.

"I won't have this." Her voice was close to a cry "I will never have this in my name." They were silent. "I will not have violence, I will not have mobs, I will not have exclusion and hatred of anyone who believes different, do you understand me?" Her voice was shaky. "I will never, ever have you do to anyone else what was done to me."

There was a silence for a moment, and then Abel spoke

"No, no, this isn't right," his voice was quiet, he spoke to himself and not the crowd. She turned to look at him, his face was pale. "The angel came to me, he showed me what you are."

"He isn't an angel, not anymore." She replied. There was a spark of recognition in his eyes. He swallowed and shook his head.

"No, he would never trick me, never."
The crowd grew restless as they saw him backing away from her. A slow murmur of booing rang out. Abel's wife took the microphone out of his hand and stepped forward to address them. She held up a hand for silence and they obeyed.

"We have witnessed a great change in the world today, God has shown us the extent of his love!"
They cheered. Abel furrowed his brow.

"What is she doing?"

"My husband and I made a mistake. But God is forgiving." She took a step back and ushered belle forward to her side.

Belle felt the strongest déjà vu as she swept an arm around her shoulder.

"I'm sure this brave young woman will be able to forgive us too." Her smile was brilliant and the crowd cheered. "Perhaps this is a sign, that women are the new leaders of the faith." Another cheer rang out. She turned to Belle and smiled. "Can I hold him?"

For a moment, Belle was stunned. Then, in her blue eyes, she didn't see an ounce of sincerity. It was the same expression she wore watching Belle getting arrested at Adrian's house. Her anger burned. "No. Not you. You don't lead me."

Her face faltered. She looked back at her husband.

"If you truly feel sorry then I forgive you all." Belle continued, addressing the crowd again. "You go home and you speak to yourself and to God about what you believe. Can you do that? Please, just reflect on everything you've seen. Just go home. Just go home and let me and my son live. Just promise me you will never cause any pain in mine or my son's name."

There was silence for a moment, she shielded Yeshua against the coldness of the air.

"What should we do with him?" Asked a man still clutching the shirt of the shooter."

She looked at him, his face crumpled and he began to sob.

"Just take his gun, send him home."

Others in the crowd pulled the man to his feet and threw him out. He stumbled away, and one of the people who had formed a ring of protection ran forward to check his injuries

Belle breathed a sigh that misted and curled in the frigid air. Abel turned to her and spoke in a hushed voice.

"Look, I've only ever done what I thought I needed to do to protect people."

Belle still felt a ball of rage that had not abated.

"I was attacked by your followers, forced to run, you spied on me, threatened me, I feared for my life, and my sons'." She stepped closer to him. "I have every right to sue you, at the very least. I have every right to send you to jail, too. Film you picking up trash in the rain."

He swallowed.

"Are you sorry?"

"What?"

"I'm asking you, are you sorry for what you did, truly?"

His face looked set to either laugh or cry. He briefly met his wife's stormy expression.

"I followed scripture, I did what I was supposed to."

"I just gave birth in a biker hideout surrounded by a mob because of you."

He swallowed his doubt.

"I have nothing to be ashamed of."

She spoke in a quiet voice, close to his face.

"Well, I hope you find shame soon, before it's too late.

She stepped off the platform and Abel watched as hands belonging to his flock reached out to touch her clothing and Yeshua's blanket as she passed them. He stepped forward but stopped as he saw several phones with their lenses facing him.

"If anyone else wants to meet my baby, we'll be in this building." The crowd parted for her to walk through, and she reentered the hideout.

Later that night most of the house was asleep. A few members of the crowd had taken Belle up on her offer, and come in to see the child. Some had prayed, some had been unaffected by his presence, some had wept, and some had cooed over him the way they would any newborn. He had been fussing in his sleep, and Belle took him outside to soothe him without waking anyone else. The crowd had completely dispersed, and most of the platform had been dismantled. She held him close against the still, freezing air, and shushed him as she rocked him. Eventually, he fell silent apart from his soft breathing.

"You're a natural already."

Gabe walked up beside her, Carl at his heels.

"It's weird," she said "this whole time I felt like I had no idea what I was going to do next, and I thought that when he got here it would just make everything more chaotic and confusing. But now he is here, it's like I know exactly what to do."

"And what are you going to do?" He asked.

"I'm going to go back home with my mom for a little while, and then I'm gonna try and build some kind of life. I cared for Adrian's mom, I could do that for a living. And I'm going to help my son try and make the world better. Starting with making sure Kitchering doesn't get re-elected."

"Sound ideal."

"And what about you, Gabe?" She asked, turning to him.

He took a breath of the icy air and exhaled, the steam of his breath lingering.

"I have to go back to my home too."

She nodded, swallowing the bud of a lump in her throat.

"And what about Carl?"

He picked the old dog up in his arms.

"He's coming with me. The poor old guy is tired."

She smiled.

"I always knew dogs went to heaven."

"Would it be heaven if there were no dogs?"

She stooped a little to meet Carl's eyes.

"Bye, Carl."

Gabe put him back on the ground and he stared up at his master, awaiting instruction. Gabe moved some of the blankets away from Yeshua's face and kissed his forehead, then Belle's.

"You are going to do great."

He began to walk away, and Carl followed him. He looked back briefly.

"If you're stuck, just pray. I'll be listening."

He walked away, and Belle stayed outside until he completely disappeared down the empty, frozen street.

MGM Grand Hotel Detroit

Lucifer sat on a tall, hard barstool and kept one eye on the elevator. He glanced at the clock, 11 pm, *Abel is an early bird so he'll be trying to sleep but it will be tough on the couch, especially for a man not used to it.* The elevator pinged and out he walked, in blue jeans, a salmon pink button-up and brown loafers. Hastily thrown on. Outside the glass-fronted lobby, the snow fell in silent flurries, looking like TV static when viewed from the corner of his eye.

Abel sat about ten feet from him and ordered a diet coke. Lucifer rolled his eyes, *damn goody two shoes.* He sipped his beer and observed him for a moment. He stared right ahead, looking as though he was trying to read the label of each bottle behind the bar.

He picked up his drink and walked over to Abel, not taking the neighbouring stool just yet.

"The caffeine in that will keep you awake you know," he commented as the coke was poured for him. Abel gave him an awkward half-smile and returned his eyes to his drink. His shoulders were hunched up against the stranger talking to him, which Lucifer willingly ignored. He pulled up the adjacent stool and sat like they were old friends.

"I was there today, you know," Abel turned to him, wide-eyed " – and I'm on your side."

He sighed, but not from relief.

"Glad someone is."

He rubbed his hand on a stiff neck.

"So what's the next move?"

Abel furrowed his brow.

"My next move?"

"Well you have to have a plan, your wife acted pretty fast,"

He winced at the reminder.

"What is it to you anyway?"

He handed Abel a business card from an inside pocket. *Andrew Mulaney, Public relations.*

"Used to work for Kitchering before the shit hit the fan. I can help you out. You have a good presence down in Tennessee, you may have to adapt, but we can make it work."

Abel handed the business card back.

"God doesn't adapt."

Lucifer stifled a laugh.

"I said you have a good presence, I didn't say you were God. Let's say this girl really is all she says, this baby is some kind of messiah. You can get in at the beginning. Imagine that, the Temple of the Staff starting a whole new religion."

Abel laughed.

"I doubt she'd want me as her spokesperson, you saw the way she told my wife where to stick it."

"You don't need her permission, you can piggyback off her. She has the credibility, you have the power. She's a tool, Abel, you can make any message sing with her."

He sighed again.

"You don't get it, do you? That girl never understood me either."

"Get what?"

"I'm a man of faith." He pointed to his heart. "All my life that's all this has been about, maybe I stepped on a few necks but it was all for God. I don't know what she is but I can't be a prophet for her because I don't believe in her."

Lucifer laughed.

"Oh, come on, Abel, you're not a monk, you're a showman. You flew here privately, remember?"

"It's never been about the money – "

"Bullshit, it's always about the money here."

"I mean it. I lost my flock last night but until I figure out what I lost it to, I can't jump back into being Brother Abel."

"So what, you retire?"

"I don't know." He drained the last of his coke. "What I saw today... Gosh, I don't know what I saw. He was just a baby, an ordinary innocent baby, and then this... miracle that makes no sense. It can't be."

"What can't be?"

"She's too... unsuitable. She worked in a gas station. She's out there breaking the law with her biker friends and convicts. God doesn't work through people like that, especially not women. How can she be mother of the whole world, an unmarried 19-year-old? It's against all the teachings of the faith." Lucifer saw real fear in his eyes. "But then the bullet. I saw it with my own eyes. I just can't square it with what I know."

"Well, you did say she could be working with the devil."

"No, not the devil."

Lucifer bit his tongue.

"That baby was nothing evil, that much I'm certain of. But I've never not known. It's like..." He struggled to find the words "If she's been telling the truth this whole time then I have to throw the scripture out of the window. I already lost my temple, my wife too, probably, I can't lose my God."

He stood up and walked back in the direction of the elevator. Lucifer dug his nails into the bar stool.

"So you just let some knocked-up teenager win?" Abel hailed the elevator.

"Fuck you."

He stepped in and disappeared behind the doors. Lucifer was almost impressed he had it in him. He sighed and sipped his beer. Perhaps Kitchering would be a better route, there was plenty of time to decide.

Belle

Belle stayed in the safehouse for two more nights. The lady Cynthia had met while grocery shopping showed up with bags of clothes, bottles, and blankets. Her name was Sarah. She cried as she held him.

They bid farewell after those two nights and Belle travelled back in a car with Cynthia and Vivienne. When they arrived home, the steps to the front door were smothered with flowers, gifts, and letters. It seemed word had spread to the faithful in Memphis. As Belle unstrapped Yeshua she saw Becky approaching the house with a young man she recognised.

"Tamir?"

"Hey, Belle!"

She felt a little out of sorts. She hadn't seen him since they went to prom together. Looking at the expression on Becky's face she knew she was behind this. He went to hug her but pulled back when he saw she was carrying the baby.

"Oh, man, I'm sorry, I could have squished the little dude!"

"He's tougher than he looks."

"I'm gonna leave you two to catch up," Becky announced and left to assist Cynthia and Vivienne in getting the stuff out of the car before Belle could protest.

Tamir seemed to have grown up a lot since high school, although it may have just been his more manicured facial hair and the fact he was wearing a smart shirt. He was still tall and skinny and had a constant goofy smile on his face, which Belle found hard not to imitate in his presence.

"So, what has Becky told you?"

"She didn't have to tell me anything, I've been following it all in the news."

He put his hands on his hips.

"I was worried about you, dude, that crazy guy after you, and Becky told me the whole deal with -" he pointed to the sky "- and everything."

"And that didn't freak you out."

"Well sure, but I'm not surprised they picked you."

He flinched a little at his honesty.

"Do you want to hold him?

He grinned.

"Could I?"

"Of course, come inside, I'll make a pot of coffee."

"Don't worry about it, I can do that for you."

Belle, Tamir, and the three women walked into the house, something Belle was worried she would never do again. At last, she breathed in the smell of the air freshener her mom always used and relished Yeshua crying out for the first time within those four walls.

The end.

Annunciation

Acknowledgments

Novel writing can be a pretty lonely pursuit, it turns out, but I'm a true believer that no one creates anything on their own and no life is without influence. My first thanks go out to my family, my mum and dad who encouraged my love of storytelling, my late stepfather David who did the same, my siblings Róisín, Fergal, Celeste, and Marcella, my stepsister Helen, my boyfriend Dan, and all my close friends who have helped me to get this thing finished and out into the world, too numerous to name

A special thanks to my aunt Jean Houghton Beatty, (or 'AJ' as I know her), for being the first to read it and helping me 'Americanize' my dialogue. To my Grandma too, I extend my thanks, I only wish she had been able to read it. Thank you too, to Andrew Rainnie, for his beautiful cover design.

To my high school English teachers, thank you for encouraging me to pursue writing, you made a huge difference. To my university tutors, thank you for telling me what I needed to improve. Thank you too, to the other writers I've met and for the feedback you gave me. Given the nature of this story, I also need to thank the religious leaders who helped me understand what it was all about – the nuns, priests, monsignors, and schoolteachers.

And finally, I want to thank all the acquaintances, well-wishers, work colleagues, online friends, strangers, and basically anyone who ever gave me a word of encouragement. It was heard, and it meant a lot.

Thank you all,

Ciara.

Printed in Great Britain
by Amazon